Howard Carter

in

The Adventure of
the Stolen Treasure

TANIA EDWARDS

TANIA EDWARDS

For Howard Carter

TANIA EDWARDS

I was born in London. I have been intrigued by time travel ever since I was a child. The past fascinates me, and I would dearly love to go back in time. Egypt and Tutankhamen came into my life when I was ten years old, and I have visited Egypt a few times following in the footsteps of my heroes Howard Carter and Giovanni Belzoni. Alas, at the time I visited, Howard's home was yet to be opened as a museum, although I do hope to visit it one day.

This is the first book I have written, and it's my way of travelling back in time and meeting Howard. Although part of the book is based on reality, for the most part it is fictitious, apart from Howard, the cast of characters all stem from my imagination.

I have my own YouTube channel where I have posted a number of videos dedicated to Howard Carter.

PROLOGUE

Egypt, 1924

She slowly opened her eyes and immediately wished she hadn't, as a sharp pain in her head made her flinch. Gently rising to her feet, she began to feel dizzy and a bit queasy. Taking deep breaths she looked up into the sky, it was darker now; she wondered how many hours she had been unconscious. She turned around and there was the house she had been visiting earlier in the day, she began to remember how a strange mist had seemed to envelope her just as she had been leaving.

Walking towards it, it gradually dawned upon her that there was nothing but desert surrounding the house. The garden, the trees, the neat paths, even the sign proclaiming this to be "Carter's House" were no longer here. There was an old-fashioned car parked next to the property, very strange she thought to herself.

A curtain was undulating gently from an open doorway, peering into the gloomy interior she cautiously stepped inside and found herself in the hallway with a domed roof at its centre. Walking further inside, she heard a noise, which seemed to be coming from a room whose door was slightly ajar. She peered through the crack and saw a man bending over something. As she watched he straightened, she noticed he was a man of medium height, he had bushy eyebrows, black searching eyes, and a dark closely cropped moustache. She must have made a noise because he suddenly became aware that he was not alone, she noticed he was as pale as a

1

ghost and there was a look of terror in his eyes.

Curious, she moved inside the room, and peered at what the man had been staring at, she gave a loud gasp and her hand automatically covered her mouth. There was a body, a very dead body, splayed out upon the floor. It was badly wrapped in bandages, only the face remained partially uncovered, the eyes bulged like two inflated balloons and the mouth was distorted into a horrible rictus grin. Slowly shaking her head, her voice barely a whisper, she said, 'Oh Howard, what have you done?'

CHAPTER ONE

London, Present Day

The cemetery was beautiful in the afternoon warmth; there were no clouds in the azure sky and just a hint of a breeze. No one else was in sight, only the chatter of the birds in the trees gave a reassuring sign of life. Charlotte Hambleton walked slowly along the path, noting the various names engraved upon the tombstones, until she came upon the one she was looking for.

The grave was very old and unassuming, the small grey headstone covered in lichen, the surround was a mass of weeds and yellow flowers, a neglected and forgotten aura surrounded it. Charlotte knelt in front of it; she could just make out the faded inscription.

Howard Carter
Archaeologist and Egyptologist
May 9th, 1874 – February 23rd, 1928

Howard had lived the remaining years of his life a lonely man, estranged from friends and colleagues. Rarely leaving his London flat, shunned by society, and ridiculed in the popular press of the day. Some say he had given up on life and simply died of a broken heart. Most newspapers barely acknowledged his passing. It seemed the triumph of his early career in Egypt had been overshadowed by accusations of theft and misconduct. Only two people had attended his funeral, his brother William, and his nephew Stanley.

A tear rolled down Charlotte's cheek as she placed a small bouquet of blue and purple carnations upon the grave. Gently touching the headstone, she whispered 'Oh, Howard, I wish I could have known you.' Then, taking one last look at the grave, she turned and slowly walked away.

Charlotte sat upon a bench and looked around, it was so peaceful here, and she found it hard to believe that just a few yards away cars thundered along a busy road. Charlotte's thoughts returned once more to Howard Carter. She was sure he had been innocent and from the books she had read about the incident, she had a pretty shrewd idea as to who the guilty party was. It was so long ago though, the people involved had disappeared into the mist of time. Howard was nothing but dust; his soul had departed to wherever it was souls went. Charlotte sighed heavily, if only she had been born a hundred years ago, she could have met Howard, and lived in his time. Charlotte loved history; she spent her days thinking of the past. She hated modern glass buildings and modern flats; they looked so clinical, like waiting rooms in a surgery. They had no personality, they lacked ambience. The old buildings in contrast were full of character, the detail in their design was quite astonishing from the pattern of the brickwork to the statuary, to the shape of the windows, so much thought and effort had gone into designing them, and they were still in use to this day. Even trains and ships used to look far more elegant, now ships were box-like in shape and resembled giant blocks of flats, and the interiors of trains were designed to emulate airplanes.

That morning a book Charlotte had bought arrived in the post. It was an old book entitled 'The Story of Howard Carter' by Joseph Eldoon, published in 1960. On opening it, Charlotte found a letter attached to one of the blank pages at the front.

19 Sep. 1960
Dear Arthur & Katie,
I am sending you 'The Story of Howard Carter' by Mr. Joseph Eldoon, which you will see makes a number of references to me. See Index. Of course, the book is heavily biased towards Herr Hengel, which is a shame. If the author had taken the time to consult me, I could've put him straight on a few of his so-called "facts", after all I was there. We'll discuss the book when I see you next year. With all good wishes to you both,

Yours as always
Stanley

Charlotte couldn't believe her luck that this marvellous letter should be here in a book she had randomly bought from the internet. Of course, over fifty years had passed since the publication of the book, she wondered if this Stanley could still be alive.

Charlotte had searched the internet for Ottomar Hengel. She discovered he had been a notable collector of antiquities; he specialized in buying and selling Egyptian antiquities. Apparently, his home in Dresden was an Aladdin's cave packed with gold, jewellery, statues, sarcophagi, mummies, busts, etc. In effect, it was a private museum, any collectors who were interested in viewing the contents had to make an appointment and show impeccable credentials.

It was rumoured that Hengel was not averse to buying stolen items, and would actually employ agents to steal the treasures he was unable to buy. After the authorities had banished Howard from the tomb, for apparently stealing objects from it, they had given the concession to Hengel to continue the excavation. There were rumours to this day that some of the items in the Cairo Museum were actually fake reproductions, and the real treasures were on display at Hengel's home in Dresden. The Egyptian authorities denied this most vehemently.

Ironically, on 18 June 1963, Hengel was at home working in his office, located behind him was a tall display cabinet featuring a prominent array of stone busts. As Hengel stood up, one of these busts, reputed to be of Amenhotep IV, (who changed his name to Akhenaten, and was probably Tutankhamen's father), toppled over and bashed him on the head, killing him instantly. Poetic justice indeed.

Later that afternoon Charlotte found herself standing outside 19 Collingham Gardens, Howard had lived here with his brother Samuel and Samuel's wife Mary. This was where Howard had died, Charlotte felt so sad, it had been a tragic end for such a talented man.

Charlotte caught the early morning train from Victoria to Gatwick. She enjoyed looking out of the window watching the scenery go by as it changed from city to countryside, but To-day it was dark and cloudy and all she could see was her reflection. She had her book to read, but found she was unable to concentrate.

The train arrived at Gatwick and Charlotte alighted, she had a medium-sized suitcase with her and a rucksack. She was looking forward to visiting Egypt for the first time, especially now that Howard's house was a museum.

CHAPTER TWO

Egypt, Present Day

Charlotte had spent the morning sightseeing in Luxor and this afternoon she spent wondering around the tombs in the Valley of the Kings. Tutankhamen's tomb was smaller than she imagined it would be. A wooden ramp covered the original stone steps and inside wooden flooring sat atop the original floor. She peered over the barrier at the sarcophagus where the remains of Tutankhamen lay, alone, his possessions now enclosed in glass display cases at the Cairo Museum. She sighed, and tried to imagine Howard working here all those years ago. She wondered out into the afternoon sunshine, and made her way back to her hired bicycle for the next stop on her list.

The small domed house sat atop a hill named Elwat el-Diban, designed by Howard and built in 1911, it had recently opened as a museum and Charlotte was eager to pay a visit. It was quite late in the afternoon and most of the tourists had gone. The house, once surrounded by desert, was now next to roads, shops, houses, offices, and a café. The little dwelling stood like an island, encircled not by a sea of sand but by grass, shrubs, flowers and paved walkways.

Charlotte walked along the path towards the main door; she showed her ticket to the guide and entered the domed hallway. The whitewashed walls gave the interior a bright ambience, flimsy net curtains hung at the windows; photographs of Howard and Lord

7

Carnarvon lay scattered about, information boards told the story of the two men and their discovery. The furniture though looked cheap; some of the chairs were seat less, the whicker work having disintegrated long ago.

She wondered through the various rooms, she couldn't sense Howard's spirit though, the atmosphere felt neutral. She came to a bedroom and sat on the bed noting the shaving kit and battered homburg hat, she doubted very much that they had belonged to Howard.

Sighing heavily Charlotte stood up, suddenly she felt very sad. She didn't regret this visit but at the same time she felt sad because the house was not as it was when Howard had lived here.

She couldn't see the guide outside, although she knew he must be somewhere as he had followed her as she sauntered around inside. Charlotte suddenly realized that she was feeling tired and hungry, and on top of that, her head ached. She wondered why it was so misty. She blinked her eyes rapidly a few times, the mist seemed to be thicker, she began to panic; her head started to spin, her legs began to buckle and the ground seemed to rise up and swallow her.

Then, without any warning, the world went black.

CHAPTER THREE

London, 1923

Howard Carter emerged from his doorway and looked about him for a taxi. This morning he was in a light-hearted mood as he would be returning to Egypt To-morrow and he was very much looking forward to getting back to his work there. In the meantime, he was to have lunch with an elderly acquaintance, Elbert Merriman.

Howard entered the Grill Room amid the lunchtime bustle and made his way to the table next to the window where Merriman awaited him. His companion was about 84 years of age, with a long and craggy face, most of his hair had disappeared leaving just a few grey wisps circling the nape of his neck. Howard sat down and glanced at the view, admiring the greenery of Kensington Gardens just across the road.

'Well, my dear Carter, you're in the newspaper once more. Your 'friend' Hengel has been talking about you, not very favourably I'm afraid.'

Howard looked taken aback, 'What do you mean?'

'Herr Hengel has been rather rude about you again, not a big article, of course he doesn't deserve one, he has a big enough head as it is. He claims you've been pilfering objects from the tomb, and that you're not doing a very good job excavating it. He says they ought to give the tomb to him; it would be safer in his hands. What an odious man he is.'

'I read The Times this morning I don't recall seeing the interview.'

'No, no, it was in the Daily Sketch. Really, Carter, you ought to broaden your horizons. The Times is all very well for proper news, but for gossip of a more fruity nature shall we say, then you have to look elsewhere.'

Howard raised his eyebrows. Merriman continued, 'Hengel is up to his usual tricks, he claims you're catalogue numbering system is suspect, objects don't match up with their given numbers, or some such thing, he's becoming a veritable bore on the subject, puts me to sleep just listening to him. Of course, I don't believe him for a minute. You wouldn't steal anything would you?' Howard opened his mouth to protest but Merriman held up a hand to silence him.

'Just one of my little jokes.'

Howard retorted indignantly, 'If you don't mind my saying so Merriman, it's in very poor taste. Everything I find is photographed, numbered and catalogued; no one has any right to say otherwise. I've a good mind to instruct my lawyer to sue that newspaper for defamation of character.'

'I assure you Carter the newspaper said nothing to accuse you directly, it was that dreadful German man, and you should sue him. ' Merriman said hastily, fearing that he may have embellished the story a bit too much, 'it's all just a silly piece of flimflam.' Quickly changing the subject he said, 'Well, I don't know about you but I'm rather hungry, shall we order lunch?'

The waiter arrived and placed the soup bowls on the table before discreetly melting away. Merriman took off his spectacles to wipe them and dropped them into his soup, trying to retrieve them he made a terrible mess; Howard managed to clean the errant spectacles with a napkin. Merriman said gratefully, 'You are a marvel Carter, I expect it comes from cleaning all those old bits and pieces you keep finding.' The waiter reappeared to supply clean napkins and a fresh bowl of soup. The rest of lunch, which consisted of grilled beef with lightly boiled potatoes and vegetables, followed by dessert, occurred without any further accidents.

Taking a sip of coffee, Merriman said, 'So, you're off to Egypt to-morrow?'

'Yes, I've not been well lately, the warmer climate should help me to feel more like myself.'

'I know what you mean, my old bones are always creaking, and my wife Jean claims the noise keeps her awake. We'll be going out their later this month, staying at the Winter Palace as usual so no doubt we'll bump into you at some point. I don't suppose you'll be digging anything else up?'

'No, I'm still clearing out Tutankhamen's tomb.'

'Goodness me, it seems to be taking an awfully long time, how long have you been at it now?'

'I only discovered it last year.' said Howard, exasperated.

'It seems like ages ago and here I was thinking that you were a man of leisure now, I was beginning to envy you, free to come and go as you please.'

'Aren't you a man of leisure?'

'Oh, no dear boy, I'm married.'

Howard crossed the road and entered Kensington Gardens. He noticed the trees were beginning to change colour, their leaves fading from green to hues of yellow, brown and red. He sauntered along the Flower Walk admiring the ornamental shrubs, the beds of roses and the flowering shrubs; he found a free bench and sat down. For a while he watched the antics of a flock of pigeons as they pecked at the ground looking for some tit bit to eat, occasionally fighting with one of their companions, Howard found their cooing had a calming effect upon his unsettled mind.

Ottomar Hengel was a thorn in Howard's side. Hengel, denied the concession to dig in the Valley of the Kings in favour of Lord Carnarvon, was now a very bitter man. He craved the glory that Carter and Carnarvon had had bestowed upon them by the press and public over their glorious discovery, but it seemed he, Hengel, was destined to be relegated to a footnote in history, if that. Hengel though appeared to be at great pains to change this state of affairs and since Carnarvon's death had stepped up his campaign of malice and vindictiveness towards Carter.

Howard had devoted almost all his life to the study of Egyptology. He first went to Egypt on the staff of the Egypt Exploration Fund archaeological survey in 1890, and two years later, he was one of Professor Flinders Petrie's assistants in the excavation of Tel el-Amarna.

His studies and experience subsequently ranked him with the experts, and the Egyptian Government appointed him Inspector General of its Antiquities Department. On behalf of the Egyptian

Government, he started work in the Valley of the Kings.

The culminating point of this was reached when with the aid of Lord Carnarvon he found and opened the wonderful tomb of Tutankhamen.

For six winter seasons Lord Carnarvon and Howard had been excavating in the royal necropolis in the hills on the west bank of the Nile at Luxor in the hope of finding the tomb of the only member of the great eighteenth dynasty whose burial place had not yet been located – the boy King Tutankhamen.

They had actually decided that the 1922-23 season should be their last in the Valley of the Kings if again they drew a blank, and it was with anxiety that Howard resumed work on November 2, 1922. Two days later, he found in the debris he was clearing a stone step, which indicated the possibility of a hidden tomb. Thirty-six hours later, he obtained proof that he had before him a sealed tomb belonging to the Royal necropolis.

He cabled to his chief, then in London, and Lord Carnarvon, accompanied by his daughter, Lady Evelyn Herbert, hastened to Egypt, and on November 26 it was verified that this was the very tomb for which they had so long been searching.

The small party, which first entered the antechamber, were dazzled by the colour and glitter of the objects that confronted them. It was a first contact with a scene which had not been witnessed by man for over thirty-two centuries. Afterwards each day brought some new treasures and discovery to light.

The clearing of the antechamber and sepulchral chamber each with its annex, and the preservation and transport to Cairo of the contents was a gigantic undertaking, carried through with outstanding success.

The following day Howard left London for the Valley of the Kings in Egypt to continue his investigations into the customs and history of ancient Egypt. At Victoria Station, he encountered a large group of newspaper reporters all shouting questions at him. Howard held up his hands to indicate he had something to say, they looked at him expectantly.

'I am positive,' Howard declared, 'that I shall find the body of Tutankhamen absolutely untouched by the robbers who apparently have despoiled every other sarcophagus and left the bodies and clothing in complete disorder after removing everything of any value.

'Wonderful as our finds were during my last visit, they will, I am certain, fade into insignificance when compared with what we will see when we enter the inner chamber at Luxor.

'We will break the seals of the inner tomb and view the body of the Pharaoh Tutankhamen who has been lying in state there for 3,000 years.

'But we have not the slightest intention of disturbing the body in any way. If we did, we would be no better than the robbers of other days.

'All we shall do will be to examine the body and the manner in which it is laid, and from our discoveries we will be able probably to solve much that at present is unknown. After our investigations have been completed, we shall reseal the tomb and leave Tutankhamen to his rest.

'Although to the popular imagination the finding of King Tutankhamen's body will prove the greatest appeal, it does not follow that that will be the greatest find we shall make. There are great treasures still to be found. We have three-quarters of the work to do yet.

'We have, of course, already removed about 600 large and small objects from the annex, the sepulchral chamber, and the inner store chamber, but to complete the task will require another two or three years' hard work.

'Work, which will last about four months, will commence immediately I get out to Luxor. I am going to Egypt via Trieste, where I shall pick up the party who are to assist me in my work.'

'Was the curse of Tutankhamen responsible for Lord Carnarvon's death?' asked a reporter.

'Do you believe in the curse, do you think it will harm you as well?' asked another.

'Are you superstitious, do you think that some supernatural force killed Lord Carnarvon?' someone else asked.

'No,' replied Howard, 'I have not the slightest belief that any occult influence was responsible for the death of my late chief. I have certainly no fears for myself in that direction.

'It is rather too much to ask me to believe that some "spook" is keeping watch and ward over the dead King, ready to wreak vengeance on anyone who goes too near.

'Lady Carnarvon,' Howard added, 'is to continue the work

where her late husband left off, and when we have thoroughly explored Tutankhamen's tomb there will be other investigations I shall make.'

Howard, looking very fit and keen, entered the boat train for Dover, rather glad to be leaving London once again for his work in Egypt.

CHAPTER FOUR

Egypt, 1923

Luxor and Thebes were still half-marsh and half-desert, as the Nile flood, which was very high this year, had not receded completely, though areas, which a few days ago were submerged, were now merely moist. The river was falling fast, within a few days the inundated areas would be dry again. The Valley of the Kings remained cruelly hot, except for Howard's workmen, it was deserted.

Preparations for re-opening the tomb were well advanced, but would probably be held up for a day or two, as Howard's arrangements were not quite complete, not all the members of his staff had arrived.

A scurrying crowd of native workers removed most of the earth and stones, which at the end of last season were piled in front and on top of the wooden structure which was erected outside the actual stone door at the head of the descending passage of the tomb, to enable locks to be installed to guard the tomb entrance by night. Howard proceeded leisurely with his preparations for the resumption of work, as much of his material was still coming up the river.

He had completed the alterations to the tomb of Seti II., the exterior of which now resembled a roofless blockhouse, wherein the objects, to be brought from the tomb this season, would be photographed. Though the winter season was now supposed to be here , the sun was still decidedly summery, and the advance party of the season's tourists who had arrived during the last two days were finding the sun's welcome far too warm for their comfort.

Howard had decided to devote the coming season's work to the shrine, the huge gilded wooden case in which it was almost certain the mummy of the Pharaoh lay. The two chambers awaiting clearance, the room off the antechamber and the inner room of the burial chamber were to be closed and the contents dealt with next year.

The shrine and its secret looked like it would keep Howard and his assistants busy for the whole season. The huge casket was so close to the wall between the anteroom and the burial chamber that the wall would have to be demolished, at least in part, if the delicate work of taking the shrine apart was to be accomplished without damage to the rich ornamentation.

The wall was composed partly of solid rock and partly of stones mortared together, and it was hoped that when the stones had been taken down, the excavators would have room to work on the casket; otherwise, the solid rock would have to be demolished.

During the 3,500 years that it had lain in the dark of ages, the woodwork of the casket had shrunk so that the faience and gilding were apt to be loose.

Great care would have to be exercised when taking down the successive panels. Each plank would have to be chemically treated and probably wrapped in cloth before it could be handled.

After much delay Howard finally opened Tutankhamen's tomb, the iron gates erected last year for protection against robbers were swung back and the dark chamber illuminated with powerful electric light. Photographing the tomb took place until lunch time, and in the afternoon Howard would be kept busy completing the alterations being made at the tomb of Seti II.

The scene in the Valley of the Kings reminded Howard of last season, hundreds of tourists from the Nile steamers created a picturesque and animated scene, particularly above the tomb of Tutankhamen where they crowded peering longingly into the depths at the foot of the descending passage and wistfully asking whether just one treasure was not coming out.

However, while they were standing on the threshold of the tomb, which most of them had crossed two oceans to see, there was a busy scene in the burial chamber, Howard had found an interesting trio of candlesticks attached to a common base. The wicks were missing, but it was believed that tightly twisted linen used to be placed in the mouths of these candlesticks and burned steadily and slowly, giving a light a little stronger than the modern candle.

Also found were eleven small oars inside the outer shrine evidently laid there for Tutankhamen, when, as the ancients believed, the time would come when he would need to cross the stream to the Elysian Fields. It was believed that this passage was difficult, and all efforts were made to give the departed soul every assistance in this terrifying journey.

To-morrow, Howard would start to take down the partition wall, which separated the antechamber from the shrine. As the wall was made of stones loosely cemented together, and not of solid rock, the operation of demolition would therefore be both laborious and delicate. To prevent the rubble and stones from falling against the magnificently decorated sides of the shrine, a partition of wood would be erected between the canopy and the wall. This year's work would impose an immense strain on the excavators, owing to the confined space at their disposal for their intricate operations, and the intense heat. The electric lamps in the tomb totalled some 8,000-candle power, and the heat rays beating down from the roof upon the excavators' heads as they toiled away at this task would be almost unbearable. Howard and his assistants showed the strain as they emerged from the tomb at the luncheon interval.

The weather was overcast. The sun went down amid towering banks of purple clouds, and throughout the night, the hills surrounding the Royal necropolis were outlined in grim silhouette by flashes of lightening. The floods between Aswan and Luxor suspended all railway communications, and made the excavators somewhat anxious in view of the unsettled weather, but all precautions had been taken in readiness to sandbank the entrance to the tomb in the unlikely eventuality of the valley being flooded by a cloudburst, for such was not unknown here.

From 7 o'clock the following morning until past noon the excavators were hard at work demolishing the partition wall preliminary to taking apart the outer shrine. Howard personally carried out this very delicate operation himself, prising up each stone with a crowbar, while one of his assistants held the stone to prevent it falling inwards against the barrier protecting the canopy. The stone was then passed out to a native digger, who staggered with it upstairs into the brilliant sunlight, adding it to the growing heap beyond the wall at the back of the tomb. Some of the stones show that a yellow wash was applied to the inner walls of the sepulchral chamber.

As a result of To-day's work, the opening made by piercing the sealed door was widened to a gap of four or five yards, but another full day's work would be required before the whole partition was down.

The unsettled weather had entirely passed away, and To-day the sun blazed down out of the peerless azure sky.

Many tourists availed themselves of a brief sojourn at Luxor to visit the Valley of the Kings. They were rewarded by the sight of two trayfuls of painted plaster from the inner side of the partition wall being removed to the laboratory.

The wall above the tomb, known to all tourists who visited the scene of the excavations last year, had been rebuilt this season. It had been slightly raised, and was of much more solid construction to avoid the possibility of the stones becoming detached and toppling down into the well beneath. A large fragment of blue granite, apparently part of the ancient sarcophagus, had been effectually utilized as a corner piece.

The removal of the partition wall was concluded shortly before noon a few days later, by which time a native clad in white had carried out several basketfuls of stones, large and small, plaster, and dust. The baulks used by ancient tomb-builders have been piled up in the well of the tomb. To-morrow Howard would take down the screen which had been protecting the shrine during the demolition of the partition wall. Thereafter he would be free to set about the important task of making a thorough investigation of the outer walls of the shrine to see how it is fitted together.

The fact that the burial chamber is hollowed out of the rock at a level more than three feet lower than the floor of the antechamber greatly adds to the difficulty of this operation. Between the doors of the outer shrine and those of the second shrine there is a space of only nineteen inches and that between the sides may be even less.

The work continued with the first stage of dismantling the golden shrine of Tutankhamen when the folding doors of the first shrine were taken off their hinges and removed to the antechamber. Before work in the shrine began, however, the remainder of the scaffolding masking the shrine had to be removed and the dust left everywhere by the demolition of the wall carefully swept up. The demolition of the wall revealed nothing of interest, that is to say no broken potsherds or boxes, as discovered among the rubbish filling the well and the staircase of the tomb.

The removal of the doors, which are about five feet high, and together measure some six and a half feet across, was a long and difficult business. Howard spent from 9 a.m. until 1 p.m. in the sweltering heat of the tomb without emerging. When he and his assistant came out for lunch, both were abundantly smeared with plaster having been in close contact with the walls of the tomb.

CHAPTER FIVE

Ottomar Hengel and his valet and general dogs body Richard Bauer visited the Valley every day. Hengel greedily watching the treasures as they emerged from the tomb to the laboratory. He glared hatefully at Howard; if possible, such a glare could turn a person to stone. Howard could feel Hengel's eyes burning into his very soul, he felt uncomfortable being anywhere near the man, and could barely bring himself to speak civilly to him. Not that that mattered, Hengel didn't care for "English manners and propriety," and said exactly what he meant.

Hengel surveyed the area surrounding the tomb, the crowds of tourists gaping into the depths below, gossiping and laughing amongst themselves.

'Baur look at this madness, if I had gun I would shoot these wretched peasants. The fools have nothing better to do than sit around and gawp at that idiot Carter. I hate him, but I have plans Bauer for getting rid of him and his namby pamby assistants.'

'You are going to shoot them as well?' asked Bauer.

'No! Idiot, Carter is too well-known, I have something else in mind.'

'Something nasty?'

'May be a little bit nasty. But it will rid us of him for good, and then the tomb will be mine.' Hengel smiled to himself, imagining all the treasures that he could take. With the help of one of his men, safely ensconced as one of Carter's assistants, he had already made copies of certain objects and now the originals were in his collection.

'Good,' he said, nodding to himself with a satisfied look upon his face, 'come Bauer.'

Bauer dutifully followed his master towards the tomb and crowds of tourists.

'Ah, Carter!' bellowed Hengel in such a loud voice that it echoed from the Valley across the Nile and over to Luxor, upsetting a large flock of pigeons who erupted into the air, the birds flew about in stunned confusion knocking several people to the ground. A few days later one man swore he found a pigeon still cowering inside his turban.

Startled by this booming voice Howard almost dropped the tray he was carrying. Hengel approached him, 'Ah, my dear Carter, how good to see you so busy.'

'Hengel, what are you doing here?' asked Howard.

'I have come to see my fellow excavator, may be there is some help I can be assisting you with?'

'No thank you, I have enough help.'

'What a shame you didn't take advantage of my services last season, perhaps I could have prevented these strange anomalies concerning missing objects.'

'There are no missing objects.' retorted Howard, quite certain that if Hengel had the opportunity the whole laboratory would have been emptied by now, with the blame squarely placed upon his shoulders.

'Ah, Carter, you are a stubborn man, but I know why. You are like me. You want to do everything yourself, because only you know how to do it properly. I understand this, I am the same.' Hengel looked over a Bauer's blank face. 'I am surrounded by imbeciles, so, I am used to working alone. You cannot rely on other people, they always bungle everything, and carefully laid plans go up in smoke. You are wise to supervise the work so closely.'

'Well, I'm afraid I've a lot of work to occupy my time, so if you'll excuse me?'

'Of course, we will have dinner together soon.'

Howard was about to say no thank you.

'I will not take no for an answer.' said Hengel, in a very stern voice.

Rather taken aback, Howard gave a slight nod and hurried off to the safety of the laboratory. Hengel watched him go. 'Look at that fool, gott im himmel Bauer; I will see that man gone before the year ends.

A young man approached, he looked very nervous and pale. 'Mr. Hengel, sir, you wanted to see me.'

'Ah, Barnaby, there you are. I have a task for you to carry out. You will not make a complete bungle of it; you will make sure everything runs smoothly. Or you may find yourself buried beneath the earth. Do you understand?' said Hengel, with a hint of menace in his voice.

'Yes sir, I understand. What is it you want me to do?' stammered Barnaby.

'Good. Come with me.' Hengel steered Barnaby to his car followed by Bauer. The car sped off leaving a cloud of dust to settle upon the fascinated tourists.

CHAPTER SIX

Egypt, 1924

Elbert Merriman and his wife Jean were about to have lunch on the terrace of the Winter Palace Hotel. Their guests were Stanley Matula, a businessman from New York, and, just arriving, Howard Carter.

Standing up to greet his friend, Merriman said, 'Ah, Carter, how wonderful to see you, this is Mr. Spatula, he's from America, but we needn't hold that against him.'

'Elbert, don't be so rude.' said Jean.

'No, it's quite all right Mrs. Merriman,' said Matula, then turning to Carter, 'it's Matula. I'm delighted to meet you Mr. Carter. I've read so much about King Tut, a wonderful discovery.'

Howard, cringing slightly at the hypocorism, said, 'Thank you.'

'I'd be fascinated to hear how you found him; I understand it took many years.'

'Yes it did, I'd be happy to tell you about it someday.' said Howard.

'You're a very lucky man, Patunia, normally Carter charges people to hear him talk on that subject.' said Merriman.

'It's Matula.'

'Yes, yes, of course.' Turning to address his wife he said, 'My dear where is that waiter? We've been sitting here all afternoon; it'll be dinner time soon.'

'There's no need to be so impatient, it's not as if we have

anywhere to go.' said Jean.

'Even so, I do wish he'd hurry up, at our age there isn't very much time left.'

'Here he comes,' said Matula, 'I must say I'm looking forward to this. I've had a busy day sightseeing. My feet are killing me.'

'Where did you go?' asked Howard.

'Well, I got up at the crack of dawn; I was told it would be cooler at that hour, still, it seemed pretty hot to me.' Howard looked at the small, round man; he had a jolly face currently covered in a sheen of sweat. Matula continued, 'I visited Karnak, wow that was impressive. Those huge columns, that avenue of rams, I was bowled over by it. I'm going over to the west bank to-morrow.' Matula took out a large handkerchief and mopped his brow.

'You ought to lose weight, you can't...' said Merriman.

'Really Elbert, you can't go around saying things like that.' interrupted Jean.

'It's alright, I really don't mind, Mrs. Merriman.' said Matula. 'You know Mr. Satsuma you should get Carter to show you Tutankhamen's tomb, I'm sure he wouldn't mind.'

'Oh, that would be wonderful, if it's ok with you Mr. Carter?'

'I'm afraid I'm not able to, you require a special permit from the Ministry of Public Works, and then you'll be permitted to look around. There are many other tombs to see, some of them are really quite breathtaking. '

'Of course, I understand that, and I'll certainly pay them a visit To-morrow.' said Matula.

'I'm sure Carter can sneak you in if you were to breathe in a bit, it's quite possible nobody would even notice you.' said Merriman.

'Honestly Elbert what a thing to suggest, you know how busy Mr. Carter is, and the situation with visitors is quite a sore point with the poor man.' retorted Jean.

'Well, I thought he might have an hour or so to spare...' mumbled Elbert.

'Please,' said Matula, 'it's really not a problem, I have a guide book with me and I'm sure I can find my own way around.'

'I know, I'll show you around,' said Elbert, 'I don't know why I didn't think of it before.'

'That's very kind of kind of you.' said Matula, although he wasn't at all sure about this arrangement.

'Well, that's all settled then Bachelor, we'll go there To-morrow.'

Matula sighed heavily and looked at Jean, who raised her eyebrows in despair.

Just then, lunch arrived.

After lunch and some more desultory conversation, Howard bade farewell to his fellow diners. As he was leaving, another acquaintance of Merriman's appeared.

'My dear Barnacle, how wonderful to see you, this is…'

'This is Mr. Matula.' Jean interrupted him.

'It's Spatula.' said Matula.

'How do you do…? I'm Barnaby.' said Barnaby.

Shaking his head, Howard made his way down the stairs.

As he reached the bottom, a voice called out to him.

'Mr. Carter, please wait.'

Howard turned to see the man called Barnaby.

'My name is Leo Barnaby, I'm really sorry to bother you like this, but I need to speak with you, urgently.' he whispered. He was gripping Howard's arm.

'Will you kindly let go of my arm.' Howard said indignantly.

Barnaby lowered his voice, 'Please, you need to hear this, it concerns you …'

Howard interrupted the young man, 'If you have anything to say why not just say it, why all this secrecy.'

'I can't be seen with you, he'll kill me if he thinks I've told you.'

'Aren't you being a touch melodramatic? Who'll kill you and why?'

'I can't say, not here. Can I come over to your house this evening?'

'Mr. Barnaby for a young man with something to say, you've told me absolutely nothing. And no you can't come to my house, either you tell me now or kindly go away.'

Barnaby was just about to protest when he suddenly turned as white as a ghost. Howard turned to see what he was staring at and saw a tall, distinguished man with blonde hair, he recognized him, it was the odious Ottomar Hengel.

'Mr. Carter, Mr. Barnaby, how are you both?' Hengel enquired, tipping his hat.

'Fine.' Barnaby mumbled.

'Good, good. Barnaby I wish to talk to you about our

arrangements, you know the ones I am talking about?'

Barnaby swallowed hard, 'Yes I do, Herr Hengel.'

'Very well, if you are not busy we will discuss them now, yes?'

'Er, yes, yes, of course.'

Howard stared at the two men, one self-assured, exuding confidence, the other looking like a frightened rabbit. Howard sighed, he couldn't wait to get back to the shrines, he had so many plans in his head and he found social life to be a distraction he could well do without.

CHAPTER SEVEN

Charlotte opened her eyes, she felt a sharp pain in her head, she tried to stand and a wave of nausea overcame her. Breathing deeply, she began to feel a bit calmer, she looked up at the sky, and it looked darker. How long had she been unconscious? Turning around she saw the house, yet it didn't look the same. There was nothing but desert, no buildings, no roads, and no garden. Somehow, the house seemed smaller, and then she saw the car, it looked like an old-fashioned Ford with its roof rolled down. There was a wall missing too, in its place was an alcove, the back wall revealed two large windows, with some sort of cupboard standing just below the left window and next to the left wall a pile of what looked like rubbish.

There was an open door; a net curtain hung over the entrance. The air was still and quiet, nobody appeared to be about. Feeling nervous, Charlotte approached the door; she peered inside, and there was the domed hallway. Cautiously she walked further into the house, it looked so different, the furniture was far more tasteful, the mud-brick walls were unplastered. Charlotte couldn't understand what had happened, a thought crossed her mind though, had she gone back in time, if so, how? Suddenly she remembered the mist – had it been a time portal?

She heard a movement, it came from a room to her left, the door was ajar and she peered through. There was a man standing there, he was looking down at something. Charlotte leaned on the door and it let out a squeak, the man turned, his eyes were wide with fear. All at once she felt scared, her heart beating like a drum, she stepped into the room and looked down. A man was laying there, a very dead man, roughly covered in bandages. His face partially exposed to reveal bulging eyes and a horrible rictus grin. Her voice barely a whisper she said, 'Oh, Howard, what have you done?'

'Done? I haven't done anything,' Howard replied indignantly, 'I've just found him, and who the devil are you?'

'Charlotte Hambleton, I'm here on holiday. What are you doing here?'

Howard stared at her incredulously, 'I happen to live here.'

'I know that, but should you be here now, in this time.'

'What time am I meant to be here? This is my home! Are you responsible for this, is this some sort of joke, if so, it isn't funny. Take your friend here and leave immediately before I call the police.'

Charlotte stepped nearer to the body; she knelt down and touched it. It felt cold, the eyes were sightless, 'I'm afraid he really is dead.' She removed the bandaging from the face, 'Do you recognize him?'

Howard looked at the man, 'I know him, his name is Leo Barnaby, he spoke to me earlier to-day, he said he had something important he wanted to discuss with me.'

Howard poured himself a whisky, and sat down. Charlotte noted that he hadn't offered her a drink, so she helped herself. 'What did he want to talk to you about?' she asked.

'I don't know we were interrupted before he could say anymore. I think I should call the police.'

Charlotte looked at him; she still couldn't believe this really was Howard Carter. Maybe she was dreaming. 'Are you sure?'

He looked at her, he saw a girl with a pretty face framed by long curly brown hair, he also noticed she had beautiful blue eyes. He wasn't sure of her age, he hazarded a guess at early to mid thirties, she was wearing a red floral dress, a white cardigan, her legs were bare, and upon her feet she were short black socks and black gym shoes.

Charlotte thought that for a man of fifty he looked younger, his eyes were beautiful, brown and shining with intelligence, she wanted to reach out and touch him, just to make sure he was there. She said, 'The police might think you killed him. May be it's a warning – interfere and this is what will happen to you.' She looked towards the corpse, 'We ought to get rid of him. Dump him somewhere, or let someone else get stuck with him.'

Howard stared at her, 'I'm surrounded by mad people. Are you insane? I can't go around with a dead body, besides, people saw me talking with him.'

'Even more reason not to call the police, you'll be their chief suspect. We'll have to bury him in the desert.'

'Why are you so eager to assist with the disposal of the body, what reason do you have for being out here?'

'I just want to help; after all it won't do your reputation any good if people think you're a murderer.'

'I've just come back from a birthday celebration, lots of my colleagues saw me there, not one of them is going to believe I had anything to do with this poor man's death.' retorted Howard.

'That may be so, but you know how people love to gossip. And I bet you don't get too many corpses around here, fresh ones I mean, as opposed to ancient ones.'

Charlotte kneeled in front of Howard, 'We'll use the car, drive into the desert, you must know of a good place where we can bury him, after all you've spent decades wondering around here and digging things up all over the place.'

Howard finished his whisky, he felt a headache developing, he closed his eyes and opened them, the girl was still there, and so was the body. What a day this had been, he sighed heavily.

He thought about her suggestion, its true the police may think there had been an argument and he had unwittingly killed the man, why would he wrap him in bandages though? He shook his head, he just wanted a quiet life, one minute he was enjoying himself at his colleague Harkness' 50th birthday party, minding his own business he arrives home and what happens? A dead body turns up! Followed by a very strange girl urging him to go out in the middle of the night and bury it. He suddenly felt very tired and wondered why he was never to be allowed any privacy?

He sighed again, stood up and said, 'You'll have to help me carry the body to the car.'

Howard grabbed the top half and Charlotte took hold of the legs, they stumbled out of the room, knocking over a table and smashing a vase, water spilled everywhere and they nearly slipped over. Reaching the car, they managed to heave the body into the back.

'We'll need a spade,' said Charlotte.

Howard disappeared around the corner of the house and returned with a couple of spades and two torches. Charlotte opened the passenger door at the same time as Howard, they looked at each other.

'Aren't you going to drive?' she asked.

'I thought you were.' he answered.

'I don't know how to.'

'Neither do I.'

They looked at each other, Howard felt annoyed, after all this was her idea, now they were stuck here.

'Oh, well,' said Charlotte, 'I'm sure I can manage, it can't be that difficult.'

Howard wasn't so sure. Charlotte went around to the driver's seat, 'In you get.'

Reluctantly, Howard got in to the car.

Charlotte looked around the interior, to her left was a lever, in front was a key, and at her feet three pedals, she had no idea what any of them did. 'Hmm,' she said as she turned the key. Nothing happened; her heel hit something hard on the floor, looking down she saw a button - ejector seat maybe? Oh well, nothing ventured…. she closed her eyes, grabbed hold of the steering wheel and pushed the button - the engine started, well, that was a good sign. How to make it go forward though and what did this stick attached to the steering wheel do?

'Isn't there an instruction manual?' she asked Howard.

'No.' he said.

She pushed the lever and tried one of the pedals, 'Oh my goodness, it's moving, it's actually moving.' she cried.

Howard was unimpressed, 'At this rate it'll take a week just to reach the road.'

'I wonder what this lever does,' she pushed it forward; 'we're going faster!'

She stepped on one of the pedals, the car suddenly stopped and they found themselves flung forward.

'Do you mind, I nearly lost my hat.' said Howard.

'Well, at least we know where the break is.'

The car jerked and whined its way past the house and onto the main road.

'I'm getting the hang of it now, it's really quite exciting.' said Charlotte.

'Very exciting,' said Howard languidly, 'a donkey would be faster.'

'Well, I'm going faster now; pity the road's so bumpy.'

'It's not the road, it's your driving.'

'You know, this car reminds me of Laurel and Hardy, I hope it doesn't collapse in a heap.' she laughed

'The way you're driving it probably will.'

Charlotte said, 'You're just jealous because you can't drive.

They carried on further into the desert. 'Is there supposed to be all that smoke coming out of the bonnet?' asked Charlotte.

'Stop the car,' Howard shouted, 'it's overheating.'

'I'm not sure I can.' said Charlotte, turning the wheel at the same time as she pulled the lever back, there was a loud banging noise, and the car stopped suddenly.

'Oh, dear, I think I pushed the wrong button.'

Howard got out of the car, 'I knew this was a mistake, now we're stuck here.'

'Never mind, go and find a suitable place for the body and I'll try and sort the car out.'

It was quite dark now; at least Howard had brought torches as well as digging equipment. Charlotte shivered, from cold or from the dead body she wasn't sure. It was so quiet, nothing but desert surrounded her, she could almost be on another planet.

Howard reappeared, 'I've found a spot and made a start on the hole. You'll have to help me with the body.'

They carried the heavy body step by slow step up hills and down hills until they came to a secluded bit of desert surrounded by rocks, and there was the hole Howard had begun to dig.

Charlotte was feeling hot now, beads of sweat poured down her face and back, she sat down 'I need a breather.'

'You can't,' said Howard, 'we have to keep digging and then bury the body. We need to be quick about this.'

They dug until the hole was deep enough to conceal the body. Every muscle Charlotte had was in agony, her back was killing her and her hands were covered in blisters. They dropped the body into its final resting place and began the laborious task of refilling the hole. Afterwards they covered it with small rocks and stones. The torches were beginning to dim; they switched them off and waited for their eyes to become accustomed to the dark. Then they walked back to the car, Charlotte noticed Howard was limping a bit.

'Sorry I dropped that rock on your foot.' she said.

Howard was too tired to care, he saw what was left of his car and his heart sank. They got in, Charlotte fiddled about with buttons and levers, and miraculously the engine started. She turned to Howard.

'You see, everything's fine, it's all over and done with trust me.'

Clamping his hat down on his head, Howard stared into the darkness; he had a feeling that it wasn't going to be fine.

Somehow, Charlotte managed to drive them back to the house. They were both exhausted as they sat down, Charlotte asked Howard if he would like a drink, he said, as though in a trance, 'I think I'm going to have a heart attack.'

She poured him a whisky, 'Here, drink this; it'll put some colour into your cheeks.'

Howard stared at her as he took the proffered glass, 'Isn't it time you were going?'

'Going where?'

'Wherever it is you're staying.' answered Howard.

Charlotte hadn't considered this, but now she realized she had nowhere to go. She supposed she could reserve a room at the Winter Palace; she had no luggage, or come to think of it no change of clothes and no money. I'll think about it To-morrow, she decided.

'I don't suppose I could stay here? After all it is very late.'

Howard conceded that she had a point, as it would be morning in a few hours; reluctantly he agreed she could stay.

She settled herself inside the spare room. As she lay upon the bed, she wondered how she was going to get back to her own time. She considered her situation from all different viewpoints, she didn't care how she got here. She was sleeping in Howard's spare room, she had actually spoken to him, she didn't care if she never went back home.

The next morning Howard told her he had arranged for his chauffeur to drive her to the ferry.

Reluctantly Charlotte got into what was left of the car. The chauffeur was obviously well trained and pretended not to notice how dusty and battered the vehicle was. The ferry made its way across the Nile and dumped her on the opposite side.

CHAPTER EIGHT

Charlotte was feeling very hungry; she'd had nothing to eat since lunch yesterday. Howard had thrown her out without any breakfast and she was thirsty as well as fed up. Tears began to well up in her eyes; she pulled herself together and told herself not to be such an idiot. She marched into the hotel and up to the reception desk. The receptionist smiled at her and asked, 'How may I help you, Miss Hambleton?'

Charlotte was so taken aback that for a moment she lost the power of speech. She stood there with her mouth open but no words would come out.

'You are perhaps wanting your key?' he turned and took a key from the rack and handed it to her. 'Is there anything else I can do for you?'

Charlotte was aware he was looking at her, and then she realized she was holding his hand, embarrassed she grabbed the key from his open palm. 'Thank you, there's nothing else.' she managed to stammer. The receptionist nodded politely and started shuffling papers about, trying to look as if he had more important things to attend to.

Charlotte looked at the room number; she climbed the stairs to the third floor. She stared at the door number, then at the key, then back at the door. Her heart was beating with anticipation, with trembling hands she placed the key in the lock and slowly turned it. The door opened, Charlotte stared inside upon a beautiful room. A splendid chandelier hung from the ceiling, dominating the room was a large double bed covered in crisp white linen, piles of lilac, pink and white pillows were stacked at the headboard. On either side were two plain white bedside tables, each with a gold lampstand fitted with a white shade edged with gold trim. A vase of cut roses sat upon a small table near the window. The bathroom had black and white tiled floors; the fixtures were white porcelain with silver taps. Fluffy white towels laid out ready for use, along with beautifully scented soap. A highly polished mirror reflected Charlotte's image, she stared at herself, she looked tired and dirty. She decided to have a bath.

Back in the bedroom, she opened the wardrobe door, and there were her clothes and her shoes. She turned to the chest and opened the drawers; there lay her underwear and knitwear. She sat down in one of the armchairs, completely bewildered. A thought occurred to her, she got up to find her bag, opened it, took out her purse and the Egyptian bank notes she knew where within, looking at them she noticed they were all issued in the present day. Charlotte shook her head in amazement, she felt giddy with excitement. Everything was just brilliant. She walked back to the bathroom as though she were floating on air.

Charlotte decided to do some sightseeing. Karnak Temple was not far away and she thought she could lose herself in there for an hour or so. She walked along the avenue of recumbent rams with their proud curled horns, she admired the enormous columns that towered up to the sky, and thought they were breathtaking. She slowly continued through the ruined temple, awed by the size and beauty of it. Turning a corner, she found herself by a large lake. It was very quiet here, just the breeze whispering through the fronds of the palm trees. A few groups of people were dotted about, but she noticed one man in particular. He was tall with dark brown hair; he had a saturnine face with startling blue eyes and he was staring at her. Charlotte began to feel nervous and scared. She tried to hurry away, but she misjudged a step and fell flat on her face. She felt a hand on her shoulder and a voice asked her if she had hurt herself. Shaken and in pain Charlotte managed to get to her feet, to her dismay she saw the tall man standing beside her.

'That was quite a fall, are you OK? '

Charlotte looked down at her leg a bruise was already starting to form among the ribbons of blood. 'I'm fine, I wasn't looking were

I was going, it's grazed that's all.' She felt quite distressed by the experience and the man's stare was unsettling her.

'Can I take you back to your hotel?' he asked.

'No! No thank you, it's very kind of you to offer, I'm perfectly all right.'

'My name's Jonathan Harrison, I'm staying at the Winter Palace.' he held out his hand to her.

She shook it, 'Charlotte Hambleton, also of the Winter Palace.'

'All the best people stay there. Listen are you sure you're OK, you look very pale.'

'I'm better already, it's more surprise then anything. I wasn't expecting to fall flat on my face.'

'Well, you did it very well, it was really quite something. I was rather hoping for an encore.'

'I'm afraid I'm going to have to disappoint you Mr. Harrison.'

'Jonathan, please, no need to be so formal, we're practically roommates.'

Charlotte smiled at him, feeling her face redden. He was so handsome, why did she have fall over in front of him? It was so undignified.

He was looking at her again with those blue eyes; she felt her legs turning to jelly. Then she realized he had said something and was waiting for her to reply. 'Sorry,' she said, 'I wasn't listening.'

'I could see that, it doesn't exactly do my ego any good, when an attractive lady finds me boring.'

'I really am sorry; I don't think you're boring at all.' Charlotte felt nervous like a teenager, it was amazing the effect a strange man could have on her.

He smiled down at her, 'I was going to do some sight seeing, I have a horse drawn carriage waiting outside, would you like to accompany me?'

Charlotte didn't know what to say, the word came out before she could think about it any longer, 'Yes!'

'Great, well let's go.' He took her by the arm and led her through the temple towards the waiting carriage.

The ride was a wonderful idea. Charlotte found herself mesmerized by the Luxor of 1924. Compared to the modern day it was still unspoiled. There were not nearly as many buildings or cars for that matter. Steamers and feluccas plied up and down the Nile. The ladies looking chic attired in their colorful dresses, with very low waistlines and shorter hem lines to show off their delicate ankles, or not as the case may be. So many fancy and elaborate hats - cloches, and turbans draped or helmeted. Some women had their hair bobbed very short and straight, others had waves and pin curls. In addition, of course, the wonderful shoes with their wide heels and straps. Charlotte thought she ought to buy herself a pair. She wasn't too sure about the dresses though, she wasn't exactly skinny and she felt if she were to wear one she would probably be mistaken for a sack of potatoes. She favoured the style of summer dress worn during the 1940s, she felt they flattered her figure, and she loved floral patterns.

They stopped for lunch and walked down a very narrow side street, packed with shops, selling seemingly everything from fabric to shoes, beans and pulses, to beads and jewellery. The tables fairly groaned under the weight of their merchandise. Charlotte peered through the narrow shop doorways, the interiors though were invariably in deep shadow, but she was sure they were just as packed with goods. Everywhere people were haggling, the noise was so loud she could barely hear herself think. As they walked on the sellers thrust their wears into their faces, excitedly extolling the virtues of their items over their neighbour's inferior items. Charlotte began to feel claustrophobic. Harrison steered her towards a small café, they went inside, where it was mercifully cool and quiet.

A Waiter showed them to a table and as they sat down, they looked at each other and started to laugh. It had been such an enjoyable day; Charlotte realized she was actually very hungry indeed.

'Let me order for you.' said Harrison.

'If you like.' she replied.

'I think you'll like this, it's called Kushari, have you heard of it?'

'No, I haven't.'

'Its rice, spaghetti, macaroni, and vermicelli with fried onions and black lentils all topped with thick tomato sauce, garlic, vinegar and chilli sauce, mixed together in a very artistic way. It's delicious!'

'It sounds interesting, all right then, I'll try it.'

'Good, what about a drink?'

'A soft drink, something cold.'

Harrison gave their order to the waiter, in Arabic. Charlotte was impressed, also a bit embarrassed as she only knew a few very basic words, while it was true that a lot of Egyptians spoke English, she did feel that as a guest in their country she ought to be able to converse with them in their native language.

The drinks arrived, a Turkish coffee for Harrison and a lemon juice with water and sugar served with ice for Charlotte. The waiter served the Kushari; it looked and smelled very appetizing. Charlotte tried a mouthful, she closed her eyes, and savoured the taste, it was absolutely divine.

She looked over at Harrison, who was grinning at her, 'Do you like it?' he asked.

'It tastes wonderful, a very good choice Mr. Harrison.'

'Jonathan.'

'I'm afraid I shall always think of you as Harrison, with or without the Mr.'

He raised a glass of water to her, 'I shall always think of you as Charlotte, but without the Miss.'

'I should hope so, Miss Charlotte makes me sound like the owner of a plantation in the southern part of America.'

'I don't suppose anyone would dare to call you Lottie?'

'No, they wouldn't, and if you want to eat your dessert and not end up wearing it you'll refrain from even thinking about calling me Lottie.'

He held his palms up in supplication, 'I promise to always refer to you as Charlotte, Scout's honour. Now, about dessert…'

Charlotte interrupted him, 'I think this time I'll make the recommendation.'

'All right then, what do you recommend?'

'Mahalabiya.'

'Sounds delicious.'

The dessert duly arrived and they both tucked in.

'Sublime, absolutely sublime.' said Charlotte beaming with contentment, she scooped up another large tasty mouthful of the milky custard topped with nuts and chocolate.

On arrival back at the Winter Palace, Harrison and Charlotte slowly climbed the steps to the terrace. 'I was wondering if you'd like to accompany me to the tomb To-morrow. I have a couple of press passes and well, it would be a shame to waste one.'

Charlotte looked at him, 'How on earth did you manage to get them? I didn't realize you were a journalist.'

'I'm not, I sort of work for Ottomar Hengel, and he's very

influential.'

'Is he not going then?'

'No, it'll upset him too much.'

Charlotte looked a bit taken aback. Harrison laughed and continued, 'He thinks the tomb should be his by rights, he's a very bitter man because the concession was not handed to him. Simply put, he hates Carter, and tries, if possible, to avoid him at all cost.'

'I see, poor man.' said Charlotte. 'From what I've read though I think Howard is doing a very good job. I'm sure Hengel couldn't do any better.'

'Don't let him hear you say that. So, do you want to see the shrines or not?'

'Of course I do! I wouldn't miss this opportunity for the world.'

'I'm glad that's settled.'

Jean Merriman had just finished a cup of tea, and was wondering what had become of her errant husband, Elbert. She noticed Harrison and called out to him. Charlotte turned and saw a distinguished white haired woman. She and Harrison walked over to her table; Jean motioned them to sit down. 'Cup of tea?' she asked. 'Yes please,' answered Charlotte.

'Help yourself to biscuits, what about you Harrison?'

'No I'm fine, thank you.' He helped himself to a biscuit though.

'I was saving these for my husband, but Lord knows where he's got to so you may as well eat them. By the way,' she said, turning to Charlotte, 'I'm Jean Merriman.'

'Charlotte, Charlotte Hambleton.' she said very quietly through a mouthful of biscuit.

'People don't call you Lottie by any chance?'

Harrison choked on his biscuit as he tried to stifle a laugh.

'No,' said Charlotte, 'nobody calls me Lottie.'

'Just as well, it's a terrible diminutive. I remember when I was at school there was a girl there called Lottie; she had a weak bladder and spent most of her days in the toilet. Everyone, including the teachers, called her "Potty Lottie".'

Harrison by now had turned a rather fetching shade of beetroot in his attempts to stifle his mirth. Charlotte glared at him, which only made matters worse.

'Luckily I've never had that trouble.' said Charlotte, with as much dignity as she could muster.

'Here on holiday I suppose, come to see the Tomb?' said Jean.

'Yes, I'm visiting it To-morrow, looking forward to it.'

'Have you met Carter yet?'

'Err, yesss, sort of.' replied Charlotte anxious not to reveal too much of what had happened when she'd met Howard for the first time.

Jean looked at her quizzically and was about to say something when just in the nick of time she was distracted by someone climbing up the stairs.

Charlotte too looked, she saw a distinguished elderly man dressed in white. He waved his walking stick in greeting to his wife and joined her at the table.

'Where have you been,' Jean asked him, 'I've been waiting for over half an hour.'

'I've just seen Maturin, I've invited him to dinner. Hello, who's this?'

'Charlotte, meet my husband, Elbert. You needn't pay any attention to him, I never do.'

'Good day.' he raised his hat and dropped his stick at the same time, 'haven't I seen you before somewhere or other?'

Harrison bent to pick up the stick and bashed his head on the table. The cups, saucers and plates all rose in the air and came crashing down.

'My dear man, are you hurt?' cried Merriman.

'No, just my pride.' said Harrison, rubbing the painful bump on his head.

Now it was Charlotte's turn to laugh, she picked up a napkin to wipe away her tears and smeared honey all over her face.

'What? How on earth?' she spluttered.

'Sorry that was me, I was dipping my biscuits into a dish of honey and I spilt it.' said Jean.

'It suits you.' said Harrison, handing her a clean handkerchief.

'I think I'd better go upstairs and tidy up.' said Charlotte. Saying her goodbyes she left, she could hear Harrison saying his goodbyes as well. She wondered if he would follow her but when she turned around, he was walking away in the opposite direction. She sighed heavily and went to her room.

'I thought we were having tea?' said Elbert, surveying the wreckage in front of him.

'I've already had my tea. You ought to have turned up on time; I've been sat here like a lemon waiting for you to show yourself.

The teapot's still intact you might find some tea left in it.'

'Charming!' He found a cup that wasn't cracked and poured himself a dribble of tea, tasting it, he lamented, 'Ugh, stewed tea.' Perhaps if he dunked a biscuit in it the flavour may improve, looking around all he could see was a broken plate piled with soggy biscuits topped by a damp pink chrysanthemum.

Howard had spent the following days dismantling the numerous sections of the first three shrines. The 14 sections of the outer shrine had been dismantled without mishap, although due to the very confined space there had been some difficulty. Fortunately, no harm had come to them and they were now resting against the walls of the burial chamber, wrapped in cotton wool to protect the fragile gilding and blue faience decoration. They would have to remain in the chamber until the smaller sections of the inner shrines had been dismantled. At the tomb, Howard looked taken aback when Charlotte went over to say hello to him.

'I'm afraid I'm rather busy To-day, the press are visiting as you can see,' he nodded over to a group of waiting men, 'anyway, what are you doing here?'

Very formal thought Charlotte, you wouldn't think we'd spent a night together, well, all right most of it was out in the desert burying a body, even so, he could be a bit friendlier. Maybe he's embarrassed, she thought.

'I'm very well thank you, and yourself?' asked Charlotte.

Howard looked at her, 'I'm happy you are well, I am busy, kindly leave me to my work.'

'Of course, I wouldn't want to get in your way. I'm here to look at the tomb.'

'No, you're not. I told you, To-day is the press visit, and no one else is to be admitted.'

Charlotte waved her pass in his face. He took hold of it, 'Where did you get this from?'

'From me.' answered Harrison, returning the piece of paper to Charlotte.

Howard glared at them and walked towards the tomb's entrance. Charlotte smiled after him; he really was a dear man.

'What are you smiling at?' asked Harrison.

Charlotte sighed, 'Isn't Howard wonderful?'

Harrison looked at her as if she had lost her mind, 'Yeah,

absolutely wonderful.' he replied, rather sarcastically.

At the top of the steps Charlotte hesitated, these were the famous steps discovered in November 1922. Charlotte had visited the tomb in her own time but then they were covered by a wooden ramp and no longer visible. This was her first sight of them and she wanted to savour every moment of her visit. Slowly placing one foot in front of the other, as the steps were narrow and uneven, she descended downwards, counting the sixteen steps as she went.

At the bottom she peered into the antechamber, the original contents had now been removed to be replaced by the roofs of the first and third shrines and the doors of the second shrine, which were propped against the walls. She turned right to look into the burial chamber or as Howard called it the sepulchre, it appeared to be overflowing with scaffolding. Moving nearer, she became aware of how tiny the chamber was and how difficult the work of dismantling the shrines must be. Her admiration for Howard grew even more.

Charlotte could just about see the sides of the first shrine, swathed in cotton wool, propped up against the sidewall of the chamber. Suspended from slings in the air were two of the gleaming gold cornices of the second shrine. The well of the second shrine was still in position, minus its doors of course, Charlotte had already seen them packed up in the antechamber. The sides of the third shrine were visible; they were beautiful, decorated with a series of figures in light relief on gold. Charlotte couldn't see the top of it though as it was covered by scaffolding.

She noticed Howard busy at the far end with a paintbrush and some glutinous substance, fixing the gilding, which had become detached in places. Some parts of the pall, still on the rack, enveloped in linen wrappings, stood beside the shrine.

It was obvious Howard was busy and had no intention of talking to her, or indeed anybody. Feeling disappointed she followed Harrison out of the hot, stuffy tomb and into the hot, sweltering desert.

Later that evening Charlotte made her way to Howard's house. She found him in his study; sat at his desk busily writing.

'Hello,' she said, 'I'm back. I thought we could go for a walk.'

Howard, peering at her over his glasses, said gruffly, 'I'm afraid I'm rather busy, there's nothing to stop you going for a walk alone.'

'That wouldn't be any fun. Come on; don't be so grumpy, it's too lovely an evening to be stuck inside.'

Sighing, Howard put down his pen and removed his glasses. 'Is there any chance you'll go away?'

'No!' Charlotte sat down and looked around the room. There were books everywhere, mostly about Egypt; some were biographies, and some pertained to historical events. 'Have you read all of these?' she asked, waving her hand in the direction of a bookshelf.

'Of course I have, they're not here to decorate the room.'

'It's a wonder you found the time, what with finding all those tombs and digging everything up. Don't you ever go anywhere?'

'What exactly do you mean by "anywhere"?'

'Well, like the theatre, cinema, museum, that sort of "anywhere".'

'As a matter of fact I do, I lead a busy life, socially as well as professionally.'

Changing the subject Charlotte asked, 'Tell me about Ottomar Hengel?'

'He's an archeologist; he's worked in Egypt for many seasons. He collects antiquities, the rarer the better. Hengel is an opportunist; he's also sly and conniving.'

'So, he's not a friend of yours than?'

Howard gave her a look of disdain. 'Hardly, I loathe the man. He's an arrogant fool.'

'I hear he says the same of you.' said Charlotte sweetly.

Howard glared at her.

'He sounds very creepy.' she said, 'just the sort of man who would commit a murder, don't you think?'

'Quite probably.' Howard stared into the distance, thinking. 'You think he murdered the man we found?'

Charlotte tapped her fingers on the arm of the chair, thinking. 'I'm not sure,' suddenly she had a thought; 'do you know a man called Stanley Matula?'

'As a matter of fact I recently made his acquaintance.'

'Brilliant! You can introduce me to him.'

'Why?'

'Because I think he has some inside knowledge about Hengel.'

'What makes you think that?'

'The letter in the book, accept the book doesn't belong here, not yet anyway. Nevertheless, it will and Mr. Matula knows something. Trust me.'

'I feel a headache coming on,' said Howard, 'you mentioned something along those lines before, as I recall it was "what are you doing here, you shouldn't be here now."'

'Err, yes, pay no attention to me, I'm finding it all a bit confusing. I'll try and explain one day, maybe.'

Howard started at her, sighing, 'I wish I'd gone to Greece.' he said.

Outside the house Charlotte looked longingly at the car, 'Can't we go for a drive? I've more or less got the hang of the controls?'

'I've only just had the car fixed, I'd rather like to keep it one piece, if you don't mind.' replied Howard.

'Pity, I did enjoy our last trip.'

He looked at her, and shook his head, 'When I'm with you I'm rather of the opinion it's safer to walk.'

Therefore, they walked. They climbed up into the cliffs that looked down on orange sand and ancient ruins. In this wilderness, time was neither present nor past. They walked in companionable silence, each buried deeply in their own thoughts. Charlotte still felt as though she was dreaming, yet the man next to her was real. She could hear him breathing, smell the faint aroma of cigarette smoke from his clothes, the scent of his aftershave. Charlotte wanted to stay in this time for the rest of her life; she didn't want to go back or should that be forward, to the future and her life there, not now. She had always felt out of place in the modern era, felt as though she had never quite fitted in, here though, she felt at home.

Howard regarded Charlotte as rather a strange person; he had never met a female quite like her. He wasn't sure why he had gone along with her suggestion to bury the body, and why he was out here now. Perhaps it was because she had brought excitement into his life. He actually quite liked her, he had been surprised when she had turned up at the tomb earlier that day. He had wanted to talk to her, but she was with Harrison and he decided to keep himself to himself. Howard would certainly never admit it to Charlotte, but he had been delighted when she had turned up unannounced at his door.

CHAPTER NINE

Sitting in his luxurious hotel suite Ottomar Hengel was feeling very pleased with himself. He stretched his long legs and stood up, he was very tall and slender, with piercing pale blue eyes, his pale blonde hair cut very short. It's true that his onetime associate, Leo Barnaby, had tried to double cross him, but that minor matter had been taken care of. It was just a pity that Howard Carter had not been implicated in the man's death as he had hoped.

That interfering girl was another matter. He had made enquiries and found out barely anything about her. He knew she had helped Carter to dispose of the body; he had a feeling that she may prove meddlesome. Well, if she crossed him again.... He smiled to himself, a very cruel smile indeed.

Hengel thought about his plans, he knew he could easily dupe the Antiquities Service and the Government. Flattery and money always helped, of course. In addition, Carter had made it easy for him. In the tomb of Ramses XI, used by Carter's team as the lunch tomb, one of Hengel's undercover workers who was masquerading as one of Howard's assistants, had found a Fortnum and Mason box. When opened the box was found to contain a small wooden sculpture of a young boy emerging from a lotus flower. As far as could be ascertained this exquisite object had not been registered. Hengel thought of the delightful possibilities this find would give him to get rid of Carter.

This little sculpture would give Hengel the advantage he needed; he would use his considerable guile and charm to convince the authorities of Carter's ill-suitable nature to continue work at the tomb. Once he had laid the seeds of doubt, it would be an easy task to put forward his own impeccable credentials. The Antiquities Service and the government representatives would hand the tomb over to him. Then he would have the pick of any desirable object that caught his eye.

He would have to be subtle of course; smaller objects would be easier to smuggle out, slighter larger objects could be copied and the originals kept by him in his museum, those fools at the Cairo Museum wouldn't even notice they were looking at replicas.

Life, so far, had been very good to Ottomar Hengel and he wasn't going to let anything or anyone spoil it. There was a knock at the door and Bauer went to answer it. Hengel heard the voice of Stanley Matula and hoped he hadn't brought that old fool Merriman with him. Matula entered the main room, mercifully alone. The room was light and airy, the doors to the balcony opened out to a view of the mighty Nile. Matula couldn't help but be impressed, his own room was very modest with a tiny balcony, in between his hotel and the building opposite was a narrow road congested with people and horse-drawn carriages.

'Sit down Matula, I will not offer you a drink as you will not be staying.' said Hengel.

Matula sat; he mopped his brow and then ran a finger between his neck and collar. 'I did everything you told me to do,' he whined, 'how was I to know that the girl would turn up at Carter's house?'

'It is your business to know, that is why I pay you. I do not forgive those that fail me.'

'Please, I'm sure I can rectify the situation,' Matula stammered, 'just give me a chance.'

'Ha, you have already had your chance and bungled it.'

'What will happen now?' Matula asked, nervously, 'I mean to me.'

'I am not decided yet.' Hengel stared at the little man, he was covered in sweat, the smell of fear radiating from every pore. This pleased Hengel, he liked it when people were scared, and he loved the power he had over them. 'Get out of my sight,' he spat and turned away.

Bauer materialized as if from nowhere and showed the frightened man out. When Bauer returned Hengel turned to him, 'You know what to do?' The valet bowed his head and disappeared once more.

Matula fled from the suite, as he reached the top of the stairs, he turned to make sure no one was following. In his haste, he missed the first step and tumbled all the way to the bottom landing in front of a pair of dusty shoes. 'Ah, there you are Matuman, just in time for a drink.' exclaimed the dulcet voice of Elbert Merriman.

Picking himself up, he followed Merriman to the bar.

'Sit down, goodness what have been doing?' said Merriman.

'I lost my footing, I guess I wasn't paying attention.' replied Matula, suddenly feeling a twinge of pain from his right ankle.

'Were you in a hurry? I usually find in those circumstances a lift is very useful, throwing yourself down the stairs is a bit extreme, don't you think?'

'I don't think there is a lift here.'

'Ah, there you have it, next time you ought to be more cautious. Now, where are our drinks?'

'Err, you haven't ordered yet.'

'Upon my soul, where is that waiter?' Looking around vaguely Merriman called out, 'I say two whiskies over here.'

'Make it a double.' said Matula, looking wearily around.

'Make them doubles.' shouted Merriman. 'You don't look well, a touch of the sun probably.'

The drinks arrived. Matula gulped his in one go. Merriman regarded him suspiciously, 'You're not about to keel over are you?'

'I feel a bit light headed; I think I'll step outside.'

'I can't say I'm surprised, you do seem to lead an active life. I'll stay here in the shade, if you don't mind, at my time of life I try to stay inside as much as possible, only Mrs. Merriman doesn't approve. She insists the sun is good for me, drags me around in it for an hour or so and when I've turned a shade resembling that of a boiled lobster allows me back inside.'

'I know what you mean,' said Matula, edging away, 'I'll try and keep in the shade, maybe I'll see you at dinner?'

'Quite probably, dear boy, I'm always here, except of course, when I'm out.'

'Yes…' Matula managed to hobble his way outside; breathing a sigh of relief, he made his way back to his hotel.

Charlotte observed the dusty and rumpled figure as he made his way down the street, she wondered why his hat looked like it had been sat upon. He looked like he was trying to hurry but a rather pronounced limp was preventing this strategy allowing her to easily catch up with him.

'Mr. Matula,' she called, this seemingly innocuous phrase had rather a profound effect on the little man. He turned to face her, clasping a hand across his heart and looking as if his last breath was about to be exhaled. Upon seeing it was she, a look of repose settled upon his face, 'Oh, Miss Hambleton, you scared me.'

'I'm so sorry, Mr. Matula, I hadn't intended to scare you. I was only trying to attract your attention. May we sit over there in that café?'

'Yes, of course.' Taking her by the arm he hobbled her across the road to the small café, he took her inside and finding a table right at the back, they settled themselves in the not very comfortable seats.

Matula asked for Turkish coffee and Charlotte opted for lemonade. The waiter returned with the drinks and snacks and discreetly left.

'What is it you want, Miss Hambleton?'

'Please call me Charlotte. It's about the body found by me and Mr. Carter; I think you may know something about it.'

Matula slowly sipped his coffee, 'I'm afraid I can't help you.'

'I think Hengel is involved in some way, I'm trying to find a way to prove that. Don't ask me how I know, but I know that you're somehow involved. You seem like a decent person, I'm asking you to help.'

'Miss Hambleton, Charlotte, it's not that I don't want to help, I can't. That body found in Carter's house, do you know who he was?'

'I know his name was Leo Barnaby, that he worked for Hengel and he wanted to tell Carter something important.'

'Exactly, and looked what happened to him. Now you may not realize this but I also work for Hengel, not willingly I hasten to add. Hengel has certain information about me and he will tell the police if I don't co-operate. So you see I have no choice.'

'Did you kill Barnaby?' asked Charlotte, she felt horrified that this seemingly jolly and polite man could be capable of murder.

'Rest assured I did not kill him. My job was to arrange to have the body placed in Carter's house, call the police with a cock and bull story about a fight and a gunshot, they were then supposed to arrest him. They turned up to an empty house, no Carter and no body.'

'So what will happen now?'

'I expect Hengel is at this very minute plotting my demise, whether he blames you or Carter for my death I have no idea. One way or another my days are numbered.'

'Can't you get away? What about the embassy, surely they must be able to help?'

'No, he's a very powerful man and a very rich one. It doesn't matter where I go he'll find me eventually.'

'I'm so sorry.'

'That's very kind of you, Charlotte, but don't be. It's my own fault, but if you take my advice, you and Carter should leave well alone. Don't cross Hengel, he's a very dangerous man. Go back to England and forget about this.' He stood up, threw some change on to the table and hobbled out without a backward glance.

CHAPTER TEN

Charlotte decided to go for a walk, she wanted to think and she always found walking alone very helpful. Wanting peace and quiet she boarded the ferry and crossed the Nile to the west bank. Seeing all the donkeys for hire, she thought she would like to hire one for the afternoon. As soon as she approached, a crowd of boys engulfed her, all shouting that their donkeys were the best. Charlotte didn't know which way to turn, a hand grabbed her arm, it belonged to a scrawny looking boy who appeared to have a tea towel wrapped around his head, and she could swear the words "Winter Palace" were just visible.

'My name is Jabari, I have very good donkey, very quiet, just right for lady like you.'

He led her over to a donkey whose coat was a sort of brown/white/grey colour. The donkey looked at her with a complete lack of interest. 'Well, she looks very quiet', said Charlotte.

Jabari held out his hand and money was exchanged.

Charlotte climbed aboard, 'What's the donkey's name?' she asked.

'Suzy.' replied Jabari. 'You will be safe with her, Suzy will look after you.'

Charlotte nodded her head and steered Suzy towards the cliffs that towered above the Valley of the Kings. Suzy had beautiful intelligent eyes, and Charlotte had already fallen in love with her. They wondered through the cultivations and on into the desert. The very few people were around, mostly ignored her, although some children ran after her shouting for baksheesh, she gave them some coins and they disappeared.

Suzy meandered along the path; it was obvious to the donkey that her present rider had no idea where she was going, so Suzy decided to walk to her favourite spot, it was lovely and cool there, with bushes and bits of grass to munch. Normally Suzy tried to get rid of her 'passengers', she found them to be very annoying, always shouting at her to hurry up, she also hated it when the people were fat and sweaty, she usually got rid of them straight away and if she was lucky they would choose one of her friends instead. The one she was carrying now was quiet enough, yes, a trip to the cave, a little snack and perhaps a snooze. Happy with these thoughts she picked up her pace.

Charlotte was thinking about Hengel, she needed to find out what he was up to. Stanley Matula wouldn't help her. Despite his fears of being murdered, she knew he would live until 1960, but maybe history was in flux, which meant that anything was possible. She was far too scared of Hengel to confront him directly; she had heard so much about him, according to Jean Merriman, a sense of evil radiated all around him. She shivered, cold icy fingers walked up her spine. Shaking herself out of her reverie, it suddenly dawned on her that she had no idea where she was going. She only hoped Suzy knew her way back.

Charlotte could hear men's voices coming from around the corner of the cliff face. They appeared to be shouting at each other, then she noticed the carriage, her heart stopped, it must belong to Ottomar Hengel, she remembered Elbert Merriman joking about Hengel and his carriage. For a moment she panicked, she tried to turn Suzy around, but the donkey stubbornly continued to walk forward. She dismounted, nearly falling flat on her face as she did so; she stood in front of Suzy and held out her hand, the donkey stopped in her tracks. Suzy opened her mouth to bray her annoyance but before she could utter a sound, a hand wrapped itself around her jaws. She was so taken aback at this effrontery; she kicked Charlotte in the shin. The pain shot through Charlotte's leg and she just managed to stifle a scream. Shushing Suzie Charlotte moved back a few feet to assess the situation.

Suzy was not happy, she bit Charlotte on the bottom, and Charlotte said in a shouty whisper, 'Will you stop that, if they hear us we're doomed, keep quiet and follow me.' If a donkey could shrug its shoulders than this one certainly would, humans Suzy thought, they're all daft. Suzy was accustomed to being shouted at in Arabic, but she was a clever donkey and she also understood English, so she decided to go along with these shenanigans - this was turning into quite an exciting day.

Suzy followed the girl to the corner of a boulder. Charlotte peered around it, not a soul was in sight, which meant the men must be in the cave. Keeping close to the rock face she crept towards the entrance, there was still no sound. Cautiously she peered inside; there were torches hanging from the walls. She still couldn't see anyone; it must be a very deep cave. Stealing her courage, she slowly walked inside. Despite the torch light, the air inside the cave felt chilly, or maybe that was her fear. The air smelt musty and there was something else, a very pungent, eye-watering smell. Continuing forward she heard a noise and something whacked her in the face; she cried out in alarm and immediately covered her mouth. She heard footsteps echoing towards her, damn it. There was nowhere to hide. She turned and ran as fast as she could veering left at the entrance, she hid behind a large rock. A man came running out; he turned right and suddenly disappeared from view.

Suzy, after her snack, had lain down for a rest. Here she was minding her own business, dreaming her little dreams, when some oaf tripped over and fell on top of her. The man swore at her and scrambled to his feet. Suzy, indignant at this rude interruption, gave a loud 'Hee-haw', turned and kicked the man as hard as she could. The man flew into the air and landed on the rocky ground with a thump he then rolled down a steep hill and disappeared from sight, his cries growing fainter every second.

Charlotte had never seen anything like it. Suzy went across to inspect the cave entrance; more men were coming out to see what all the commotion was about, seeing them approach her Suzy lowered her head and butted the first unfortunate man, he stumbled backward and those behind him went down like bowling pins. Suzy's shrill 'Hee-haw' echoed angrily through the cave, she pawed her front hoof across the ground and charged. Charlotte heard an almighty crash; the sound of objects scattering and bouncing across the floor reached her ears. This woke the bats, not wanting to be left out, they started flying and crashing into those unfortunate souls still inside. Screams and curses reverberated around the cave's rocky walls. Judging this was probably a prudent time to retreat, Charlotte went in search of Suzy.

Suzy was having a very good day indeed; she had taken the opportunity to tread upon the waving appendages of the fallen men, and had bitten some of them for good measure. Once the bats started flapping about, she thought it was time to leave; she ambled outside and ate a well-deserved snack. To-day had definitely been a very productive day. Suzy decided she liked her new friend very much, and wondered if there would be other days like this. Charlotte, ignoring the pain of her bruised shin, spotted Suzy and climbed into the saddle, before she could say anything Suzy was off like a bullet, she hadn't had so much fun in ages.

The bats and the dust began to settle revealing the carnage of the broken pottery, battered statues and scattered jewels. Wooden crates lay strewn about, straw and broken lids littered the floor of the cave. Hengel, blood streaming down his face from lacerations caused by the bats, staggered to his feet and bellowed, 'Bauer, where the hell are you?' No answer was forthcoming, 'Bauer, if you are not here in five seconds I will shoot you.'

One of the workers stumbled forward and in a stammering voice said, 'Herr Hengel, he, Herr Bauer I mean, he's gone sir.'

'Gone, what do you mean gone, gone where?' shouted Hengel, the bats, who had only just settled themselves back to sleep, began to stir ominously.

The frightened man replied, 'I, I, don't know, I saw him flying through the air, and then he was gone, sir.'

Hengel shoved the man out of the way, 'I'm surrounded by incompetents, find me Bauer, and clear up this mess.'

The bats had had enough, they erupted around the cave squeaking and banging into each other and any poor soul who happened to be in their way. Men ran for their lives, unfortunately for Hengel he was standing in their way and in their panic they ran into him, he fell flat on his face and they all fell on top of him, the bats dived into the heap of bodies.

Crawling painfully outside, Hengel was dazed and could barely walk in a straight line. He shouted orders at the men to secure the treasure and move it to the new site; it was then he noticed a strange battered figure crawling towards him. 'Bauer, is that you? Gott im himmel what has happened to you?'

Bauer, arms outstretched, cried, 'Help me, save me.' before collapsing in a heap.

Hengel went over to the stricken man, he shouted orders and two of the workers came forward, they picked up the dirty, stunned man and threw him into the waiting carriage. Climbing in after him, Hengel yelled at the driver to take them back to the hotel. What a day, he was covered in blood, dust and bat droppings. When he found out whom was responsible for to-day's events there life wouldn't be worth living.

Suzy had now slowed down and was reluctantly walking slowly along the track, she didn't want to go back home. Charlotte wanted to go to Howard's house; but she had no idea where it was in relation to where she was now. She sighed, 'Oh, Suzy, if only you could understand me. I want to go to Howard Carter's house, can you take me there?'

Charlotte tried again, 'You might know him, he's English, he usually wears a homburg hat and carries a walking stick.' Suzy pricked up her ears; she knew the grumpy English man, she had passed his house many times. She thought for a second, then turning right she trotted off down the dirt road.

Charlotte wasn't sure if this was the right way, but Suzy seemed to know where she was going so she decided to place her trust in the donkey's navigational skills. After a bit, appearing in the sunlight atop its hill Charlotte saw Howard's house, Suzy picked up her pace hoping there may be some carrots or hay waiting for her upon arrival.

Leaving Suzy next to the car, Charlotte barged her way into Howard's study, 'I've found a cave full of treasure, boxes and boxes, I'm not exactly sure where it is though, I think it may be somewhere over there.' she cried out, knocking over another vase as she gesticulated wildly, fortunately this one was empty.

Howard lowered his glasses, 'Good afternoon, Miss Hambleton, nice of you to drop in.' he said, eyeing the broken vase.

'Sorry about that, I had to come and tell you straight away. You should see it, I have no idea where it comes from, but it's all hidden away in this cave. Hengel and his men were there, I've no idea what they're up to, but it's obviously nothing legal.'

'Yes, do you think you could start at the beginning, that way I may be able to grasp what you're trying to tell me.'

Sighing and collapsing into a chair Charlotte tried to compose herself, 'It all started with Suzy, she's the one who found the cave. When I looked inside, I saw Hengel and his men, they were shifting crates.'

'How do you know they contained treasure?'

'Well, there was a small contretemps involving Suzy, bats and lots of dust, the crates got dropped and broke open and the treasure spilled out.'

'I know I'm going to regret asking this, but who is Suzy?'

'She's a donkey I hired for the day, she's very clever, she literally beat everyone up, flung one man up into space, and kicked the rest of them into semi-consciousness. She's absolutely wonderful!'

'She sounds a bit too violent for my liking.'

'No, no, it's only because some idiot tripped over her and she got annoyed, she's very gentle I can assure you.'

'Where is this paragon of virtue now?' asked Howard.

Charlotte looked round in a shifty manner.

'She's here, isn't she?'

'Yes, but I promise you she's very sweet natured, she won't hurt anyone, or damage anything, I promise.'

Howard wasn't convinced, but decided not to think about that for the moment.

'I'll take your word for that. There was no indication where this treasure came from?'

'Err, I have no idea, it's just treasure, admittedly some of it is a bit broken now, it's possible it's from a tomb. Suzy knows where the cave is; we could go back and take another look.'

'Hengel's probably moved it by now.' Howard thought for a minute, 'On the other hand, maybe not. Very well, we'll take a look.'

'Brilliant, this is so exciting!'

'It won't be so exciting if we bump into Hengel.'

'I think he may be in hospital, he did get a bit battered, especially by the bats.'

Howard opened his mouth to say something, thought better of it and changed his shoes instead.

Outside, Suzy was disappointed that no carrots or hay had been forthcoming; she had had a drink of water and chewed one of the car seats while she waited expectantly. The girl came out of the house followed by the grumpy man; he disappeared around the other side of the house. Charlotte walked over to Suzy and gave her a hug and a kiss on the nose. The donkey snuffled her ear and gave a contented 'Hee-haw', a very quiet one. Charlotte noticed the eaten seat, 'Oh Suzy, I promised Howard you'd be good. May be he won't notice it. We're going back to the cave; we need you to take us there.' Charlotte looked into Suzy's beautiful brown eyes, 'Do you understand?' Suzy brayed affectionately. Howard arrived upon his donkey, whose name was Amherst, with Suzy leading the way the little party started for the cave.

Meanwhile, Hengel had taken the semi-conscious Bauer to hospital. Doctor Shafie reported that Bauer's injuries consisted of four broken ribs, a fractured left femur, a broken right arm, fractured wrists and concussion. Looking at Hengel, he asked, 'Has there been a battle? I confess I was not aware of any discord taking place to-day, a play maybe, or one of your reenactments perhaps?'

Hengel gave him a cold stare, 'No, Doctor Shafie, no battle took place, just, how shall I say, a slight accident.'

Shafie raised his eyebrows, but decided against further comment. 'Mr. Hengel, Nurse Magdy will look after your injuries, they are mostly scratches and you will have some bruising, particularly around the eyes. The good news is that you have no broken bones. After treatment, you will be free to leave.'

'And Bauer, how long will he be kept here?'

'It is difficult to say, I will of course keep you up to date with his progress.'

'Thank you, Doctor Shafie, I appreciate that.'

Arriving back at the hotel Hengel ignored the stares of his fellow guests. Seeing himself in the mirror, he wasn't surprised by their curiosity. His white suit was grey with dust; the streaks of blood added an additional touch of colour. As for the state of his face, well he couldn't do anything about that. Cursing under his breath he was about to call for Bauer to run him a bath, 'Damn him, damn them all, it appears I have to do everything myself. Incompetent fools.'

Downstairs in the lobby Merriman emerged from behind his newspaper, 'I say, Jean did you see Hengel? He looks as if he's been in a fight.'

'Can't say I'm sorry, wonder what happened to the other chap?'

'There's a very large bandage covering his head, blood everywhere, plus he had a black eye.'

'Humph, wretched man deserves everything he gets as far as I'm concerned. Pity somebody hasn't bumped him off yet.'

'I'm sure it's only a matter of time. What a shame I missed it. I wonder who it was; you don't think it was Carter?'

'Highly unlikely, I'm sure Carter would just shout and insult him, can't see him getting physical with a man like Hengel... No, it's probably some poor suffering native, or even that valet of his, honestly the way he talks to his staff it's a wonder any of them stay.'

'Dear, oh dear, all this excitement, I think I need a drink. Waiter, a large brandy please.'

Jean countered that with 'Make that two large brandies.' The waiter nodded in acknowledgement.

'I say,' complained Merriman, 'that's not like you.'

'I'm celebrating.' Jean replied happily.

Back in the desert, Howard and Charlotte had arrived at the cave. Everything was quiet, even the bats had gone. Leaving the donkeys outside, they entered the vast interior, the torches barely penetrating the darkness. It was as if nothing had happened. The tidying up had been very thorough, nothing was left, not a crate nor a piece of broken pottery.

'We're too late, they've moved everything, even the broken bits.' said Charlotte.

'It's hardly surprising, after what happened they would be very foolish indeed to leave everything here. If you hadn't blundered in we could have recovered the treasure.' said Howard sourly. Suddenly he realized what Charlotte had said, 'What do you mean by "broken bits"?' he exclaimed.

'I'm sure some pieces are still intact.' Charlotte replied, and then quickly changing the subject, she said indignantly, 'Pardon me, if it hadn't been for us you'd be none the wiser there was even a cave here. All right, the treasure's gone, but at least we know Hengel hasn't spirited it out of the country. He can't have moved it far, I'm sure we'll find it again.'

'We?'

'Yes we, I mean us, me and Suzy. Actually, it was more Suzy than me so you ought to thank her.'

Howard replied incredulously, 'Thank her, that donkey did heaven knows how much damage. Broken bits indeed, those artifacts are quite probably thousands of years old, they've survived burial and robbery, the Ancient Egyptians never in their wildest dreams thought that those precious artefacts would encounter a marauding donkey, or I'm sure they would have made contingency plans. And don't think I didn't notice she chewed my car seat.'

'There's no need to get so worked up. You should be happy, I didn't notice you discovering lost treasure, and I'm sure we'll find them again, maybe even more. On a happier note, most of Hengel's men were pretty battered, so at least they'll be recognizable, just look for men covered in bruises and bandages.'

'Very funny, well, there's nothing we can do here now,' said Howard.

'Are you going to tell the authorities?'

'Tell them what? I have no proof, what do I tell them, "a mad donkey and his companion found some treasure, but now it's disappeared" they'll think I'm mad.'

'Suzy is a she, not a he, and despite your insults I'm sure she won't hold a grudge against you.' Charlotte turned to look at Suzy, who was eyeing Howard in a very unfriendly way.

'See that look on her face, she likes you.' said Charlotte.

Howard who was well aware of the donkey's malevolent stare, backed away slowly towards Amherst, who was standing placidly by a rock, and enjoying the little scene playing out in front of him. Therefore, he was a bit disappointed when his owner climbed aboard and steered him towards home.

Suzy took the opportunity to bite Howard's leg as he passed her, Howard yelped. Before Charlotte could say anything, Suzy was off, Amherst trotting behind in her dust, while Howard muttered dark curses under his breath. As they trotted along the track Howard found himself thinking about what had happened these last few days, he had been busy at work in the tomb, which took up a good deal of his time, but since Charlotte had appeared in his life he found he liked being in her company. Even that crazy donkey and her antics made him smile because they reminded him of a beloved donkey he had once owned. The donkey, named San Toy, used to wander through the house trying to find Howard, as soon as San Toy found him the donkey would bray with delight. Sadly, in the summer of 1902, a cobra bit San Toy in the mouth and Howard's cherished donkey had died three hours later.

A few days had passed since the discovery of the cave, and, this time, with Howard's blessing, Charlotte visited the tomb once more. Howard was about to embark on the dismantling of the third shrine, the roof having already been removed a few days earlier. Aided by his assistant and members of his staff good progress was made. The fourth golden shrine was now revealed, elaborately inscribed with texts probably taken from the Book of the Gates. A bundle of staves discovered between the walls of the shrines came as something of a surprise to Howard and his colleagues, as they had not expected further discoveries of this nature.

The complete dismantling of the third shrine took place the following day. Now only the fourth shrine remained. Howard explained to Charlotte that the shrines had been put together in a very careless manner, many of the joints were not properly closed and a number of hammer marks were apparent where the sections had been forced together.

A cold and windy Saturday dawned, Howard was busy all morning ensconced in his house with his lawyer who had arrived, unexpectedly, from Alexandria. Charlotte gathered it was something to do with the long-drawn out negotiations between the Egyptian Government and the excavators regarding the conditions of control of the tomb. Howard was back at the tomb in the afternoon, the lid of the fourth shrine was raised revealing the lid of the sarcophagus.

By Sunday the weather had turned wild, the excavators were busy inside the tomb dismantling the fourth shrine, while outside a high wind swept through the Valley of the Kings, raising clouds of dust. The revealing of the sarcophagus was, for Howard, especially poignant. After long years of excavation, during which he had unearthed many interesting and important tombs, it had never before been granted to him, or indeed any other excavator in recorded Egyptian history, to look upon the unviolated sarcophagus of one of Egypt's kings. Howard would later write.

As our light fell on the noble quartzite monument, it illumined, in repeated detail, that last solemn appeal to gods and men, and made us feel that, in the young king's case, a dignity had been added even to death. With the profound silence that reigned the emotion deepened, the past and present seemed to meet – time to stand and wait, and one asked oneself, was it not yesterday that, with pomp and ceremony, they had laid the young king in that casket? – So fresh, so seemingly recent, were those touching claims on our pity that the more we gazed on them the more the illusion gathered strength. It made one wish that his journey through those grim tunnels of the Underworld might be unperturbed until he attained complete felicity! – As those four goddesses, sculptured in high relief at the corners, seemed to plead as they shielded their charge. For in them had we not a perfect Egyptian elegy in stone?

The great pink sarcophagus now stood majestically in the centre of the burial chamber, a magnificent piece of workmanship. Within lay the secret of old, how were the Pharaohs laid in their graves?

That night the wind continued to howl through the Valley and through Luxor itself, whipping up the brown Nile into angry waves.

On the following day, Howard had invited some of his colleagues to view the sarcophagus and Charlotte had permission to accompany them. The burial chamber was strewn with mallets, wedges and planks; it looked like a carpenter's shop. The doors of the fourth shrine had already been placed in boxes and were now in the antechamber awaiting removal to the laboratory, some sections from each of the four shrines remained in the burial chamber making the space between the walls and sarcophagus ever narrower. The roof of the fourth shrine hung suspended by overhead winches above the sarcophagus. The men were discussing the problem of how to raise the lid, they had discovered that the lid was not made of the same crystalline sandstone as the sarcophagus, instead it was carved from granite, and it was cracked in half. The crack had been filled with plaster and painted over to match the rose-coloured crystalline sandstone of the body.

Looking at the sarcophagus Charlotte was struck by the simplicity of the decorations. Three broad bands of inscriptions ran the whole length of the lid. Four protective goddesses carved in bold relief encircled the sarcophagus with their widespread wings. There was no elaborate decoration to distract attention from the exquisite modelling of these figures. There was also a narrow frieze covered with religious texts, while towards the base of the sarcophagus there was a dado whereon a series of symbols represented strength and support.

The wind was still blustery and the days were still very cold. The Valley was swarming with visitors, every day more visitors arrived in Luxor by train and by the Nile steamers. It was the height of the tourist season, approximately two hundred sightseers had crossed the Nile the previous day and more than three hundred had arrived this morning. Howard was still ensconced in the burial chamber, copying out the bands of hieroglyphics on the lid of the sarcophagus. Five boxes containing the cornices and the two doors of the fourth shrine were dispatched to the laboratory.

The workmen who had put the shrines together had made a very shoddy job of it, sections had been forced into position upside down, and there were hammer marks on the gesso and orientation marks scratched on the gilding. Then of course, there was the cracked lid, another instance of carelessness, thought Charlotte. That evening Howard left for Cairo, he would be absent for some days.

While Howard was in Cairo procuring tackle for the raising of the lid and arranging the details of the opening ceremony with the Egyptian Government, the tomb remained closed. Howard's colleagues were busy in the laboratory restoring and cleaning the second of the life sized statues of the king from the antechamber.

The day after Howard returned to Luxor, Charlotte visited the tomb again. Outside Howard's workmen were taking down coils of rope for use with the different pulleys with which the lid was to be hoisted up. In the course of the morning a great flat-packing case, borne by four perspiring men, arrived, containing a sheet of stout glass cut exactly to the measurements of the sarcophagus. After the lid was raised, the glass would be laid over the coffin to allow visitors to gaze into the casket, and protect the contents damage.

Howard and his assistants spent the morning shifting the roof of the fourth shrine, which was suspended from slings above the sarcophagus, to the antechamber, where it would be packed up and stacked with the roof sections of the other shrines, which were awaiting removal.

Rumours were floating about that a certain disagreement had arisen between Howard and the Egyptian Government. Apparently, due to Howard's American lecture engagements, he intended to leave Egypt at the end of February and resume work next winter. However, in view of the fact that the digging season usually ended at the beginning of May the Egyptian Government was thinking of transferring the tomb to the custody of the Antiquities Department.

Howard spent a strenuous day supervising the sawing of planks, cutting lengths of rope, and other humdrum jobs necessitated by the erection of the scaffolding all around the sarcophagus and placing in position pulleys to raise the lid, before he took a very brief lunch break.

Starting at 8.45 this morning, when Howard's assistants opened the tomb, it had become the scene of the greatest activity. The existing scaffolding used for the dismantling of the shrine had to be removed and the new scaffolding to take the tackle for the raising of the lid of the sarcophagus, as well as to provide a platform for the excavators to stand on, erected. The scaffolding, which had been made in sections in the carpenter's shop, was carried into the tomb, which throughout the morning and afternoon resounded with the ring of hammers, the whine of the saw, and the clink of chisels, on the stone lid of the sarcophagus.

Two carpenters were kept busy all day sawing up planks or cutting little wedges, and at one moment great lengths of hempen cable were brought out into the sunshine and cut off into lengths for use with different pulleys for raising the lid.

Howard was determined to make sure that everything was in working order for the official opening, to which leading Egyptologists and Egyptian Government officials had been invited, at 3 o'clock To-morrow afternoon. He ordered his men to test the pulleys. Slowly, almost imperceptibly, the massive lid, which had not been moved for over three thousand years, left its sockets. Then he abruptly ordered a stop. The lid, which had been lifted about one inch, was lowered downwards once more.

Howard worked in the tomb later than he had ever done before. It was past five o'clock and the daylight was already fading from the Valley of the Kings when the tomb was finally closed. As Howard left, he gave a last lingering look, he felt happier than he had for a long time past, assured that To-morrow all would work according to plan. He journeyed home through the sunset to his house on the edge of the Royal Necropolis. The day's work had been most successful.

At home, he sat in his favourite chair, cradling a glass of whisky, a cigarette smoking in the ashtray next to him. To morrow would be the day when Tutankhamen would give up the secret guarded for over thirty centuries. Howard was confident that his hopes, which so far, had been so splendidly upheld by the bewildering series of magnificent treasures he had successfully discovered since that day, more than fourteen months ago, when he had first entered the tomb, would not be deceived by the contents of the sarcophagus.

The day of the opening ceremony had arrived. Howard opened the tomb at 10.15 that morning. Shortly afterwards, the police guard above the tomb stood to attention as the Under-Secretary of State for Public Works accompanied by the Provincial Governor arrived, and at Howard's invitation, entered the tomb and inspected the sarcophagus and the gear ready for this afternoon. Afterwards they paid a visit to the laboratory.

There was great disappointment though amongst the several distinguished Egyptologists and archaeologists who had been invited to be present to attend the opening of the sarcophagus at the Government's decision to keep the operation strictly private. A statement issued by the Under-Secretary for Public Works stated that:

"For To-day the only persons who will be admitted to the tomb will be myself, M. Boivin (Director-General of the Government Antiquities Service), the Chief Inspector of Antiquities for Upper Egypt, two sub-inspectors, the Governor of the province, Mr. Howard Carter and his staff."

This resulted in the humiliation of the eminent would-be spectators, who had been kept waiting, much to their consternation, in the terrible heat after having been asked to come. One or two world-famous explorers found themselves the temporary victims of this decision.

The expectant crowd had also been disappointed by this

decision and the bulk of them had decided to go elsewhere. Seemingly taking advantage of this favourable moment, without any public notification some of the eminent would-be spectators were privately admitted with the party a few moments after the descent. This was the result of much mysterious comings and goings on the part of some minor officials.

The noonday sun beat down, the people still present were taking no chances, and decided they were not going to leave for lunch, no matter how hungry they felt. Every movement to and from the tomb was watched with feverish interest. Three o'clock arrived, along with the party of excavators and officials. The others in whose favour the Government decision was revoked, and Charlotte, followed shortly afterwards.

Charlotte looked around as everybody settled themselves inside, when they were ready; Howard delivered a short address, displaying all the while an emotion only natural at the triumph of his long task. Then, the biggest thrill of the day, the rasp of the pulley chain, the intervals between the grating of the line over the wheel became suddenly longer. Charlotte realized that the lid was being raised, her heart began to beat faster in anticipation, the long-hidden secret was about to be revealed. Everyone in the tomb was now holding their breath as the stone lid, weighing over a ton, swayed slightly under the first irregular pull of the chain. Howard finding it impossible to stand aside and watch lent the workmen a hand. It took approximately twenty-five minutes for the slab to be hoisted high and clamped safely, Howard, Charlotte and the others were the first people for thousands of years to feast their eyes on the wonder within.

A magnificent mummy case dazzled Charlotte's eyes. The glorious promises of the earlier discoveries around the body was fulfilled, the splendour of the heavily gilded cover astonished them all. The case was about nine feet long, and the portrait of King Tutankhamen was traced on the uppermost side.

Howard's first glimpse inside the sarcophagus revealed but little of the splendour with which the Monarch was laid to rest, further inspection would hopefully defy imagination.

A dark brown cloth covered the coffin as a shroud. With hands trembling with excitement, Howard turned back the covering fold by fold, revealing gradually the radiant beauty of the dead king's coffin. Beneath the cloth, covering the entire surface was a sheet of pure gold modelled in statue relief form to represent the ruler lying beneath it. The face of the King was youthful and singularly handsome. Above his head was depicted the Royal Crown of Egyptian Kings, with the heads of a hawk and a serpent, encrusted in lapis lazuli. Tutankhamen lay with folded arms, and in his hands were clasped a golden sceptre and flail. A band of inscriptions, displaying the King's cartouches, ran round the figure beneath the forearms, and around either side of the body appeared the outstretched wings of the protective goddesses.

The most remarkable feature of this amazing sight though, was a wreath of natural flowers placed around the heads projecting on the crown. Howard thought this perhaps the most touching by its human simplicity, this tiny wreath of flowers placed around these symbols, as it pleased him to think, the last farewell offering of the widowed girl queen to her husband, the youthful representative of the "Two Kingdoms."

After a thorough inspection of the wonders before them, the party stopped their work and came to the surface. The lid of the sarcophagus had been left suspended in mid-air, but was to be lowered again into position once a record of the contents of the coffin had been made.

To-days revelations had surpassed all Howard's expectations. Charlotte, the excavators, archaeologists, and officials emerged from the tomb in silence. They had been confined in the hot and stifling atmosphere of the tomb for over an hour and a quarter, they had seen the golden coffin, a masterpiece of art unparalleled in magnificence and treasure no excavator in the history of digging had ever found.

Thrilled, but exhausted by the strain of the excitement of their unique experience, Howard, his assistants and Charlotte made their way to the luncheon tomb for tea.

CHAPTER ELEVEN

A bleak wasteland of rocks, mountains and endless sand lay spread out before him. The sun radiated heat and the sky was cloudless. In the distance, a large group of native men and boys were digging. Baskets of rocks and debris were passed along an endless line of hands, emptied and passed back again. Ottomar Hengel sat under the large canopy attached to the front of his tent. A medium-sized table, piled with bits of broken pottery and statuary, stood by his side. An overflowing ashtray spilled its contents over more bits of pottery. Hengel took out a large linen handkerchief and mopped his face and neck; he took a long swig of water from a green canteen. For ten years, he had been excavating in the barren areas surrounding the Valley of the Kings, and he had found nothing but rubbish. When the concession to dig in the Valley had become available in 1914, Hengel had desperately tried to obtain it. However, Gaston Maspero, the Director of the Antiquities Service, had given the concession to Lord Carnarvon. Hengel had ended up in the back end of nowhere. He glared balefully at the pottery shards, Flinders Petrie may find them fascinating and full of importance, but Hengel wanted to find something more substantial. When Howard Carter had stumbled across the steps that led to the final resting place of Tutankhamen, Hengel was furious. When all the beautiful treasure were being removed from the tomb, Hengel was there, standing in the crowd and watching with greedy eyes. It was at this point that his plan had begun to form. With a sweep of his arm, he swept the pottery pieces off the table in disgust.

Hengel had placed six men amongst Carter's workforce. One of them, Apep, was tasked with removing the sculpted wooden head of Tutankhamen that had been hidden away in the Fortnum and Mason box. Having been smuggled away, it was now residing in Hengel's hotel suite, waiting to make its impact upon that interloper, Howard Carter. Hengel had already ingratiated himself with the new Chief Inspector, Monsieur Boivin, who had assured him that if Carter ever breached the agreements of the concession the clearance of the tomb would pass to him. Hengel smiled to himself.

The small wooden head carved with the beautiful features of the young Tutankhamen, sat on top of a crate. Hengel couldn't take his eyes off it. It was beautiful, it depicted the head of the boy Pharaoh emerging from an open lotus flower, the base, painted blue, represented the water in which the flower grew. Hengel thought it one of the most exquisite pieces he had ever seen. He was loathe to part with it, but needs must. He carefully buried it within the Fortnum and Mason box and nailed the lid shut. With a final flourish, he attached an address label: 19 Collingham Gardens, London, S W 5, England.

'Bauer, you are certain the writing matches Carter's?'

'Yes sir, Monsieur Gagnier is an excellent forger.' replied Bauer, still swathed in bandages.

'Good. Now, you will secrete the box in Carter's house. I will inform the Antiquities Service, and we shall see what happens. If all goes according to plan, Carter will be deported and I will take charge of the tomb.'

'What if they don't deport him, maybe they will send him to prison instead.'

Hengel shrugged, 'It makes no difference, one way or another he will be out of my way for good.'

Later that night, or very early the following morning, depending on which way you preferred to look at it, Bauer, carefully clutching the box, crept towards Carter's house. He slowly walked around the building, making sure there were no servants lurking outside. Everything seemed very quiet. Coming back to the front door, he cautiously opened it, and stepped over the threshold. He had no idea where he was going to hide the box; he stood still, waiting for his eyes to adjust to the dark.

The time passed, a clock ticked, how long had he been standing in one place? He wasn't sure, but decided he ought to make a move before the sun came up. If he bungled this… he really didn't want to think about it. Slowly making his way through the interior, he could see the dark shapes of furniture, he stood in a room turning around in circles trying to find a suitable place to leave the box, but he couldn't see one. He began to panic; he tried another room, no, nothing here either. As he was leaving the room, his foot caught on a table and a vase came crashing down. Bauer froze, he felt cold with fear. He thought he could hear someone coming and he knew he had to escape. Still clutching the box, he hurried out of the room and tried to find the main door, but he panicked and in the darkness he had become disorientated.

Then he noticed what looked like a small cupboard set into the lower part of the wall. He opened its door, felt around inside – it appeared to be empty. He shoved the box into the bare space and slammed the door without thinking. More by luck than judgement, he found the main door and ran outside as fast as he could.

Very early the following day the Chief Inspector of Antiquities, Monsieur Jean-Jacques Boivin, along with an armed guard turned up at Howard's house and demanded access. Howard, who had recently left his bed and only just finished dressing, was affronted by this show of force.

'Mr. Carter, I am sorry that it has come to this, but my men are here to search your home. We believe you have, err how shall I put this, 'borrowed' certain items from the tomb, items which have not been catalogued.' said Monsieur Boivin.

'Have you taken leave of your senses? How dare you come here to my home with armed men, you have no right.' shouted Howard, he was very angry.

'Monsieur Carter, I have every right. You are here by permission of the Egyptian Government, you are working in an Egyptian tomb, I am representing the Government, and so I have every right. If you are stealing treasure from this country, you will be punished accordingly. Just because you are English does not mean you will be allowed to walk away.'

'You've had it in for me ever since I discovered that tomb. You've done everything in your power to make my life here as difficult as possible. You've insisted on allowing visitors to trample inside, potentially causing irreparable damage to the treasure therein. You've made irresponsible demands on my time, preventing me from completing my task. I am doing my best working in very small, cramped and stifling conditions, and all you do is swan around and make unreasonable demands.'

At that point, one of the guards came into the room and whispered into Boivin's ear. Howard couldn't hear what the guard said, but from the triumphant look on Boivin's face, he knew it wasn't going to turn out well for him.

'Monsieur Carter, it appears we have found a box, a Fortnum and Mason box no less, hidden away in a cupboard and addressed to your London home. Ah, here it is, open it.' instructed Boivin to the guard.

The guard prised open the lid to reveal, the exquisite wooden sculpture. 'Well, Monsieur Carter, how do you explain this?' he said, with a triumphant smile on his face.

Howard stared stupefied at the box, he fell into a chair, he tried to speak but his throat had become so dry he couldn't make his voice heard.

Boivin poured a glass of whisky and handed it to Carter, who took a few sips. Howard closed his eyes and tried to think. 'I have no idea how that box came to be here. The statue is very delicate, please be careful with it. I don't understand any of this.' Howard felt his mind was a befuddled mess, he just couldn't think clearly.

Boivin signalled the guards to leave, picking up the box he himself began to leave.

'What are you going to do?' asked Howard, anxiously.

'The sculpture will be taken to the Cairo Museum for preservation. As for you Monsieur Carter, as yet I do not know what your fate will be.' He raised his hat and left.

Howard tried to think, but his mind was in confusion, he had no idea why the box was in his cupboard. He remembered finding the sculpture amongst the filling of the tomb's entrance passage. It was in a perishable condition and had taken some time to salvage it, not to mention the painstaking work of picking out the fragments of its painted decoration from the dust and rubble. The head was carefully packed away in a box and then stored in the luncheon tomb - tomb no. 4, until he had an opportunity to record and preserve it.

Howard pondered upon this puzzle and only one solution

seemed to make sense. Someone had deliberately placed it in his home, the same someone who had left a dead body in his home. Somewhere deep inside himself Howard could feel his anger growing, the humiliation of being thought a thief added to that anger.

Howard roused his chauffeur to drive him to the Metropolitan House. He had been invited to take breakfast with his American colleagues and their wives. Over the meal, he explained to them what had happened. Every one of them was furious at this latest insult from the Government. Howard informed them that he was going to close the tomb.

He returned to Luxor and wrote the following communication.

Owing to impossible restrictions and discourtesies on the part of the Public Works Department and its Antiquity Service, all my collaborators, in protest, have refused to work any further upon the scientific investigations of the discovery of the tomb of Tutankhamen. I, therefore, am obliged to make known to the public that immediately after the Press view of the tomb this morning between 10 a.m. and noon, the tomb will be closed and no further work be carried out.
- (Signed) Howard Carter.

He posted it on the noticeboard of the Winter Palace Hotel. The events of this morning had come like a thunderbolt especially after yesterday's sensational discovery. For a long time now there had been disagreements between him and the Egyptian Government largely arising from the contract Lord Carnarvon had concluded with The Times newspaper whereby he had promised them priority of all news from the tomb. This had created considerable resentment amongst the Egyptian, British and world press, Howard had endeavoured to carry out the contract despite all of this and frequent interference from the Egyptian Government, who were anxious to maintain their rights over the publicity surrounding the discovery.

Inside the tomb, King Tutankhamen continued his slumber. The great golden effigy of the Pharaoh stared up at the raised granite lid of the sandstone sarcophagus; meanwhile, the doors of the tomb remained padlocked.

A specially strengthened police guard, with loaded rifles, patrolled the precinct with strict instructions to prevent access to the tomb to anyone, no matter who they were. Howard, meanwhile, remained in his house. The note he had posted up in the hotel lounge the day before had been taken down by the hotel management, who claimed they were unaware it had been put up, and they considered its tone offensive towards the Egyptian Government

The next morning Howard decided to visit the tomb; he still retained the keys and wanted to make sure that the locks were intact, and also to collect various articles from the laboratory. On arrival he was met by the local Chief of Police at Luxor, who was now on daily duty in the Valley, he showed Howard a written order from the Egyptian Government refusing admission to the tomb of anyone whatsoever. Howard turned and left.

The Egyptian Minister of Public Works sent an ultimatum to Howard informing him that his excavation license would be immediately cancelled if he did not resume work at Tutankhamen's tomb in forty-eight hours.

Howard telegraphed a protest:

I regard the action of the Director-General of the Antiquities Department as both insulting and illegal. It is essential to ensure the safety of the sarcophagus and its contents that I be granted the access to which I am entitled.
The arrangements made for suspending the sarcophagus cover are temporary, and I must be given an opportunity to take full precautions.

The Minister of Public Works replied:

I am profoundly astonished to learn that when you closed the tomb you did not take all necessary precautions to ensure the safety of the sarcophagus which is so valuable to science and the world. I reserve my rights in the event of any damage.

The situation in the Valley of the Kings rumbled on. The representatives of the Antiquities Service continued to be in possession of the tomb, with the support of an armed guard, and Howard was still unable to obtain entrance.

Charlotte, like everyone else, waited anxiously to see what the next move would be. It was understood that the Government were prepared to force the door in order to allow the public to view the sarcophagus; an official notice had been posted though to say that all visits to the tomb had been suspended until further notice. Howard had applied formerly to the Government to be allowed to enter the tomb and the laboratory in order to carry out certain precautionary measures, but so far had received no reply.

Howard sent another telegram to the Minister of Public Works:

> In order to safeguard the contents of the Tomb I am commencing proceedings in the Mixed Courts To-day. If the Director-General of Antiquities apologizes for his insult to me, and if an undertaken is given that all vexatious interference shall cease, I will reopen the Luxor Tomb for ten days in accordance with agreement.

Howard's lawyer visited the Minister of Public Works and unsuccessfully endeavoured to reach a compromise. The Minister declared that the Government could not tolerate Mr. Carter's "browbeating attitude," and that Mr. Carter must remember that he was dealing with the Government.

Howard felt that the Ministry of Public Works and the Department of Antiquities in Cairo had treated him with disdain. He found he could no longer stomach the petty and irritating insults which he had borne for months. During the last few months alone, Howard had lost no fewer than seventeen out of fifty working days visiting Cairo to argue, plead, expostulate and remonstrate with officials.

He had spent thirty years in Egypt, first as a draughtsman then as an excavator, the search for Tutankhamen's tomb, which others had given up as hopeless, might never have been discovered without his tenaciousness. Throughout the clearance and investigations of the tomb he had adhered most scrupulously to the contract with the Government, carefully observing the strict letter of the laws on excavation, and, in acting for the widow of Lord Carnarvon, who now held the concession, he knew he had never exceeded his rights.

The Egyptian Government cancelled the licence; Howard felt his world disappearing around him. Just when his work was to be crowned, he had been denied the right to continue his work. Seventeen years had elapsed since he and Lord Carnarvon had begun digging, and most of those years were dull and uneventful. Howard thought back, his career had not been uneventful. He was not only an archaeologist, he was also a painter. He had inherited his talent from his father, who had been an animal painter of some repute. Indeed, Howard might have been an artist if he had not enjoyed excavating so much. Years before he became known as an excavator his watercolour illustrations were the bright touches of many books on archaeological matters. Howard possessed a singular knack for reproducing the spirit of Egyptian art. He could sit down in a temple and copy some timeworn wall painting, reproduce the faded colours, and generally restore a fragment without losing the touch of the original. Howard was fond of wildlife and had created several watercolours of birds and beasts; he was also a Fellow of the Zoological Society.

One afternoon Charlotte decided to pay a visit to the tomb. She had heard rumours that it was about to be reopened, and decided to investigate. Finding Jabari, To-day's tea towel wrapped around his head definitely had "Luxor Hotel" printed upon it, she wondered if he had friends who worked in the local laundry who dished out hotel tea towels for some reason or another. Maybe he was paid to advertise the hotel, she shook her head, and asked for Suzy.

'Suzy she miss you very much, she likes you. I may have to charge you more.' he looked at Charlotte sternly.

Charlotte, taken aback, was about to stammer a protestation when Jabari burst out laughing.

'I am very funny, yes? The look on your face, I wish I had a camera.'

'You're quite the comedian aren't you?' Said Charlotte, feeling a bit foolish, she handed over the money. Jabari called Suzy over. The donkey ambled towards them, looking very unenthusiastic, then she saw Charlotte and her face lit up, she gave a huge donkey grin, shouted 'hee-haw', and ran to Charlotte, almost knocking her down.

A few tourists were lingering in the Valley of the Kings waiting to see if anything exciting was going to happen. An armed guard of police surrounded Tutankhamen's tomb, Charlotte counted twenty of them. She settled down with Suzy to wait and see what may happen. She had brought a picnic and a blanket. The two friends tucked into their food protected from the heat by Charlotte's umbrella.

Two officials from the Antiquities Service arrived, Charlotte discreetly followed behind, and she saw them examining the locks of the outer door. There was a heated discussion, and one of the men left. He was back later accompanied by two workmen with tools. M. Boivin, Director of Antiquities arrived accompanied by the Chief Inspector of Antiquities for Upper Egypt. There was no sign of Howard, he was meant to be here to hand over the keys. 'Over my dead body', Charlotte recalled him saying to her over dinner last evening.

The locks were forced without too much difficulty with the aid of chisels, hacksaws, and crowbars. The officials entered the tomb and spent some time in there, presumably listing the contents and taking additional precautionary measurements to avoid the possibility of damage. Charlotte assumed their priority was to safeguard the sarcophagus and the coffin.

Charlotte and Suzy spent the next few days visiting the tomb, observing the comings and goings of officialdom. One particular day though, turned out to be quite interesting. M. Boivin had turned up as usual, only now Hengel accompanied him. Apart from making an inventory of all the objects in the tomb, it appeared that Hengel had been busy erecting wooden railings around the sarcophagus and the parts of the shrines which were still inside the tomb, in order to protect them from possible injury by the hundreds of people who were expected to visit the tomb within the next week. Charlotte looked around; along with their donkeys, there were already hundreds of people here.

Meanwhile Howard was in Cairo bringing his action in the courts to clear his name of the accusation of theft, and to appeal to the Government to renew his concession so he could finish his work. Charlotte felt a pang of dread, it looked like Ottomar Hengel had already wormed his way in, and she worried what effect it would have upon Howard when he found out.

Meanwhile, Howard was having a disappointing time of it in Cairo. The referee of the Mixed Courts had found in Howard's favour on all legal points. The Government then appealed. The

Appeal Court decided that the Mixed Court was not competent to deal with the case, and the original ruling was reversed and the cancellation of the concession remained.

The court case was the sole topic of conversation in Luxor. There had been a great buzz of excitement when the Egyptian Government had reopened the tomb to great ceremony. Three special trains were provided to bring a distinguished party of two hundred guests from Cairo. The streets of Luxor had been decorated with flags and thousands of Egyptians crowded together cheering and singing to the accompaniment of Egyptian bands.

First to arrive were the Ministers and members of the Egyptian Cabinet who assembled under a huge tent and were entertained by Sheikhs performing feats of horsemanship upon their beautiful Arabian horses. The second group to arrive were the foreign diplomats, members of the Houses of Parliament and press representatives.

At about two o'clock, a large Government boat conveyed the party across the Nile. Thirty cars stood waiting for them, specially sent from Cairo for the occasion, to take them to the Valley of the Kings. After about half an hour the party arrived at the tomb, there was a great tent where refreshments were served to them. They were split into groups of eight; one group at a time was allowed to descend the steps into the tomb to view the sarcophagus, the lid of which had been removed when the Government took charge of the tomb. A large platform had been erected allowing an excellent view of Tutankhamen's gold-covered coffin. Round about six o'clock, the party returned to Luxor to attend a banquet followed by an Egyptian fete and fireworks.

Charlotte noticed Hengel amongst the dignitaries, he looked like he was having a very good time, laughing and joking with the officials and ministers, at that moment Charlotte thought that she had never hated anyone as much as she hated him. He turned and looked straight at her, her heart froze, he said something to the group of men he was with and made his way towards her. Grabbing her arm, he made it quite clear that her life, and Howard's life, would not be worth living if the pair of them didn't stop poking about in his business. He rained down so much fire and brimstone upon her that she deemed it prudent to leave town. She thought of Howard and her heart broke. She made up her mind that she would take the overnight train and join him in Cairo.

CHAPTER TWELVE

The gentle breeze stirred the dust that covered the streets. Trams travelled along their well-worn routes, pouring out groups of passengers at each stop and embarking many more. Cars sped by tooting their horns impatiently at the poor souls who were trying to cross from one side of the road to the other. The population of Cairo - citizens and tourists alike – scurried or gently strolled along the pavements intent on fulfilling whatever purpose had brought them outside. Howard and Charlotte were sitting upon the terrace of the Continental Hotel observing these activities.

Before this little mise en scène, Charlotte had found Howard sitting on his own in the hotel's bar. He looked as though he had given up on life, his colleagues, people he had thought of as friends, he had been ostracized by them all. He was treated as if he were a leper, a person to be avoided at all costs, certainly not someone you would want to be seen associating with. People gathered in their cliques and whispered about him, trying unobtrusively to stare at him, but Howard was well aware of all that was happening around him. He felt the loneliness of his position acutely. When Charlotte had turned up with a big grin upon her face, he had been momentarily paralyzed by fear that she was going to sweep past him to greet someone else. She sat by his side, and placed her hand on top of his. He felt comforted by this gesture, he wanted to say something but the words wouldn't come; he was not a man who easily expressed his emotions, at least those emotions that were not motivated by anger and a sense of injustice. They had sat like that for a while, people around them staring and whispering, one woman haughtily exclaimed, 'Well really, I don't know what the world is coming to, people like that should never be allowed in respectable establishments such as this.'

Charlotte turned to the woman and said, 'No, I quite agree, I'll call the manager and ask him to escort you and your friends off the premises.'

The woman's eyes opened wide in indignation, 'How dare you, I've never been so insulted before.'

'Maybe not, but I'm pretty sure you've insulted many other innocent people before. You and your friends are a disgrace, I certainly wouldn't wanted to be acquainted with such a rude person as yourself and I'm sure Mr. Carter is absolutely delighted that he doesn't possess any friends as ugly in mind and spirit as you are.'

Before the shocked woman could gather her thoughts, Charlotte had taken Howard's arm and propelled him out onto the terrace.

The pair had spent the next morning visiting the Cairo Museum. It was far larger than Charlotte had imagined and one morning was not enough to view all the exhibits the veritable old building proudly displayed. Tutankhamen's treasures were indeed magnificent, more so in real life than she could have imagined. The work that had gone into creating the various pieces was awe-inspiring; the skill of the ancient artisans, the artistry and brilliance of their creations was a true work of art and virtuosity. Howard had proved to be an excellent orator; his knowledge and enthusiasm were infectious, also revealing an unexpected sense of humour. Charlotte found herself ever more enchanted by this slightly pompous yet diffident man.

Howard was pleased that the morning's visit had gone so well, he had worried that the young girl may have found ancient Egypt to be a rather dull subject, but she had listened to his stories with an eagerness that had delighted him.

Howard had never married or indeed had any close relationships, he was happy with his own company, the bachelor life suited him and he did not miss family life at all. That was not to say that he didn't enjoy being in female company, the opposite sex amused him, he loved how they listened so intently to his tales of discovering the tomb and the years of hard work that followed. Unfortunately, Howard had an acerbic sense of humour which some of his gracious lady hosts did not appreciate, and more often than not he found dinner party invitations were not forthcoming a second time.

The next morning, after an early breakfast Howard met Charlotte in the lobby, she greeted him warmly. Howard thought she looked very charming in a red and white floral dress, her long, wavy hair loosely hanging around her shoulders. Howard told her he had arranged a visit to the pyramids.

'Let's go by tram,' Charlotte pleaded, 'I always feel sick in taxis and I'm sure it'll be more fun.'

Howard was not so sure though, the idea of squashing into a tram did not appeal to him at all, he was a man who liked his comforts and at his age, he appreciated them even more. Seeing the look upon his face, Charlotte said, 'come on, don't be such a stuffed shirt.' She had a winning smile and Howard succumbed and reluctantly agreed.

They didn't have long to wait until the tram clanked and squeaked its way towards the stop. Upon boarding Howard was relieved to see it wasn't very crowded and they found a couple of vacant seats very easily.

The tram trundled towards the river, crossing over the Bulaq Bridge and making its way across the island of Gezira, it groaned its way across the Zamalik Bridge and continued to squeak south past the zoological gardens. At each stop, more passengers boarded, the air became fetid with the smell of sweat and garlic. Howard noted that none of this discomfort seemed to have any effect on Charlotte's cheerfulness. He wished he could be like her, instead he had sweat pouring down his face, his three-piece suit was stifling him and he longed for the comfort and privacy of a car. Eventually, after what seemed an eternity of stopping and starting the tram arrived at the terminus near the Mena House Hotel, whence it disgorged its passengers. Howard felt very sick, his legs had turned to jelly, his head was spinning and he thought he might pass out at any moment; in fact, he didn't care if never travelled on or saw a tram again.

Charlotte turned towards him full of enthusiasm and was shocked to see the state he was in.

'Howard, oh my goodness, what have I done to you? You look like you're going to faint, you're as white as a sheet.'

She sat him down and gave him a drink of water from her flask. With shaking hands Howard managed to swallow the slightly tepid liquid, breathing slowly he found he was beginning to feel himself once more.

'Are you feeling better now?' Charlotte asked anxiously. Howard was silent for a moment.

'Yes, I think so, you know you were absolutely right, it was quite an experience ' he said, sardonically

Charlotte felt terribly guilty for insisting they go by tram, she apologized profusely to Howard and promised him they would make the return journey by taxi. With Howard more or less recovered, they bought their tickets and made their way towards the pyramids. The noise of chattering tourists and the shouts of beggars pervaded the air, dealers trying to persuade gullible tourists to part with their money for rather dubious looking 'antiquities' scampered from one group to another. The smell of donkeys and camels and their ordure suffused the atmosphere. Charlotte found it all delightful; a warm, happy feeling filled her heart.

The Great Pyramid towered before them; crowds of tourists were climbing up the large stone blocks, pushed and pulled by groups of Bedouin. Charlotte suggested they climb to the top; Howard though, refused to go, 'I'm far too old, my climbing days are behind me, I shall find a nice shady spot and wait.'

Charlotte began the ascent unaided, the climb was tiring and she found she had to rest a couple of times to get her breath back. At last, the summit appeared, a number of other visitors were already there, and some of them were sitting down and admiring the spectacular view, Charlotte sat down as well. She felt so free; she could see the other pyramids; an Arab village in the distance; the majestic sphinx; fields and trees sprawled below her looking like miniature models. She sat there staring lost in thought, the world carrying on without her. She was not sure how long she had been sitting there, but she thought of poor Howard alone, and began the long descent back to terra firma.

Finding Howard, she joyfully recounted her experience, he was very happy she had enjoyed herself so much. She managed to persuade Howard to visit the interior of Khefre's pyramid. Once they entered the passageway, they found they had to crouch down as they descended the narrow corridor, every now and then tourists leaving the pyramid would appear from the opposite direction, so

Howard and Charlotte would have to squash themselves against the wall to let them pass by. It reminded Howard of his younger days, excavating deep down below the earth, with just candles to light the way, removing vast quantities of shale and rock, barely able to breathe in the stale and rancid air that became filled with fine particles of dust, at least now the air was breathable, if very stuffy, and electricity lit the way.

The corridor continued ascending and descending until they finally found themselves in a rectangular chamber, empty but for a black granite sarcophagus sunk into the floor, its occupant long gone, the lid propped against the wall next to it. There was nothing else to see, except on the south wall, engraved in large graffiti were the words: "Scoperta da G. Belzoni. 2 Mar. 1818."

They sat next to the sarcophagus to have a rest before beginning the trip back through the narrow corridors to the outside world. As they came out into the daylight, a wall of heat engulfed them. 'That was breathtaking,' laughed Charlotte, 'I don't think I've had so much fun for ages.'

Having tired themselves and feeling hot and thirsty, they returned to the Mena House to partake of a light lunch. Looking at the pyramids through the haze of heat Charlotte felt as though her life back in England was a distant dream.

Charlotte woke up the next morning feeling that life was wonderful, how lucky was she to have met Howard, her idol. She wondered if she was still asleep and this was all a vivid dream or perhaps she was unconscious and hallucinating. She didn't care, it seemed real enough, she was going to enjoy every minute of it. To-day Howard was taking her to Khan el-Khalili bazaar, so she hurried to get dressed.

There was a knock at the door and the bellboy handed her a message. It was from Howard, he had met an important acquaintance and needed to discuss some aspects of the pending court case with him, rather than delay their visit she should make her way to the Khan el-Khalili and wait for him at El Fishawi's coffee shop. Sighing with disappointment, Charlotte gathered her bag and made her way downstairs. She got into a waiting taxi and settled back in the seat, trying not to succumb to motion sickness.

Arriving at the café, she sat at a table near the door, so she could be sure to see Howard when he arrived. Ordering a glass of lemonade, she looked at her watch, then took out her book and started to read. She became aware of a shadow looming above her. Eagerly she looked up, hoping it was Howard, instead she saw a strange man leering at her. He had a stubbly chin and rotting teeth, his yellow piggy eyes raked over her face. She gave an involuntary shiver.

'Come with me.' he rasped.

'What? I'm not going anywhere with you.' said Charlotte, appalled, perhaps he thought she was waiting here for custom. Oh, god, where was Howard? She'd been waiting over an hour now.

'It is not a request; you will stand up and come with me now.'

Charlotte was about to say something when she realized another man was behind her.

'We can do this quietly, or not so quietly, it is up to you. You are very pretty, it would be a shame to break your face.' the first man said lasciviously.

Charlotte felt sick, she couldn't move because her legs felt like jelly. The other man held her arm firmly and pulled her up. She was so frightened, she wanted to scream for help but her voice had deserted her.

She was taken out to a waiting truck, the man holding on to her pulled her into the back, as the truck began to move she lost her footing and everything went black.

She opened her eyes, her head felt very groggy, she threw up violently. Where on earth was she? She tried to stand up, but the world started spinning and she quickly sat down. Charlotte tried to look around, she couldn't seem to see anything, and semi-darkness surrounded her. There were torches along the walls, proper torches with real fire flickering in the eerie silence. Charlotte got to her knees, she still felt very dizzy, she looked around, it looked like a small room.

Turning to her right she saw something in the shadows. She crawled towards it and with rising hope realized it was a door, she couldn't open it though, the damned thing was locked. Charlotte hammered upon it until her fists became too painful. She called out for help, nothing but silence answered her. With a terrible dawning of the reality of her situation, Charlotte understood that she had been imprisoned. She sat down and started to cry, she wished Howard would come and rescue her, yet she knew he had no idea where she was. She was all alone in this horrid room; clutching her knees to her chest, she cried until she had no tears left to cry.

CHAPTER THIRTEEN

'I am so very sorry Mr. Carter, Miss Hambleton checked out over an hour ago.' said the receptionist.

'Checked out,' exclaimed Howard, 'how, why, where did she go?'

'To the train station, I believe she was travelling on to Alexandria.'

'I don't understand, are you absolutely sure it was Miss Hambleton.'

'Oh, yes, Mr. Carter, it is a memorable name, there is no mistake.'

Howard turned away, dazed. He couldn't believe it. Charlotte hadn't said anything to him about leaving. For goodness sake, they were supposed to be spending the day at the bazaar. Was it something he had said? Perhaps he had bored her so much, that she had fled rather than spend another day with him. Slumping into a chair, Howard suddenly felt very old, what a fool he had been.

He sat there very quietly for a long time, going over yesterday's events in his mind. He felt something was wrong, he was certain that Charlotte would not have left without seeing him first. Howard went back to the reception, 'Were you on duty when Miss Hambleton left?'

'Yes, Mr. Carter, I was.'

'How did she seem to you, was she distressed in anyway?'

'I did not actually see her' admitted the receptionist, 'it was a friend of hers who paid the bill.'

'What did this "friend" look like?'

'If truth be told he was looking very unpleasant, not the sort of friend a young lady like Miss Hambleton should have. I was quite surprised that she knew a person such as this. He looked dirty, very bad teeth, not shaven for days, most unpleasant.'

'She left no message for me?'

The receptionist checked the box, 'No message, I am sorry, Mr. Carter.'

'Thank you.' Howard turned and walked outside. He needed time to think this through properly. Someone had taken Charlotte, almost certainly against her will. He had a pretty good idea as to who had arranged it, but to what purpose. Had Hengel taken her? But why, surely he wasn't going to kill her? Howard felt annoyed with himself; he should have looked after her, especially following the unpleasantness in Luxor, he knew Hengel was a dangerous man, why hadn't he been more alert to that danger?

Charlotte opened her eyes; she had had the most terrible dream. Turning over to get out of bed, she bashed her head on the stone wall, practically rendering herself unconscious. Managing to focus on her surroundings, she discovered she hadn't been dreaming at all, she really was locked up in this horrid room. Through blurred vision she thought she saw a tray near the door, she stumbled towards it, it contained a plate of stale bread and a jug of water, no cup though. She drank the water, but couldn't face eating the bread. Charlotte shouted out, no reply, she shouted again and again, hoping that somebody would come, nobody did. Her voice became hoarse and her throat felt sore, she drank some more water.

She needed to go to the toilet, looking around she could see nothing suitable. God, she was going to have wee on the floor. Charlotte tried to make a hole using her hands to scrape the sand away. The ground was too rocky, and she barely managed to create a shallow depression. Desperate now, she crouched down, she felt so undignified, humiliation burned inside her. Fortunately, they had not taken her bag away, finding her tissues, she tidied herself up and replaced her clothes. She hoped they wouldn't keep her here too long. Please, please let someone find her, She collapsed upon the floor and holding her head in her hands tried to conjure up an image of Howard in her mind, she thought very hard to make a telepathic connection with him, she knew she was clutching at straws because she didn't even know where she was.

The man with the rotting teeth peered through the door, he watched as Charlotte removed her underwear and went to the toilet, leering at her lustfully, he was about to open the door, when someone clouted him around the head with a crutch. Olaf turned ready to punch the lights out of whoever dared to hit him, and stopped abruptly when he became aware of whom it was. At this point, he turned into a gibbering wreck: 'Herr Hengel, I wasn't expecting you.'

'So, I see. I hope you were not planning to harm our guest, because that would make me very angry.'

'No, no, sir, I wanted to make sure she was all right, nothing else, I swear it.'

'Good, I would hate for any misfortune to happen to you, you understand?'

'Yes, yes, Herr Hengel, I understand.'

'Good, now get out of here.'

'Yes sir.' in his haste to escape from Hengel, Olaf tripped over his feet and fell flat on his face. Hengel sighed; you really couldn't get the staff nowadays.

Entering the room he said, 'Ah, good morning Miss Hambleton, or may I call you Charlotte?'

'I might have known you'd be behind this.' said Charlotte. 'How long do you intend to keep me here?'

'That is up to you. You have caused me a great deal of inconvenience, my employee Bauer was in hospital because of you, and as you can no doubt see, I too have suffered injuries because of your interference. It must stop. You will return to England, without your influence Carter will not obstruct my plans.'

'You can't make me leave; you have no authority to do that. You're just a bully, you surround yourself with henchmen, but I bet without them you're a coward.' said Charlotte angrily.

'You are not in a position to be so brave; I could keep you locked up for good. Nobody would ever find you; this room will be your tomb.'

Swallowing hard, Charlotte's heart was beating so loudly she was sure Hengel could hear it. She had to placate him somehow, once she escaped this room she may have a chance to get back to the hotel and to Howard, 'What do you want me to do?' she asked.

'You will copy this note and I will deliver it to Carter, you will then be escorted back to London.'

She bowed her head. Hengel smiled, 'Good, come with me.'

Charlotte thought this might be her chance to escape, but the rotten tooth man tied her hands behind her back and pulled a hood over her head. Grabbing her elbow, he pulled her along the uneven surface. Her feet kept tripping over small rocks, and once or twice, she nearly fell to her knees. Charlotte felt the air and noted the change of atmosphere, outside at last! Unceremoniously she found herself thrown into a car, which then proceeded to bump its way to heaven knows where. By now, she had lost all sense of time; she was also feeling very indignant at the way they were treating her. Who on earth did this man think he was? Charlotte was no longer feeling scared, she was bloody angry. Just wait until she was free, they would have to untie her hands to write the note, then she would show them, by the time she finished with them they would be wishing they had left her alone.

Finally, the car came to a halt. Pulled from her seat, Charlotte could smell it was the yellow-eyed man with rotting teeth steering her into a building or something. With the hood removed, she blinked a few times until her eyes began to adjust bringing a study into focus. Untying her hands, Hengel told her to sit down. He placed a piece of paper and a pen in front of her, along with another bit of paper inscribed with the words she was to copy. She read it through, it was a letter supposedly written by her telling Howard that she was leaving to return to England.

'Howard is never going to believe that I wrote this.' she said.

Hengel smirked at her, 'My dear Miss Hambleton, it makes no difference what he believes.'

'I refuse to write anything, it's all nonsense.'

'You would be very wise to co-operate in this matter. Do you think I don't know it was you who did this to me.' he pointed at his bandaged head, 'and poor Bauer, who was stuck in hospital for weeks. I know you were responsible; you will not have the opportunity to spoil my plans anymore. Instead of killing you I am giving you the opportunity to leave this country, you will take it.'

'Yes, I was conscious the first time you mentioned it, there's no need to repeat yourself.' said Charlotte.

'I want to make sure that you understand that I am not a fool, I do not have a zip in the back of my head. I will not tolerate any further impudence, do you understand?'

Charlotte tried to say something.

'I will have no argument.' shouted Hengel. 'If you wish I can arrange for that troublesome donkey to meet with a fatal accident.'

Charlotte stared at him in disbelief, how did he find out about Suzy?

'Oh yes, I know all about that donkey, Bauer will be scarred for life because of that miserable creature. So, write the note, sign it, and do it now.' he banged his fist down on the table so hard a large crack appeared.

Charlotte practically jumped out of her skin. Thinking about her situation in as rational a way as she could under the circumstances, and hoping to buy time so she might find an opportunity to escape, she said, 'You leave me no choice'.

Picking up the pen, she copied out the words. Hengel watched over her shoulder, making sure every letter was correct.

Charlotte noticed Hengel's crutch propped against the table, would she be able to grab it before he could stop her. Suddenly, the telephone began to ring, startled for a moment by the noise, Charlotte gathered her wits together and just as Hengel was about to pick up the receiver, she grabbed the crutch and whacked him over the head, just for good measure she belted him across the knees as well. He was down for the count, he groaned and fell silent, she worried she may have killed him. She checked his pulse - he was still alive. The bloody phone was still ringing, picking it up she threw it against the wall, and it smashed into pieces. She heard someone approaching, it must be Rotten Tooth. Still holding the crutch, she flattened herself against the wall, the door slowly opened, and a greasy round head appeared. She let him come further in to the room, and walloped him across the back of his knees, he went down like a leaden lump.

Charlotte ran like mad, where the hell was the front door? She ran outside, bloody typical, a fifty/fifty chance and she had to find the back door. No, no, no, running back inside, she raced down the hall and out of another door – yes, there was the car. She jumped inside and started the engine, she had no idea what direction to go in, all she wanted to do was to get as far away from here as possible.

CHAPTER FOURTEEN

Araminta Fazakerley had lived in Egypt for a very long time, she liked to tell anyone who cared to listen that the climate was good for her lumbago. She was a large woman, (she delighted in tasting the local cuisine and frequenting the local drinking establishments), her skin was of a rather doughy appearance, her blue eyes were slightly rheumy, and she had a mop of untidy grey hair. As for her age, well, let us just say she had reached three score years and ten, perhaps even beyond that.

Araminta's husband, Bartholomew, had built their mud brick house in a small suburb not far from Cairo; a largish garden full of colourful flowers and shrubs surrounded the property, paved with grey flagstones, in pride of place stood a giant sycamore tree, which provided some well-needed shade. The house, or bungalow as Araminta referred to it, had large interior rooms that were crammed with furniture, books, lamps, tables, rugs, and a rather plump black and white cat that went by the name of Theodora. The floor, at least the part that could be seen, was covered with orange coloured stone tiles. Once upon a time, the flat roof had been used as a sun terrace, for afternoon naps and lunch, that sort of thing, unfortunately, Araminta was unable to climb the stairs, and so the roof had been left to its own devices and was sadly in a state of neglect.

Araminta had been a widow for some fifteen years; she was a sociable person though and had a large coterie of friends, so she never felt lonely. She drove herself around in a car that had seen better days, and once a month she visited Cairo, to see if anyone she knew had arrived and was staying in one of the smart hotels there and might possibly invite her to tea or maybe even dinner.

One particular afternoon, Araminta was driving along the dusty road, her large hat sitting askew on the top of her head, her ample bosom wedged against the wheel making steering a tad difficult. Up ahead she saw an automobile lying askew across the verge, from its angle she surmised it had hit the palm tree.

'Dearie me,' she muttered to herself, 'looks like a nasty accident, I hope no one is hurt.'

Almost colliding into the unfortunate tree herself, she stopped her automobile, got out and went to investigate. Smoke was gently billowing from the bonnet; she could hear a low hissing sound coming from somewhere inside the engine. Lying upon the front seat was a young girl, blood trickled from a gash on her forehead. Araminta checked her pulse - she was still alive.

'My dear, can you hear me?' Araminta asked.

Charlotte tried to speak, but she couldn't seem to form any words, her brain felt like cotton wool.

'Are you able to stand?' Araminta said in a loud voice.

Charlotte tried to move, her head started to spin though, and she collapsed further into the seat.

'What am I to do? I can't leave her here. I wonder...?' Araminta got back in to her own automobile and moved it as near as possible to the damaged one. After a lot of reversing, forwarding and crunching of gears she eventually managed to get her passenger door next to where Charlotte was sitting. Her idea was to push Charlotte into her automobile; there was one tiny flaw though - the automobiles were too close together and she was unable to get the door open.

'How frustrating, what ridiculous things doors are.' She looked about, a bewildered expression upon her face.

Looking at the girl, she thought to herself, 'I'll just have to find another way, now let me see. My dear,' she said loudly, 'I need you to try and stand up, just for a moment, can you manage that?'

Charlotte, startled by the loud voice, gradually began to understand what the elderly lady was saying. Gathering all her strength, she heaved herself up and fell out of the car.

'Bother!' she managed to say.

'Never mind,' said Araminta, 'here, give me your arm, it's not far.'

She dragged Charlotte to the car and propped her into the passenger seat. Araminta peered at her passenger who now resembled a bag of laundry heaped upon the seat.

'Off we go then.' she said cheerfully.

The gears grinded and the engine moaned. The car shot off down the track with Araminta singing "A Wand 'ring Minstrel I'" in a loud tuneless voice. Mercifully, Charlotte was oblivious to the in car entertainment.

At the Continental Hotel, Howard waited in the vain hope that Charlotte would reappear. He had telephoned the Winter Palace in Luxor to enquire if she had by any chance turned up there, the answer had been no. He was reluctant to leave Cairo, and spent his time searching for her. He had visited El Fishawi and spoken to the proprietor, who vaguely recalled the English girl, but couldn't say when she left, or indeed, if anyone had been with her.

Howard was at his wits' end, he had no idea where to look for Charlotte, he had also discovered that Hengel had left Luxor the day after she had. He felt a great weight of responsibility, after all Charlotte had been helping him, and now she was gone, and it was his fault. Howard knew he couldn't go to the police, they would ask too many questions and the murky story of the stolen sculpture and the current court case was bound to come up, he was sure they would find a way to implicate him. No, the police were out of the question.

Then he received a note, he read it. So, Charlotte had returned to England after all. Howard stared at the words upon the paper, very cold and informal words, not the sort of communication he would expect from a friend. He felt hurt and foolish, and sad to know that he had been right, he had bored her and she had run away.

Araminta had made Charlotte comfortable upon one of her couches, which converted into a bed. A doctor had diagnosed mild concussion, and said to leave her to rest in peace and quiet. Charlotte, fortified with green tea, and Mrs. Fazakerley's beef broth, and bread and butter pudding, began to make a slow recovery. One day, Araminta asked her if she would be all right on her own for a few hours.

'I have to go to Cairo; there are supplies I need to collect and I'm sure I'm meant to have an appointment to keep with someone or other. I've left you something to eat,' she gestured to the table next to the couch, 'and plenty of water. If you want tea, I'm afraid you'll have to make it yourself, you'll find everything you need in the kitchen.'

Charlotte replied, 'I'll be fine, please don't worry about me, take as long as you need, I can manage on my own.'

'Well, if you're sure, my dear. There are some books lying about somewhere, and I daresay I may have a newspaper or a magazine lying about.' she looked vaguely around, not seeing anything resembling a magazine or a newspaper, although was that a newspaper Theodora was sleeping upon? Araminta shook her head, maybe not.

Charlotte noticing this said, 'I think I'll just sit quietly out in the garden.'

'Yes, you do that, you're looking a bit peaky, and the sun will do you good.'

Araminta bustled around gathering her belongings in her arms, dropping them, and picking up the scattered objects that had fallen out of her voluminous bag, until finally she was ready. Theodora, obviously used to such goings on didn't even bother to open her eyes, only her ears moved around like two separate radar dishes.

'Cheerio!' shouted Araminta, waving her stick and then she was gone. From outside came the noise of whining and grinding as the car lurched and bounced on it's way to the city. Charlotte thought to herself how lovely it was here, peace and quiet, all alone with just a cat for company. She leant down to stroke her, Theodora turned herself in a haughty manner and settled back to sleep, Charlotte sighed.

Charlotte wondered around the house, it was very homely and exuded an aura of tranquility. She had no idea how long she had been here, or what had become of Hengel and that silly note. Had he sent it to Howard? Would Howard believe it? No, Howard was an intelligent, astute man; he would know at once that she hadn't sent it. She wondered where he was now. Had he returned to Luxor or was he still in Cairo. Her befuddled mind suddenly reprimanded her – idiot! Mrs. Fazakerley was on her way to Cairo, why oh why had Charlotte not thought to send Howard a note letting him know she was all right. It was too late now. Charlotte wanted to scream in frustration, what a complete and utter fool she was. The opportunity had been there for the taking and she'd muffed it. She slumped back down upon the couch in despair.

The drive to Cairo usually took about 35 – 40 minutes, depending on the whims of the car and the other traffic. Araminta had listened to the story of how Charlotte had ended up in a crashed automobile with a great deal of interest. A villain, treasure, a handsome hero, it all sounded very exciting indeed. In fact, this was the reason why Araminta had been looking forward to her trip to Cairo. If this Howard Carter, where had she heard that name before? If this Carter person was still at the Continental, she could let him know about Charlotte, and maybe even bring him back with her. She found the whole idea thrilling, Charlotte would so happy to see her friend again. She, Araminta Fazakerley would be the one to reunite them. Araminta was so busy with these thoughts that she found herself drifting into an indignant camel, who bellowed loudly and spat in her eye.

'Really,' she retorted, 'camels have no manners.'

The Arab, to whom the camel belonged, shouted out something to her, she only caught the last word, 'ya sharmouta!' She tutted to herself, muttering 'How rude.'

Araminta arrived in Cairo without further mishap, parking haphazardly, she pulled down her hat and gathered the spilled contents of her bag, thrusting everything back inside and squashing it closed. Crossing the road, the Giza bound bus service almost knocked her over; the driver appeared to shout something that certainly wasn't very polite. She waved her stick at him and continued to the other side unaware of the cacophony of car horns and the irate shouting of angry drivers.

She flung herself through the entrance door of the Continental Hotel, marched up to the reception desk and demanded to see Mr. Howard Carter forthwith. The receptionist, stunned by the apparition in front of him, for a moment forgot who he was and why he was there.

'Well, my good man,' demanded Araminta, 'didn't you hear what I said?'

Pulling himself together the man said, 'Forthwith?'

'Mr. Carter! For goodness sake man, are you heard of hearing?'

'Err, yes Mr. Carter, forgive me madam, I will telephone.'

'You do that.' she turned around and spotting a comfortable armchair said, 'I'll be sitting over there.'

'Yes, madam.' the receptionist eyed her warily, really these English women were so strange, he thought to himself. He shivered at the thought of having a wife like that; he shook his head and lifted the receiver.

'Yes,' said Carter's voice.

'There is a strange woman to see you, waiting in reception.'

'Do you know her name?' asked Howard.

The receptionist, who had forgotten to ask her name, and didn't care one way or the other replied, 'I do not know her name, she is an elderly lady, your mother perhaps?'

Howard bridled at this, 'I'll be down straight away.' and slammed the receiver back in its cradle. His mother had died many years ago, his mother indeed, impertinent man!

Making his way to the reception area, he looked around. He wasn't sure whom he was looking for, then his eyes alighted upon the large figure of an elderly lady, her hat had fallen over her face, her bag had spilled its contents over her shoes, and he could hear some faint rumblings coming from somewhere underneath her hat.

'Hello, my name's Carter.' he said, giving her a prod.

There was a loud grunt, the hat fell off, and her eyes opened. Peering at him she said, 'Who are you?'

Sighing deeply, he answered, 'Carter, you asked to see me.'

'I did? Oh, yes, of course I did. Goodness me, I'd forgotten all about it. Sit down; I had something to tell you.'

Howard helped her gather her belongings. They eventually settled down, just as a waiter arrived with a pot of tea and sandwiches, which he placed upon a nearby table.

'Shall I be mother?' said Araminta, without waiting for an answer, she poured the tea and they each helped themselves to a sandwich.

'My name is Fazakerley, Araminta Fazakerley.'

Howard choked on his tea.

'Are you all right?' she asked, handing him a napkin.

'Yes,' he spluttered, 'swallowed it the wrong way.'

'You ought to be careful, there's no need to gulp it down, my advice is to always sip tea gently, that way you can appreciate the taste.'

Howard smiled half-heartedly and wondered why he was

destined to attract mad, eccentric women.

'You wanted to talk to me' he said, hopefully.

'Of course, yes, I remember now. It's about your friend Charlotte.'

'Charlotte? She's gone back to England' said Howard, sadly.

'Nonsense, I left her at my house, she's perfectly well, although she did have a slight accident with an automobile.'

Howard looked alarmed.

'There's no need to upset yourself, she's quite recovered now'

'Where is she? I don't understand, she sent me a note saying she had returned to England, are you sure she's at your house? ' Howard thought the lady looked a bit vague and wasn't entirely sure if she had a complete set of marbles.

'Of course I'm sure, my dear man I'm not a half-wit. She told me her name was Charlotte Hambleton, and she told me about you, Howard Carter. If you are indeed Mr. Carter, then you're the person I'm looking for, if not, I shall finish my tea and take my leave.'

'I am Howard Carter, and I assure you Charlotte Hambleton is a very good friend of mine.'

'Well, in that case what are we arguing about? These really are very good sandwiches.'

Howard sighed, 'Can I see her?'

'She's not here, she's at my house.'

'Yes, you told me. May I ask where your house is so I can visit her?'

'Of course you can see her, my dear Mr. Carter. That's why I'm here, to take you to her. Didn't I explain that?'

Howard thought, she had confused him so much he couldn't remember if she had or hadn't.

'Probably.' he answered. 'How soon can we leave?'

'You're very eager I must say.' said Araminta, becoming caught up in the moment and forgetting all about her shopping and the appointment. 'I have an automobile you know.'

'You can drive it I hope?' asked Howard suspiciously, remembering Charlotte's attempts at driving.

'Of course I can young man, how on earth do you think I arrived here, by balloon?'

Howard wasn't sure what to say to that, he then found himself propelled out of the hotel and into the street.

'Goodness me, now where did I leave it?' murmured Araminta. Howard's spirits dro0ped, he opened his mouth and suddenly found himself dragged across the main road with cars and buses bearing down on top of him, insults hurled left, right and centre, horns blaring, brakes screeching, and his heart pounding in fear for his life.

'Here it is! I knew I must have left it somewhere, otherwise how would I get home again '

At a loss as to what the correct reply was to this logic, he climbed into the passenger seat, Araminta wedged herself next to him, the vehicle started with a loud bang and Howard found himself enveloped in black smoke. Coughing and spluttering, he was suddenly thrown forward as the vehicle gave a violent jerk and he banged his head on the windscreen, the momentum flung him back into his seat, Howard clutched at his nose to make sure it was still in one piece, and began to have serious misgivings about the whole trip.

'We're on our way at last, Mr. Carter', said an enthusiastic Araminta.

'How far away do you live?' he enquired, hoping it wasn't going to be a long journey.

'Oh, about forty minutes I should imagine, of course, I could drive faster and then we would arrive earlier, if you'd like.' she said, smiling at him genially.

Howard didn't like the sound of that, 'No, no, there's no rush, take your time'.

'Well, if you're sure.' Araminta replied, sounded rather disappointed.

Howard mopped his brow; he could feel another headache developing.

The old car wheezed, clanged and banged its way along the road. The car's suspension was non-existent causing it to bounce to such an extent Howard feared that any minute he would become airborne. Mrs. Fazakerley was oblivious to the discomfort, indeed so wedged in was she that the bouncing had no effect on her whatsoever, she cheerily sang, if that was the right word to use, "Climbing over Rocky Mountains".

'Do you like Gilbert and Sullivan, Mr. Carter?'

Howard had never given it much thought, 'I'm not sure.' he replied, cautiously.

'Wonderful operettas they wrote, of course they all tell the same story only the names of the characters and locations change. Gilbert wrote some very clever lyrics, I do enjoy the Major's patter song from Pirates of Penzance, would you like me to sing it for you?' asked Araminta, hopefully.

'If you must.' said Howard, closing his eyes and sighing with a heavy heart.

'Wonderful!' Mrs. Fazakerley went at it with gusto, it seemed clear to Howard that she had forgotten most of the words and was repeating what she did remember over and over again. He could a feel dull throbbing pain in his skull and wondered how much longer it was until they reached her home.

It appeared as if Araminta was performing the entire operetta for his benefit, Howard wasn't sure his equilibrium could take much more. Up ahead he could see an Arab and his camel, the Arab appeared to be gesticulating wildly with his arms. The camel, which had been standing quite placidly, suddenly turned very nasty when he saw the car and began to charge towards it. Howard looked on in alarm, what on earth was going on?

'Oh, don't worry about them Mr. Carter, just some old acquaintances of mine.'

The car swerved onto a verge to avoid the pair and partially demolished a stone wall; it then lurched and bumped back onto the road.

Just when Howard thought things couldn't possibly get any worse Araminta began to sing again. He began to wish he had never got out of bed that morning, being in prison would surely be better than this.

He was saved from further vocal torture when without any warning; the car lurched over to the right and screeched to a halt. Araminta, her hat hanging over one eye, exclaimed, 'Here we are, home safe and sound.'

How he survived the journey Howard didn't know, were all women drivers like this, he asked himself. Stumbling from the car, dusty and dishevelled, he looked around at his surroundings, he found himself in a slightly unkempt garden, unexpectedly, a loud voice bellowed in his ear, causing him to jump out of his skin,

'This way Mr. Carter, mind the broken paving stone, I usually forget and trip over it, it's a bit of nuisance I'm afraid.'

Howard gingerly walked behind her; he observed that from this angle Mrs. Fazakerley rather gave the impression of a large galleon sailing off to war.

Inside Charlotte had heard the car return, she stood up and waited for Araminta to make her entrance.

'My dear Charlotte,' called out a loud voice from the doorway, 'I've brought you a surprise, oh, I've lost him! Where are you Mr. Carter?'

Howard, who had caught his foot on a piece of trailing vine, was vainly trying to remove it, when Araminta grabbed him and propelled him inside.

'Here he is! I've found you're friendly hero for you.'

Charlotte jumped up and hastened forward to hug Howard, he was about to hug her, yet he also wanted to keep up a sense of propriety. While trying to make up his mind whether he should shake her hand or kiss her on the cheek, Charlotte leaned towards him, and they bashed their heads together, Charlotte fell back upon the sofa, Howard lost his hat and tripped over Theodora, who gave a piercing scream of disapproval. Araminta, overcome with joy at the reunion, became quite giddy and had to be settled down upon the sofa with a glass of brandy to steady her nerves.

After dinner, Howard and Charlotte went out into the garden; they sat side by side on a bench looking up at the waning crescent moon hanging in the evening sky. Charlotte told Howard of her kidnapping and subsequent escape. Howard was horrified at the way Hengel had treated her. She also told him about the letter he had forced her to write. Howard thought about this, he felt despair that he had ever doubted her and wondered if this situation would never end. Charlotte saw the worry writ large upon his face.

'We have to prove your innocence, we have to find some way of exposing Hengel as the treacherous man he is.'

'How?' asked Howard, 'Where do we even start?'

Charlotte thought about it, 'I'll follow him, he must have the treasure stashed somewhere. If he's in Cairo that may mean it's here as well.'

'I won't hear of it, you know how unstable he is, it's far too dangerous an undertaking.'

'Well, you can't go, Mrs. Fazakerley certainly can't go. What about Mr. Harrison?'

Howard shivered in distaste at the thought of the elderly lady becoming involved. 'Why Harrison?' he asked.

Charlotte answered, 'Well, he works for Hengel, but he doesn't like him, neither does Matula. Unfortunately, Matula is too scared of Hengel to be of any use to us. No, if we could get Harrison on our side we may have a chance to show the authorities that you're innocent.'

'Well,' said Howard, 'I don't think it's a good idea at all, you've already been kidnapped by him, and I don't trust Harrison. If I were you, I'd leave well alone. I'm sure we can find another way to prove that I didn't commit any indiscretions. I'll have to return to Cairo To-morrow, the court case is dragging on, if by chance anything may happen I don't want to miss it.'

'I can come with you. After all, you need someone to protect you from those dreadful women at the hotel.'

'Very funny,' replied Howard, 'No, I think you should stay here. That way we can make it difficult for Hengel to follow us. He doesn't know about Mrs. Fazakerley so you'll be safe here.' he thought for a minute, 'Providing of course you don't let her drive you anywhere.'

'All right, we can keep in touch by telephone; you can try and contact Harrison, and find out, subtly, if he's willing to join us.'

'I'm beginning to feel like I'm starring in a kinema crime drama.'

Araminta bustled outside beaming at the two of them, 'I couldn't help overhearing your conversation, and I am willing to do all I can to help. If you need me to do any sleuthing on your behalf or even to follow someone discreetly, you may count on me.'

Charlotte and Howard looked at each other in astonishment, not sure whether to laugh or cry.

'I thank you very much for you kind offer of assistance, Mrs. Frazel…' Howard came to a halt.

'Just call me Araminta.'

Charlotte could barely hold in her laughter, Howard glowered at her.

He cleared his throat and tried again, 'Araminta.' he said, barely able to bring himself to say it. Charlotte by now had turned red with suppressed laughter.

Howard struggled on, 'If we find we need any extra help we will of course turn to you.' he said as diplomatically as he could.

Araminta patted his hand, 'I've been very lonely since my

Bartholomew died you know. You're not married are you, Mr. Carter?'

Howard stared in horrified silence at the expectant expression upon Araminta's face. Charlotte let out a laugh and tried to turn it into a cough, Araminta turned her attentions away from Howard, to his relief.

'My dear Charlotte, are you quite all right?'

Charlotte nodded her head, unable to speak.

'I think you've been out in the night air too long, you still haven't fully recovered after your dreadful ordeal, come inside both of you. I think some hot cocoa will help to revive us.'

Araminta drove them to Cairo, Howard had wanted to take a taxi, he pleaded and begged to be allowed to phone for one, the indomitable lady would not hear of it, 'Of course I'm going to drive you, what kind of hostess would I be if I didn't make sure my guests arrived safely at their destination. Taxi Indeed!' 'With that she chivvied the reluctant man into the passenger seat.

Howard, not wishing to offend her after all the help she had been, reluctantly gave in. Charlotte, who had been semi-conscious during her trip with Araminta, was unaware of what lay ahead. Howard and Charlotte braved the mercifully short journey with a courageous spirit General Kitchener would have been proud of. When they were finally decanted out of the vehicle, Howard had almost lost the will to live, and Charlotte threw up her breakfast all over the shoes of a passing policeman. Having spent hours polishing them to a lustrous shine that blinded anyone who stared at them for too long, the policemen was, to say the least, rather put out by this turn of events. Strong words issued forth from his mouth, Araminta fussed around him trying to clean him up and only succeeded in knocking off his hat, which rolled out into the road and was flattened by a passing bus. This was too much for the poor man, his face red with apoplexy, he streamed forth all the curses of hell upon them and their families and their ancestors, and was only placated when Howard gave him a large sum of money to cover his hurt feelings, and to pay for the damage to his property.

CHAPTER FIFTEEN

In his hotel room, Hengel was gazing at his reflection in the bathroom mirror. He hated growing old, he still thought of himself as a young and virile man. He was sure he could see new creases and wrinkles upon his face, damn it, they were not there last night. It was this business with Carter that was ruining his visage, not to mention the strain upon his nerves. Then there was that wretched girl, he felt the bump on his head and winced. She would pay; he would find her, eventually.

'Bauer!' he shouted.

Baur limped into the bathroom, 'Yes, sir, you called.'

'How old do you think I look?'

Bauer wasn't sure what to say, he thought very carefully before answering and decided to tell the truth, 'Err 57, I think.'

Hengel glared at him, 'I don't want to be 57, I want to be 40.'

'But Herr Hengel, you can't be 40 if your son is 35.'

'Well, make him 25.'

'But his wife is 30.'

Hengel pushed past Bauer and made his way to the main room, 'I want…' just at that moment he tripped over a footstool and fell flat on the floor.

Bauer rushed over to help him up.

'I can manage,' snarled Hengel, jumping to his feet, 'don't put me in a wheelchair yet.'

'No sir.'

'Now, what was I saying? Ah, yes, the boxes, I wish to inspect them, we will go to the site To-morrow. Make sure all is ready for me.'

'Very well, Herr Hengel.'

'Good. Now bring me some refreshments.'

Back at Araminta's bungalow, Charlotte was bored. She missed Howard, but she knew he was preoccupied with the court case. Araminta fussed around worrying about her, she invited Charlotte to her friends little get togethers, which Charlotte dutifully attended. Here, she met many of Araminta's acquaintances, including her closest friends, Hettie and Emily, and recent recruit Susan. They were lovely people who enjoyed a good gossip, and playing cards. Charlotte was not very good at card games, and consequently didn't join in as much as she would like, as she always managed to lose no matter how hard she tried.

One day Araminta suggested to her that she ought to visit the outer lying areas around the Giza pyramids, she said there was a lot to see and Charlotte could hire a donkey and make a day of it. Araminta would make her a packed lunch, and it would be an interesting experience she was sure. Charlotte liked this idea and willingly acquiesced.

Early the next morning she made her way to Giza, to explore the area around the pyramids, where the old cemeteries, temples and unfinished pyramids were located.

Charlotte walked over to the stand where the donkeys were waiting. A crowd of boys ran towards her all shouting and gesticulating towards their donkeys, she was dragged from one side to the other, 'Quiet!' she shouted. The boys stopped talking and the donkeys pricked up their ears, wondering at the audacity of this newcomer. The donkeys hoped there might be an altercation and if so, they were rather hoping to take part in it.

'I'm looking for a friendly, reliable donkey.' said Charlotte.

The boys looked at each other and the shouting started once more. Charlotte sighed, where was Suzy when she needed her?

Then one of the boys shouted, 'Lateef, come here.'

A boy with the biggest grin Charlotte had ever seen stepped forward, with him was a donkey that eyed her suspiciously.

'I have very good donkey, very reliable and fast.' said Lateef.

The other boys started to snigger.

Charlotte patted the donkey on his head; the donkey nuzzled

her palm, wondering if there was a tasty titbit there, to his disappointment, there wasn't. Charlotte thought he looked very placid, the complete opposite of Suzy, but that may be no bad thing; after all, she was only out for a leisurely ride.

'Very well, I shall hire him for the day. What's he called?' asked Charlotte.

'Sam.' said Lateef, holding out a dirty hand.

Charlotte handed over the money; Lateef grabbed it quickly and pushed Charlotte up onto Sam.

'Shukraan,' she said, waving him goodbye.

'Afwan, miss.' answered Lateef, and all the boys started to laugh again.

Charlotte encouraged Sam to trot away. The scenery was yellow, the sky was blue, the desert sand was a sort of orangey yellow, yet somehow it was very beautiful and had a calming, almost hypnotic effect upon her. Her bag contained her lunch, a treat for the donkey, water and her camera. There were people about, but not crowded together, just sporadic groups over here or there. Donkeys and camels, either working or resting in what little shade there was, and the occasional car would thunder past. Up ahead were four men riding horses. The one in the middle seemed to be quite tall and thin, Charlotte looked at him again, it couldn't be could it? Hengel! Or was her overactive imagination playing tricks on her mind. The men were talking loudly, she couldn't quite make out what they were saying, but she recognized one voice, it was definitely Hengel. What was he up to? No good, she could be sure of that. She would follow him and find out.

Sam, a very placid donkey, was certainly no Speedy Gonzales, no matter how hard Charlotte tried to encourage him, he never deviated from his gait – a combination of a bit of trotting followed by a longer period of walking then back to the trotting and so on. Sighing, Charlotte strained her eyes to see the dwindling figure of Hengel far away in the distance, at least she thought it was him, the way things were going it would probably turn out to be a rock.

The journey seemed never ending, where on earth was he going? She had lost him, now what was she to do. Then she heard the sound of voices, at first Charlotte thought to attract their attention and ask them where she was, but she thought better of it, you never could tell who was friendly or who was likely to bash you on the head and lock you up.

Dragging herself and Sam behind a rocky hill type thingy, she peered over the edge; the men were too far away though so she was unable to get a good look at their faces. Sitting down, her back against the rock, Charlotte looked around, desert, sand, and sun burning down from a blue sky. She was sweating profusely; she cursed herself for being a fool in coming out here in the first place. Well, she couldn't sit here forever, standing up, she decided to trail behind the group of men she had seen. With any luck, they were heading back to civilization, and hopefully to somewhere she recognized.

The men were quite obviously in no hurry, Charlotte had difficulty concealing herself, as the rocks became scarcer and she worried one of them may turn around and see her, one of the men, not one of the rocks. She had a blinding headache, the sun was beating down giving a good impression of a furnace. She was probably going to die of sunstroke, and nobody would even notice, nobody would know where to find her. She felt the tears well up and her nose began to run, she couldn't find a handkerchief, so used her sleeve to wipe her face. Looking ahead, to her horror, the men had gone, disappeared into nowhere, she began to panic.

Up in the distance, she could see a rocky area, encouraging Sam to put some speed into his trot/walk routine, as she drew nearer she noticed a couple of entrances hewn out of the rock face, judging by the look of them, probably many millennia ago. The entrances as far as Charlotte could estimate were approximately 350 to 400 feet apart. Presumably, the group had gone inside one of the caves.

Leaving Sam tethered to a bush, with a dish of water and a bunch of carrots, Charlotte went to peer inside the nearest entrance, it seemed very quiet, she wondered inside a few steps and listened, no sounds came from within. Stepping outside she walked over to the second entrance, like the first cave, this one also had torches placed at intervals along the walls. She went inside, and stood still, she thought she could hear faint voices in the distance. She stealthily made her way further inside, despite the torches some parts of the cave remained in darkness. Reaching out her hand to feel the rough wall, Charlotte slowly followed it further into the interior. Suddenly, her hand felt nothing, she had been so intent on her task she hadn't realized how dark it had become. Scrabbling around with her arms now, trying to find the wall, she lost all sense of direction, panicking, Charlotte was about to cry out for help when her feet disappeared from under her and she fell down for what seemed like an eternity before landing at the bottom of a shaft.

Charlotte lay quite still. She had no idea how long she had been down here, whether it was minutes, hours, days or even weeks. She tried to move, it seemed she had no legs, at least she was unable make them move, had they dropped off in mid-fall? Don't be silly, she said to herself, they must be somewhere.

Very, very, gingerly she sat up, a sharp pain shot through her back, she cried out. Grimacing she tried to manoeuvre herself into a more comfortable position. As she leaned forward, her head hit the side of the shaft, wonderful, as if she didn't have enough pain. Actually though this was quite fortuitous, she shimmed her bottom towards the wall and propped her back against it. The pain from her leg was excruciating, Charlotte felt along its length, there were sticky patches all over, and her foot was bothering her as well. She swept the hair out of her eyes and smelt the tangy iron of blood upon her hand.

Charlotte hoped that her leg wasn't broken; she wiggled it about, no, probably just badly bruised. Her other leg appeared intact; it felt badly bruised as well. She looked up; she thought she could see the hole vaguely outlined in the dim torchlight, maybe that was wishful thinking though, and how was she ever to get out of here? Swallowing, her throat dry and dusty, she tried to call out, 'Help, is anyone up there?' she croaked. This was no good, nobody could possibly hear her. She tried again, 'Help, please, somebody get me out of here.' Only silence met her ears.

Crying now with anger and frustration, Charlotte slammed her fist on the ground. No, she wasn't going to die down here, she couldn't, please not here and not all alone. She thought of Howard and Suzy; how she longed to see them, touch them. And what about Sam, what would happen to him? Perhaps this was all a terrible nightmare and she would wake up and find herself back in Araminta's spare room, with Suzy outside causing her usual chaos. Charlotte sniffed, it just wasn't fair, and why had fate picked on her and then dumped her down a whacking great hole?

Charlotte must have nodded off because she suddenly woke up with a start. She could hear something, someone moving about, was somebody up there. Was she imagining it? Pulling herself together, Charlotte yelled as loud as she could, 'Please, if anyone's up there help me, I'm stuck in this hole.'

A light appeared at the aperture, a voice said, 'Are you hurt?'

'No, just bruised and battered.' cried Charlotte.

'OK, I'll be back in minute.' The light disappeared and Charlotte was alone once more, this time though there was a small flicker of hope in her heart.

The light returned, then more lights and the sounds of people.

'Are you still alive down there?' said the voice.

'Yes, I'm still in this world, just,' replied Charlotte, delighted because she recognized that voice.

'Good, won't be long now.'

'Have you seen a donkey? She enquired.

'Yeah, there's a donkey out here, is he with you?'

Thank goodness for that, thought Charlotte. 'Yes, he's name is Sam. Please look after him.'

'He's fine, don't worry.'

She could hear somebody scrambling down a rope, or something. Her heart was beating in anticipation of seeing daylight once more. Without warning, a large object fell on her head and bounced away into the further recesses of the shaft. 'Sorry about that, did it hit you?' shouted the voice.

'Yes,' said Charlotte, 'I thought you were rescuing me, not adding to my injuries. Anyway, what was it?'

'I think it was a piece of rock.'

'That's very comforting.'

'Hey, Charlotte, thought I recognized the voice, what are you doing down here?'

'Harrison, how relieved I am to see a friendly face and in answer to your question, I'm down here looking for mushrooms.'

'I guess that's an example of English sarcasm.'

'Well, ask a silly question… Anyway, how did you find me?'

'I saw a donkey ambling away on its on own, and wondered what was going on, then I heard a voice shouting for help. I saw you down the bottom of the shaft and as I wasn't doing anything else I thought I'd help you out.'

'That was very considerate of you, Mr. Harrison.'

'Jonathan, remember.' He poked her about, 'Does that hurt?'

'Ow!' she shouted.

'It's not broken, just bruised.'

'I seem to have lost my foot; it's not where it should be. Ouch!'

'I've found your foot; it's attached to your leg.'

'If you've quite finished prodding me about would you please get me out of here?' said Charlotte.

'I thought we'd take tea down here.'

'Very funny.'

Lift up your arms, she did so, Harrison tied the rope around her and called up the shaft to his colleague to begin pulling.

'Will it take long?'

'Why, are you planning on going somewhere?'

'Well, I am hungry, I think I may have missed my dinner.'

'Oh, I see! In that case, we'll try to make it as fast as we can.'

Charlotte closed her eyes as her aching body was hauled upwards, gently bouncing off the walls as she made her way up to the light. After only a couple of minutes or so the top of the shaft came into view, hands reached down to lift her out, and gently carried her into the open. Dusk was falling; Charlotte could just make out the truck.

Harrison leaned over her, 'You see, you weren't even that far down.'

He pointed a torch down the hole.

She gazed down, feeling slightly foolish, sighing, Charlotte retorted, 'Well, it certainly gave a good impression of being far deeper.' She turned with a haughty nod of her head and climbed into the truck.

CHAPTER SIXTEEN

Charlotte had a surprise waiting for her when she returned to Araminta's house. Araminta was fussing about, wondering where earth she had got to, her poor visitor had been waiting for hours. Theodora opened an eye, then deciding there was nothing to interest her, she closed it again. Charlotte wondered who the visitor could be.

'Howard, oh, how glad I am to see you.' Charlotte gave him a hug, Howard, not sure whether to hug her back or not, decided upon the latter.

'How are you?' she gushed, 'Have you got the tomb back yet?'

'I am keeping well, and no are the answers to your questions'. Howard replied, 'Perhaps I should be asking how you are?'

'Oh, don't worry about me, where's Sam, I'm worried about him.'

'Sam?'

'A donkey. He belongs to Lateef. I hope he hasn't wondered off.'

'Why would Lateef wonder off?'

'Not him, Sam, the donkey. Honestly Howard, try to keep up.'

'What is this obsession you have with donkeys?'

'Well, they're very clever and intelligent, unlike some people I could mention. And they're very loyal.'

'Yes, they're also very destructive and one in particular is a danger to the population.'

'Only to a certain duplicitous German and his gang of ne'er do wells.'

Araminta kept winking at Howard, Howard had turned red, and Charlotte wondered what was going on. Then she noticed Howard had brought with him a bouquet of flowers and a box of chocolates.

'Are they, by any chance, for me?' asked Charlotte.

'Yes, I do beg your pardon, I forgot I had brought them in all the excitement.' replied Howard with a start.

Charlotte took the flowers, they were lovely a mix of roses, chrysanthemums and cornflowers, all in different shades of red, pink and lilac.

Araminta sighed wistfully, 'Silly me, I thought Mr. Carter had brought them for me.'

Howard coughed, at the remembrance of how Araminta had embraced him in her ample bosom, and his embarrassment at telling her the gifts were for Charlotte.

'Thank you!' Charlotte was very touched by this kind gesture, she looked at Howard who had turned a deep shade of red, leaned over and hugged him, when she let go she noticed he had turned an even darker shade of red.

Howard cleared his throat, 'What have you been up to?'

'I went for a ride, with Sam. Then I fell down a hole and Mr. Harrison rescued me.'

'You fell down a hole? Could you not see it?'

'My dear girl, did you hurt yourself?' said a concerned Araminta.

'No, I'm fine, just bruised, oh, and a rock fell on my head, apart from that all is well. Oh yes, and I saw Hengel.'

'Don't tell me he was at the bottom of the shaft as well.' said Howard.

'Do you want me to tell the story or not?'

Howard sighed and nodded his head.

'So, there I was out for a quiet desert ride with Sam, when I saw Hengel and some other men. Therefore, I decided to follow them. Unfortunately Sam wasn't to keen on going faster than a trot and I lost them. Then, quite by accident we, that is Sam and I, stumbled upon the openings of two caves. And it was while I was investigating one of these caves that I discovered this whacking great hole, or shaft, or whatever it was pretending to be.'

'You're very lucky that Harrison found you.'

'I don't know about luck; don't forget Harrison works for

Hengel, so if Hengel is up to something within those caves, then it's no coincidence that Harrison was there as well.'

'Why didn't he inform Hengel about you?'

'I don't know why, perhaps he's just a nice man, I'll ask him if you like.'

'Promise me you'll look after yourself, I was worried about you.'

Now it was Charlotte's turn to redden, 'There's no need to worry, honestly, I promise I won't get into any more trouble.'

Araminta returned with cake and tea, she sat herself next to Howard and patted his arm.

'Shall I pour?' she asked. There were three slices of Madeira cake already cut and laid out upon individual plates, Araminta handed the small slice to Charlotte, the very large slice to Howard, and the not so large slice for herself. She smiled fondly at him.

'Thank you Mrs. Fazerk…' said Howard.

'It's Fazakerley! Why don't you just call me Araminta, it's a tiny bit easier to say.'

'Only a tiny bit.' he replied. He leaned over to Charlotte and whispered, 'I can't bring myself to say it.'

'Try it, Ara-mint-a, you see it's easy, just rolls off the tongue, well, almost.' Charlotte whispered back.

'Lovely cake, Araminta.' said Charlotte.

'Yes, Emily is a very good cook. She loves making cakes, and other delicacies. Mmm delicious.' said Araminta with a mouthful of cake, some of which ended up on Howard's lap.

The telephone rang, 'Oh bother!' said Araminta. 'Who on earth can that be?' She heaved herself up, dropping cake crumbs everywhere and went to answer the telephone.

'She's been threatening to go to the police and report you as being kidnapped into slavery.' said Howard. 'When she's not threatening to do that, she's dropping very unsubtle hints about how lonely she is, and how lonely I must be, and perhaps we ought to think about marriage.'

Charlotte couldn't help laughing. 'Oh dear, I'm sure you'd be very happy with her bustling about, she'd look after you and make sure you had a proper meal, and don't forget the advantages of her car, she's a ready-made chauffeur. Think of all those trips you could take driving around the English countryside, it sounds lovely.'

Howard didn't look happy, even his moustache had drooped. 'I don't think that's very amusing Miss Hambleton.'

'Oh dear, we're back to being very formal, I apologize. You're quite right though, it would never work. You're the wrong man for her.' Charlotte laughed.

The next day, Harrison came to call upon her. Araminta was out for lunch with her friends. Charlotte was happy to have company; she took the opportunity to ask him more questions about Hengel.

'I make deals on his behalf, selling and buying antiquities, I make hotel and travel arrangements, I'm a jack of all trades really.'

'What sort of antiquities?'

'Legitimate ones, mostly'

Charlotte eyed him suspiciously.

He said, 'Oh, they're bought and sold through dealers verified and approved by the Egyptian Government.'

'I see,' she said, 'there's nothing underhand going on then. I mean, it's definitely meant to be Howard who's the thief and not Hengel?'

'Well, who can say? In all honesty I reckon Hengel is just as crooked as Carter.'

'Don't say that about Howard, he's nothing like that dreadful Hengel. At least Howard has some integrity. He loves what he does, he's knowledgeable, and takes care of all the precious treasures that he finds. Your wretched Hengel doesn't give a toss about them; all he wants is money and the kudos of showing them off as part of his collection.'

They sat upon a wooden bench in the shade of the beautiful sycamore tree.

'You really like Carter, don't you?' said Harrison

'Yes, I do. I think he's a lovely man.' replied Charlotte, defiantly. 'He's very clever, sensitive, and he loves animals.'

'Ah, well, I don't think I can compete with that.'

'Don't you love animals?'

'Sure I do. I'm just not very sensitive.' he gave her a wide grin.

'Very funny. I don't understand you, what are your motives? What is it about working for Hengel that attracts you so much?'

'Money, I love money and he pays very well.'

'Yes, he also arranges to kill people. Have you killed anyone on his behalf?'

Harrison looked at her, wondering how much he should tell

her. 'I don't have anything to do with that.'

'You know about it then and you just turn a blind eye to it. What sort of man are you?'

'I'm under no illusions as to what Hengel gets up to. I have already got my escape route arranged. In fact, I'm planning to leave him in the not to distant future. Just don't tell him.'

'I won't need to, he's got spies everywhere. He probably already knows about your escape route. You should watch your back or you could end up like Barnaby.'

'I've no intention of letting that happen to me. You ought to take care of yourself as well, he's not very happy with you. If I were you, I would keep a safe distance away from him. You never know what he may do to you, he may have plans to ruin your life, or he may even kill you.'

'When you say ruin my life, you mean Hengel might frame me for some misdemeanor, like he did with Howard?'

'He certainly wouldn't want you to be happy; he'd probably make your life very difficult.'

'By spreading malicious lies about me?'

'That's about it. He's a ruthless guy; you shouldn't cross him, ever.'

'No,' said Charlotte, 'but Leo Barnaby did, and he paid the price with his life. Hengel probably has spies planted amongst Howard's workmen. They're able to come and go without suspicion; the guards recognize them as part of the team. Hengel could easily have planted the stolen treasure in Howard's home, then all he would have to do was bide his time. Unfortunately for him, Barnaby developed a conscious, and tried to warn Howard that he was about to be framed. Hengel overhears part of this conversation, kills Barnaby and plants his body in Howard's home, then tips off the police. Luckily for Howard though, I turned up at just the right time, and helped him get rid of the body.'

'I can't believe I'm hearing this. Actually I'm not sure I want to hear this.'

'Well, you'd better believe it Mr. Harrison, because I can assure you it's probably quite true.'

Harrison stared at her. He looked into her eyes; he knew she believed every word she had just told him about Hengel.

'So, Mr. Harrison, are you going to help me to prove Howard's innocence?' Charlotte asked.

'And get killed too? You must be joking. No, I'm sorry, Charlotte, I value my life too much.'

'Very well, then Mr. Harrison, I shall prove Howard's innocence on my own. But just you remember, Hengel is quite capable of killing you whether you help me or not. Especially if he knows you've been talking to me.'

CHAPTER SEVENTEEN

Mindful of everyone's warnings about the threat Hengel posed, Charlotte's idea was to disguise herself and return to the cave to find out what exactly was going on. She was determined to look for Hengel herself, and prove he was the thief.

The next morning she visited a photographic shop and left the proud owner of a 35mm camera that not only took still photographs but also moving images. In addition, by removing a lid from the back of the camera and placing it in front of a light source the camera became a projector. It was perfect! Now all she had to do was secretly record Hengel, hopefully with the missing treasure.

She visited more shops, buying various supplies from bemused traders, until, exhausted she returned to the house. She felt hot and dusty, sweat was pouring down her back and her feet were killing her. After a nice bath and a cool drink, she began to feel herself. Eagerly unpacking her purchases Charlotte spread them on top of her bed. Yes, she was sure her plan would work; she would go to bed early, as she wanted to be up and on her way before dawn.

Deep in the depths of sleep, Charlotte was dimly aware of a loud racket somewhere nearby. An incessant ringing, clanging noise, 'what, where am I…' she muzzily mumbled to herself. She opened her eyes, realized the racket was coming from the alarm clock and reached out her arm to turn it off, knocking it on the floor and banging her head on the table as she tried to retrieve it.

Dressing herself in her disguise, she looked in the mirror, not quite the effect she had hoped for. Staring in front of her was the image of a very effeminate man. Oh, well, it would have to do.

She took the bus to Giza and received some very suspicious looks from the driver and her fellow passengers. Ignoring their stares she settled into a window seat and watched the scenery go by. Then she remembered travelling in buses made her feel sick. Too late to get off now, fortunately the window was open, allowing a smallish breeze to waft over her, and helping to dispel the smell of the diesel fumes that perfumed the interior of the bus.

Arriving at the last stop, opposite the Mena House Hotel, Charlotte fell out of the bus and had to be helped up by two elderly ladies. Who sat her down, said something she couldn't understand, and left her there. Great, they probably thought she was a drunken tourist.

She pulled herself together and went over to the donkey park where she found Lateef, and asked for Sam. He looked at her suspiciously, this was going well, he hadn't recognized her.

He brought Sam over, the donkey seemed to remember her, and nuzzled her hand. Lateef handed her the reins and said, 'Enjoy your ride Miss, this time don't lose him.'

She glared at him; he shrugged his shoulders and said, 'Sorry, enjoy your ride, sir.' He bowed his head as he said this, then he and the other boys burst out laughing. Clearly, Charlotte's disguise wasn't as effective as she had hoped.

To make amends for not coming with her, Harrison had drawn her a map showing her the route to take and the correct cave she should investigate. He told her to be very careful though, because although Hengel had returned to Luxor on business, some of his men may still be in the vicinity.

Charlotte was feeling very hot. She had no idea how men coped dressed in suits in this heat, how she longed to be wearing a dress instead of a three-piece suit. What on earth had possessed her to wear one? She could have found a light linen suit, the type that Hengel favoured, but no, she had to emulate her hero, Howard. Well, there was nothing to be done about it now; she would just have to suffer.

The route hadn't seemed so far on the map, yet it seemed as if she had been out here for an eternity. Nothing but desert and rocks surrounded her; with her sense of direction, she had probably crossed the border and was now wondering about in Libya. The hills were becoming steeper; she dismounted and left Sam munching on some greenery from a bush of some sort. Rummaging in her bag for her camera, she felt something sticky. Actually, everything seemed sticky. Pulling the camera out she discovered, to her horror, that it was covered in melted chocolate. Great, this is what happens when you have a sweet tooth.

She recognized this place; these were the hills and rocky outcrops where the caves should be She made a mental note to be more careful where she put her feet upon when entering the cave. Leaving her bag with Sam, clutching the cleaner but still slightly sticky camera, Charlotte crept along the path. She came to a turning, and very, very slowly stuck her head round the corner. There was no one in sight. She continued on stealthily, and there on her left was the narrow entrance to the cave. Inside it was completely dark, she wondered if she was in the right place. Standing still, she listened intently, there was no sound to be heard, except for the faint hissing of the torches. As she was about to enter she saw a shadow moving across the lit wall.

Charlotte left the cave, retrieved Sam, and walked back down the track. A few hundred yards later she came to a slope, she and Sam scrambled their way up. At the top were a few bushes and a rocky outcrop. It wasn't an ideal hiding place; there were no trees or overhangs to provide shelter. Charlotte removed a blanket from her bag and covered Sam so the sun's fierce rays wouldn't burn him. She took off her hat and plonked it on the donkey's head, trying, unsuccessfully, to tuck his ears inside it. Living in England where it seemed to rain on a daily basis, Charlotte was in the habit of always bringing an umbrella when she went out; in Egypt she found it equally helpful to always bring a parasol when venturing into the heat of the day. She sat down and waited.

Ten minutes later Charlotte heard her stomach rumbling. She gave Sam a drink of water and a carrot, and found a rather squashed, slightly chocolate covered slice of cream cake in her bag. Five minutes later, she heard the sound of donkey's hooves on the track below. Carefully peering down, she saw it was two men, presumably heading back towards the Nile, or maybe some meeting house in Cairo itself.

Gathering her belongings back into her bag, Charlotte led Sam down the path and returned to the cave. She worried that the men may have left a guard behind; looking around though, she couldn't see a sign of another living person. Pulling her torch out of her jacket pocket, she switched it on with the beam pointing downwards, this time she wanted to make sure her feet were walking on terra firma. Charlotte stroked Sam's nose and left him another bowl of water. Satisfied that the donkey appeared to be happy now he was inside and away from the heat, she turned her attention to discovering what exactly was hidden inside.

Charlotte was surprised to see electric lights up ahead, what if someone was still here? She stood listening, but could hear nothing. Feeling a bit braver now, she continued to walk towards the light. As she drew nearer, Charlotte flattened herself against the wall, and switched off her torch. Slowly, step by step she inched her way nearer and nearer. Still she couldn't see anyone. The wall disappeared and she found herself in a cavern, stacked all along the sides were boxes. Some lay open upon the floor, straw and shreds of paper strewn all about them. Charlotte felt her heart beat faster; she had found the stolen treasure.

She filmed the general layout of the boxes, and then filmed some close-up shots of the ones that were open. Charlotte put the camera down so she could examine the objects. There were necklaces, and jars, fans, and jewellery, and linen cloth, she filmed them all. Upon examining the other boxes she found they were nailed shut, damn it, she thought. She couldn't risk opening them though; she took photographs of the closed boxes just in case.

She returned to the open boxes, and looked again at the beautiful treasures within. Some of them seemed familiar, she couldn't quite think why. Probably photographs of them had appeared in one of her books about Ancient Egypt. She gazed about her in astonishment, what was Hengel going to do with all this treasure? He couldn't sell it, could he? Perhaps there were collectors who would indeed pay a gigantic sum of money to own one of these priceless artifacts, and keep it hidden in a secret room for their own private delectation.

She stood in the entrance to the cavern and took a wide shot of all the boxes. Making her way back to Sam, still thinking about the familiarity of the objects she had just seen, she suddenly remembered why they were so familiar. Her visit to the Egyptian Museum, that's where she had seen them. She clearly remembered Howard telling her about their history and who had found them. Where these perhaps duplicates? Charlotte returned to the cavern and took a closer look. She picked up some of the objects and filmed them from all angles. Unfortunately, she wasn't an expert and she had no idea if these were the genuine artifacts or not. Howard would be sure to know, she would have to bring him here as soon as possible.

Something caught her eye in one of the dark recesses, more boxes. These ones had been filled with broken pieces of pottery and battered and bent gold plates. These must be the unfortunate pieces of treasure that had been in the cave in Thebes on that memorable day when Suzy had run amok. She wondered if these pieces were the genuine articles as well, if so, it would likely cause Howard to be more predisposed to dislike Suzy.

Unable to bear the heat any longer, Charlotte discarded the jacket and waistcoat, rolled up her shirt sleeves and headed back to Mena House, as fast as she could make Sam go. This time he was adamant that he wasn't even going to trot, and walking would do very well thank you. In fact, the donkey was in no rush to go back; if this person sitting on his back was in a hurry then she could jolly well use her own legs. Coincidentally, Charlotte was thinking the same thoughts, that it would be quicker for her to walk and leave Sam to his own devices. She remembered Lateef warning her not to lose Sam again, and resigned herself to reaching Mena House within the next week, or possibly the next two weeks.

The magnificent funerary mask made of gold and lapis lazuli was the most beautiful and unique object he had ever possessed. Inlays of black and white for the eyes and eyebrows glinted in the sunlight. Hengel stared at the exquisite creation, he marvelled at the beautiful face of the young king, the magnificent artisanship that had gone into creating this exceptional masterpiece, which was now his pride and joy. The moment he had seen it he knew it was destined for his collection. He had paid a series of artisans a great deal of money to replicate the mask, once they had completed the task he had had them all killed, retrieving his money, the mask and its fake.

The fake funerary mask of Psusennes I. sat proudly in the Egyptian Museum, the so-called "experts" hadn't even noticed - they were all stupid fools. It had been so easy; the museum had no security or proper locks. His men had gained access easily, and were able to swap the originals with the fakes at a leisurely pace. A shadow crossed in front of him.

'Herr Hengel, sir, the crates are all loaded onto the plane.'

Hengel, who couldn't take his eyes off the mask, nodded.

The man stayed where he was, 'Sir, shall I help you with the mask?'

'No, I will pack it myself, wait outside.'

The packing crates contained concealed compartments where the treasures nested within their soft bedding. Ostensibly, Hengel was removing legitimate antiquities; he was free to leave the country without any interference from local customs or other authorities.

Carefully packing the mask in its box, he attached the lid, and gentle carried the box to the cargo plane he had hired, which was waiting at the head of a wadi. Settling himself into his seat the box safely secured in the adjacent seat, Hengel gave the signal that he was ready. The plane began to taxi, gaining speed until it lifted up into the air, turned and headed towards Germany.

Charlotte was happily wearing a dress once more. She had arrived in Cairo and found Howard sitting on the hotel terrace; she ordered herself a lemonade and told him of her discovery.

'You'll have to come and see it for yourself, I can't tell if their genuine or not, I've taken photographs and film footage.'

'I can't leave until To-morrow.'

'It may be too late. Howard we should go now, it's important, it's evidence, it could help exonerate you.'

Howard sighed, the courts and his lawyers were still arguing, and he was stuck in limbo. He felt tired, he knew he should show some enthusiasm, after all Charlotte had gone out of her way to help him, and almost been killed in the process.

He looked into her eager face, 'Oh, very well, we'll leave this evening.'

Charlotte was about to protest that they should leave now.

Howard was adamant though, 'It's far too hot to be out in the desert now, and besides I have to keep an appointment with my lawyer within the next hour.'

'I can show you the film footage if you like.'

'Not now, I'll look at when I come back.'

Charlotte stood up, 'Honestly, I don't know what's wrong with you. Anyone would think you didn't want the tomb back. You've just given up, haven't you? You don't care if one day the rozzers turn up at your door and arrest you, and you'll spend the rest of your life in prison doing porridge.'

'Rozzers?' questioned Howard.

'Yes, rozzers.' Howard looked taken aback, Charlotte continued, 'Well, I haven't given up. One way or another, with or without your help, I'm going to prove your innocence, whether you like it or not.' With that, she turned to make a dramatic exit, collided with a passing waiter, and ended up soaked to the skin with various beverages, and lumps of ice sliding down her dress. She turned to glower at Howard, who sat there with a bemused expression upon his face. Turning once more for a second attempt at a dramatic exit, she managed to leave without any further mishap, the waiter, meanwhile, giving her a very wide berth.

Later that night in Howard's suite Charlotte was slumped in a chair, staring balefully at him. 'I told you we should have left earlier. Heaven knows where he's taken it now.'

'I hasten to point out that if we had arrived earlier we may very well have stumbled across them in the act of moving it. Hengel and his men could easily have either left us in the middle of the desert to die or just killed us there and then.'

Charlotte sighed, 'I know, it's just so frustrating to be that close and to have the opportunity of catching him red-handed snatched away at the last minute. Why does nothing ever go right? Why does fate work in his favour, why for a change can't it help us?'

'Never mind, my dear Charlotte, we'll get the better of him eventually. To-morrow we'll visit the museum and show the director the photographs, hopefully he will allow us to examine the objects on display and we will be able to say with certainty whether they are genuine or not. I suggest for now we go to bed and get some rest.'

'What time is it?'

'It's nearly five o'clock.'

'Mmm, not much point going to bed.'

'Why?'

'By the time I've got to my room, changed into my pyjamas and finished in the bathroom it will be time to get up.'

Raising his eyebrows, Howard said, 'Goodnight Charlotte.'

'Oh very well, goodnight Howard, see you in five minutes.' and with a wave of her hand she left the room.

CHAPTER EIGHTEEN

Makalani Hafez had been the director of the Egyptian Museum for almost eight years. He was of medium height, and very round, he had a jolly countenance and an infectious laugh. He was married with five children, four girls and one boy. His wife had once been very lovely to look out, with a sweet personality, which, somehow, over the years had disappeared. Her face was now harsh and her tongue even harsher. She had a mean right hand especially when wielding a large frying pan. He gently felt the bump on the back of his head, which throbbed with pain. He'd only gone out for a celebratory meal with some colleagues from the museum; admittedly, he had neglected to mention to her that he would be late home. However, he saw no reason for her to be so upset about it. She shouted and cursed him, claimed she had been slaving over a hot stove all day cooking for him, threw the dinner plate at him, which just missed him by a fraction of an inch. Then clanged him on the head with a pan, and told him in future he could make his own bloody dinner.

He sat at his desk, clutching a couple of aspirin and a glass of water, when a knock at the door brought him back to reality. 'Yes, what is it?'

A head poked round the door, 'A Mr. Carter to see you.'

Mr. Carter, what on earth could he possibly want? He shook his head, 'Tell him to go away, I am busy.'

There was the sound of muffled voices behind the door, the head popped through once more, 'He says he will not go away, he

121

has something very important to tell you, and you must let him in. There is a girl here too.'

Hafez's ears pricked up at this, a girl, maybe he should see Carter after all. 'All right, let them in.'

Howard and Charlotte were shuffled in to the room, and told to sit down, which they did.

'Mr. Carter, how are you? Any progress yet with your court case?' asked Hafez.

'Not yet, I'm afraid they are still discussing the matter. In a round about way, it's why I've come to see you.'

Charlotte coughed.

Howard looked at her, 'Oh, yes, this is my colleague, Miss Charlotte Hambleton.'

Hafez stood up to shake hands with her, 'I am Makalani Hafez, Director of this magnificent museum. What a pleasure it is to look at such a beautiful lady, you make my heart sing with joy.'

Charlotte blushed, 'Thank you, Mr. Hafez; it's very kind of you to say so.'

'Not at all.'

Howard rolled his eyes, 'Mr. Hafez, if I may continue?'

'Of course, of course, please say what you have to say.' said Mr. Hafez, still beaming at Charlotte.

Howard continued, 'With your permission we'd like to examine the following objects.' Howard handed Hefez the photographs.

'I originally found these treasures packed in crates and hidden in a cave in Luxor.' explained Charlotte. 'Then quite by chance I was going for a donkey ride in the desert near Giza, and I saw Herr Hengel, I followed him to another cave, then I fell down a shaft. Anyway, that's another story. I eventually found my way back and took film footage and photographs of objects that had yet to be packed away. Unfortunately by the time I returned with Howard, Hengel had already removed everything.' Charlotte stopped to take a breath.

Hefez looked stunned, his head began to hurt again, and he gingerly touched the bump and winced. 'Miss Hambleton, I am sorry for being very slow in mind this morning, but I do not quite understand the meaning of your tale.'

Howard replied, 'What Miss Hambleton is trying to say, and making a complete mess of it.' Charlotte glared at him indignantly. 'Is we think Hengel has replicated these objects and placed fake ones in the museum, we would like your permission to check if this is so.'

Hefez stared at them open-mouthed. He looked at the photographs; they showed jewellery, a couple of gold funerary masks, some beautiful ivory caskets, and bejewelled ebony boxes. He shook his head, he knew that security wasn't as strong as it ought to be, even so, how on earth would anyone be able to walk in and out of here with these treasures without somebody noticing, after all some of the boxes were not exactly small, you couldn't put them in your pocket.

'Mr. Carter, is this maybe you're idea of a joke?'

'No, it is not. I strongly recommend that you do as I ask, before it's too late.'

'Too late for what?'

'Too late to get the originals back, Hengel will sell them to private collectors, once that happens we'll never see them again.'

Hefez looked at the photographs again. He sighed, well, what harm could it do. 'Very well, come with me.'

They left the office and followed Hefez down the stairs. Although Hefez was large in girth, muscle he claimed, though his wife claimed it was the consequence of eating far too much, he had tiny feet and he didn't so much as walk but spring. Charlotte marvelled as he sprang down the stairs at a cracking pace, his feet moving so fast they were almost a blur. Howard trotted after him, and Charlotte tried to keep up, but was wary of missing her footing and landing at the bottom in an undignified heap.

Howard spent hours going from one display cabinet to another, he minutely examined each object until he was satisfied and only then moved onto the next object. Charlotte having nothing to do but wait, had become bored and impatient, so she and Mr. Hefez had gone back to his office and treated themselves to a very nice cup of tea for Charlotte, a Turkish coffee for Hefez and some delicious little butter cookies stuffed with dates and nuts and sprinkled with sugar.

After tea, they went back downstairs to look for Howard. He had just finished looking at the last object, his face took on a serious expression as he looked up and saw them approaching.

'Well,' asked Hefez, 'what have you discovered?'

'It's not good, there's no gentle way of breaking this news to you.'

Hefez's eyes opened widely, 'What are you trying to tell me?'

'That all of these objects are fakes, Hengel has the real ones.' There was a crash. Howard turned to look at Hefez, to his surprise he had disappeared.

Charlotte pointed down towards the floor, Howard looked and there was Hefez lying flat out in a dead faint. Charlotte bent down, and clasped his hand, 'Mr. Hefez, can you hear me? Are you all right?'

'Of course he's not all right, he's fainted and knocked himself out.' said Howard.

'Mr. Hefez,' shouted Charlotte, 'please wake up.' there was no reaction. 'He's not moving, maybe he didn't hear me.'

'I should think the dead heard you. The mummies upstairs are probably climbing out of their cases as we speak.' said Howard.

'I don't see you doing anything to help the poor man.' There was a groan, 'Mr. Hefez, say something, please.'

Hefez opened his unfocussed eyes, and stared blindly into the distance. 'Are you telling me my collection, the one I am meant to look after, is nothing but a fake?'

'Probably not all of it,' replied Howard, cheerfully.

Charlotte kicked him. 'Do you mind?' she said to Howard, 'Try not to get upset Mr. Hefez. Can you stand up?'

Hefez groaned again, he said in a weak voice, 'fakes.' Then he closed his eyes. With the help of a security guard, they manoeuvred the stricken man to a chair. Another guard arrived with a glass of water, Charlotte tried to get Hefez to drink, but the liquid just spilled down his chin. 'He's in shock.' said Charlotte. 'What shall we do?'

Howard called the guard over and told him to help Hefez to his office. The guard, a big, tall man, lifted Hefez as though he were a sack and threw him over his shoulder.

Charlotte and Howard watched them ascend the stairs. 'Great, now what happens?' said Charlotte.

'We pay a visit to Monsieur Boivin.' answered Howard.

Boivin was taking the opportunity to have something to eat. He had spent the last few weeks busy with lawyers, and there was also the problem of Tutankhamen's tomb. He had practically made up his mind to hand it over to Hengel, but there was some opposition to this, not from his own department but from members of the

Museum and the Government. Hengel didn't exactly endear himself to anyone, he was brash and always demanding, and quite frankly Boivin had been glad to see the back of him, even if only for a few days. Hengel had asked for and been granted a permit to remove antiquities to his private museum in Dresden, these antiquities had all been bought from official dealers and they all had the relevant paperwork attached. Boivin was looking forward to some peace and quiet; he looked lovingly at his toasted ham sandwich, the cheese melting enticingly down the sides. He was about to bite into it when there was a knock at the door. 'Yes?' he called, in voice that implied he didn't wish to be disturbed.

'Mr. Carter to see you Monsieur Boivin.'

Boivin sighed, Carter was the last person he wanted to see, he frankly didn't care if he never saw Carter again. Sighing, he motioned to allow his visitor entry.

'Monsieur Carter what a surprise to see you here.'

'Monsieur Boivin. I am here to acquaint you with some important news, indeed quite distressing news, particularly for poor Mr. Hefez.'

'He is not dead, I hope?' Boivin asked with alarm.

'No, no I can assure you he is still very much alive.' replied Howard, thinking of the prostrate body of Hefez lying on a couch in his office, and deciding not mention this to Boivin.

'We've discovered that these particular objects in the Museum have been replaced with fakes.' Howard handed the photographs to Boivin, who looked through them in astonishment.

'Fakes, what do you mean fakes? What have you been up to?'

Howard gave him a deadly look, 'I sir have been up to nothing. Indeed myself and my colleague have been risking our lives doing your job. We've discovered who hid the lotus head in my house and the boxes in my laboratory, the same person also killed Leo Barnaby and tried to implicate me.'

Boivin stared at the photographs again, he turned to Carter, 'So, who is this master criminal?'

'Ottomar Hengel.' said Howard with relish.

Boivin looked stupefied. For a few minutes he couldn't speak. 'But how can you be sure Monsieur Carter that he is the culprit?'

'Because my colleague, Charlotte Hambleton saw him in the cave with these treasures, she was the one who took the photographs. We also have a witness, Jonathan Harrison.'

Boivin stood up, 'Mon dieu, the crates, the plane.' He sat down heavily.

'The treasures are no longer in the cave Boivin, they're gone.'

'I know, and I helped him.'

'You have to do something, don't just sit there. Can't you intercept the plane?' said Charlotte.

Boivin looked about him in confusion, 'No, there is nothing I can do.'

'But Hengel will be back, he wants the tomb doesn't he? 'Said Howard.

'Yes, you're right we could arrest him then. But, ah non, we will have no evidence. He has been too clever. We will not be able to prove that it was him. Quel merdier.'

Howard's shoulders sagged; he lowered his head, so near yet so far.

Boivin sat down and placed his elbows on the table, there was a squelch, and he looked sadly at his cold and clammy sandwich, now flattened upon the plate. He lowered his head and tried to think what could be done.

CHAPTER NINETEEN

American Lecture Tour, 1924

The RMS Berengaria towered over the Cunard terminal building at Berth 44. Never in her life had Charlotte imagined that she would actually be looking at a real ocean liner. Not only that but also this berth was the one RMS Titanic had sailed from in 1912, almost exactly twelve years ago to the day. Charlotte was very excited, not only to be travelling on a steam ship on the legendary transatlantic crossing, but also because it would be her first visit to America. Admittedly, Howard hadn't exactly invited her, she had inveigled her way onto his lecture tour, and he had eventually relented and agreed that she could accompany him.

The ship's black hull seemed to sparkle in the sunlight, gentle plumes of smoke emanated from her three giant funnels in the Cunard colours of red with a black top and two black rings. There were two huge masts, one forward of the bridge, the other at the rear of the ship, a telegraph wire strung between them. The ship's cranes were busy loading very large trunks, cargo, mail and heaven knows what else into the massive forward hold. There were people everywhere, the noise of chatter, and seagulls squawking overhead. The tumult of baggage being unloaded from the steam train, the smell of the coal from the cargo trains, the whistles and sounds of shunting from the nearby goods yard, Charlotte was entranced by it all. She didn't know where to look. She tried to take a photograph of the ship, but she was too close to it and only managed to get a tiny portion of it within the viewfinder.

There were so many photographers about; Howard was in his element posing as if he were a movie star. The reporters asked him questions about the trouble at Luxor, but he refused to be drawn in, all he said was, 'I am going to America on a trip not unconnected with Egyptian exploration. Many of our warmest supporters came from America, and several of my most capable assistants were also natives of the United States, and I am responding to an invitation to visit their country.

'No doubt I will give several lectures when I am over there; that is unless the interest has completely departed from me now that I am no longer actually working in the Valley of the Kings.

'I do not know yet when I shall return to Egypt. But no doubt I will one day soon.'

A reporter asked him about his attitude towards the Egyptian Government. Howard, rather tactfully replied, 'At the moment it does not seem likely that I shall resume control at Tutankhamen's tomb, but I am hopeful.'

Charlotte was settling herself inside her first class cabin. To the right of the door was the bed. Very comfortable to sit upon, two large plump cushions one on top of the other looked very inviting. A dressing table, with an oval mirror stood next to the fireplace. A medium sized round table occupied the middle of the room, at its centre stood a pot filled with ferns, and two beautifully decorated silk covered chairs completed the scene. A bathroom was to the right of the table, with a proper bath, a sink and a toilet. It was just gorgeous, instead of portholes there were two rectangular windows, with tied back curtains. A little booklet lay upon the table giving information about the ship.

The ship had been built for the Hamburg-Amerika Line and named Imperator; her maiden voyage took place in June 1913. She spent the war lying idle in the harbour at Hamburg; she was destined never to sail for her original owners. In 1919 the US navy used her as a troop transport, in 1920 she was handed over to the Cunard Line as reparation for the loss of Lusitania, who had been sunk by a German U-boat off the Old Head of Kinsale in 1915. Imperator was renamed Berengaria and became the Cunard flagship and the pride of their fleet.

Charlotte went to see Howard in his cabin next door. He had a box that looked like a filing cabinet; within it were approximately a thousand lantern slides, and over three thousand feet of motion picture film lay in more boxes. The ships commander, Captain Irvine had invited Howard to lecture to the passengers that evening, and Howard was busy checking his notes and making sure everything was in order. Charlotte was looking forward to it, she knew he was an interesting and enthusiastic speaker, but she wondered how the audience would react.

Howard told the fascinating story about his years' of toil in the Valley of the Kings, Charlotte found herself engrossed, even though she already knew most of it, the audience too were very appreciative to have heard the authentic account from the man himself.

There arrival into New York was delayed by fog and a 30-mile wind. The ship arrived very late on Friday and everybody spent the night on board. The next morning was no better weather wise, a very dark sky and driving rain greeted the passengers as they disembarked. The weather didn't appear to affect Howard; he looked about ten years younger, vigorous and eager to talk to the New York reporters who were just as enthusiastic as their British counterparts to take as many photographs of him as possible. Howard was asked about the supposed curse that would descend upon explorers of the tombs, he answered, 'Did the Ancient Egyptians put a curse on me for disturbing their dead? They did not. Was I ill as reported? I was not. There is no such thing as superstition among the natives. They don't believe in disturbing the dead. Neither do I.'

In response to another query, he said, 'On many ancient tombs I have found this inscription, "Let all those who love life and hate death wish thousands of geese, loaves of bread and beer to my soul." This is what the old Egyptians thought of prohibition, and I believe I agree with them.'

Howard and Charlotte had settled themselves into their respective rooms at the Waldorf-Astoria Hotel. They had partaken of a delicious dinner in the roof garden restaurant, and were now sitting quietly, reflecting upon their hectic day. Howard had been talking to numerous newspaper reporters, and Charlotte had stood watching him bask in the glory of his discovery.

They had been talking about books and the conversation had somehow turned to Sherlock Holmes. Howard mentioned that he almost became a detective with Scotland Yard, Charlotte looked at him in disbelief, he had a habit of making these off the cuff remarks and Charlotte never quite knew whether to take them seriously.

She gave him a quizzical look, 'I thought you wanted to be an excavator, archaeologist I mean, where does being a detective come into the equation?'

He inhaled deeply at his cigarette and replied, 'The spirit that makes boys want to be detectives or to hunt treasure is about the same. The fever starts very early in life and never stops. It's a spell of enchantment that the lure of the unknown weaves.

'You see Charlotte when searching for a tomb; I use my brain as I would if I were solving a crime. It's a matter of deduction; I knew that the mother of civilization was the Nile Valley, and that the origin of civilization was in eastern equatorial Africa. I started to hunt, fully expecting to find the tomb, and also fully expecting to find it ninety-seven per cent looted. Instead, I was surprised to find it ninety-seven per cent intact.

'I have the same enthusiasm for my work that I had when I was a boy, hunting shells and bugs and funny animals. Now I am hunting the world's greatest treasure, but the impulse that guides me man or boy is the same.

'As a boy I hunted for the sheer love of it. But as a man, I have a deeper purpose. I know that I will be of benefit to mankind. For how can we learn of our early civilization unless we dig up first hand evidence of what that civilization was?'

Howard's first two lectures took place in front of an invited audience at the Metropolitan Museum. His first four public lectures were held at Carnegie Hall, followed by an appearance at the Natural History Museum and two lectures at the Brooklyn Academy of Music.

The following two lectures took place at the Academy of Music in Philadelphia, the first on Friday May 2nd at three o'clock, and the second on Saturday May 3rd at 2.30pm. Each lecture was different, continuing the narrative so that the entire work of discovery was related. By arrangement with the Academy, University students were given the opportunity to purchase half-price tickets to hear Howard lecture on the "Discovery of King Tut-ankh-Amen's Tomb."

In Newhaven, he spoke before three thousand Yale students on his research work. He was invited to the White House for a private audience with President Coolidge. The following day he was meant to give a private lecture for Coolidge and his family and friends but due to unforeseen circumstances, this had to be cancelled.

Charlotte's life was now a whirl of hotel rooms and train stations, there was barely time for her to get her bearings before they would be off again. She hardly had much time to talk to Howard; he was either lecturing, resting, or being interviewed. It was quite an experience for her, she made sure to take lots of photographs and she even managed to film a couple of lectures as well.

They visited the Boston Opera House, followed by Connecticut, Pittsburgh was next and they left that night for Chicago.

In Chicago Howard was scheduled to give two lectures at the Orchestra Hall: "Last Year's Discovery", on Wednesday evening, and on Thursday evening, "This Year's Discovery."

Charlotte sat at a side seat in the front row listening intently to Howard.

'King Tutankhamen was the perfect lover.' he declared. 'The Pharaoh's tomb contains numerous paintings of Tutankhamen's devotion for his wife, one painting shows the Pharaoh caressing his wife's hand; another shows him bestowing affectionate glances on his consort.

'Many of the paintings also testify to the devotion of the wife. In one of them, she is shown whisking specks of dirt from Tutankhamen's robes.

'Those were the days when men and women married for love,' Howard continued, 'when they lived in love and died together.

'That part of the wedding ritual reading "With all my worldly goods I thee endow" came down to us from Tutankhamen's days.

'Just before the ceremony the Egyptian bridegroom locked up his worldly goods. To show the promise of his worldly goods was not empty, the bridegroom presented his bride with the key.

'In this discovery of Tutankhamen's tomb we find that even in utilitarian objects therein, where art is not a necessity, refinement has always been the first consideration.'

Next was Cincinnati, then over the border to Canada. Apart from the lectures and travelling there was a great deal of socializing, lunches, teas and dinners with a wide variety of rich ladies who were delighted to invite the softly-spoken Englishman into their homes, occasionally Charlotte was invited, but on the whole she was kept in the background. The organizer of the tour, who was also accompanying them around the country, had been polite enough to her, but he wasn't quite sure how she fitted into the scheme of things, and preferred her to keep a low profile.

They spent just over a week in Canada, visiting Toronto, Montreal and Ottawa, returning to America to complete the tour.

While appearing in the Memorial Hall in Columbus, Ohio, some opportunist had broken into Howard's dressing room and pinched his hat, coat, silver cigarette case and a cigarette holder. When asked by the investigating policeman what value could be put on the thieves haul, Howard thought about it, 'Let me see now, the hat's worth a pound, the cigarette holder a pound, the cigarette case twenty pounds and the coat twelve pounds.'

'Pounds of what?' asked the policeman, as politely as possible, thinking perhaps Howard thought in terms of barter for ham and eggs or something along those lines.

It was finally explained in American and the police were tracing Howard's loss of about $140.

Back in New York, Howard was presented with a scroll featuring an old Egyptian symbol meaning, "to seek beauty" by a quartette of New York Camp Fire girls. Charlotte took a wonderful photograph of Howard holding the scroll, Howard looking very self-conscious surrounded by the four girls.

The highlight of the tour and probably the proudest moment of Howard's life took place on 18th June when Yale University awarded him an honorary degree of science; he was now Doctor Howard Carter.

Another Cunard ship, this time the very popular RMS Mauretania was to be their home for the trip back to Southampton. The Mauretania had the distinction of being the fastest ship to cross the Atlantic, she held the Blue Riband for the fastest westbound and eastbound crossings for twenty years. She was a beautiful ship inside and out, her first class lounge was panelled with richly carved and gilt old growth African mahogany, the reading and writing room was adorned with ornate gilt grilled bookcases. The dining room was layed out over two levels and topped by a large dome skylight, the verandah café situated on the boat deck was

Charlotte's favourite place, where she enjoyed sitting at a table drinking tea and eating cakes and sandwiches while looking out to sea.

One afternoon, sitting in this café, Howard told her that he was going to search for a long lost tribe on the African continent, which may still have the customs and the manner of Tutankhamen's time. Charlotte couldn't decide whether this was one of Howard's tongue in cheek stories, she said, 'Seriously?'

He ignored this comment and continued, 'I believe that in the uplands of the River Nile there lives to-day a lost race of people who still have the customs of the people of King Tutankhamen's time. I have ascertained that in the uplands of the Nile are many tribes that are practically unknown to civilization. And that the Valley of the Nile was the cradle of civilization. I cannot doubt from the investigations so far carried on.'

'What investigations, when did all this happen?' asked Charlotte, still a bit suspicious that he might possibly be pulling her leg.

'There is no doubt, that the discovery of the tomb at Luxor is the most important of its kind in connection with the history of ancient Egypt, together with being one of the most significant contributions to our knowledge of the orient.'

'So you're going to find these tribes? On your own?' asked Charlotte.

'Quite possibly I may go to Mesopotamia, or even Ethiopia.'

Charlotte stared at him wide eyed, 'Why?'

'Well, the Upper Nile is a promising field for archaeological study of the origins of the civilization of the Mediterranean region, including Mesopotamia. The early history of Ethiopia has hardly been touched. It's just an idea of mine, something to do should things not go according to plan with regard to the tomb.' he looked at her, a twinkle in his eye, and then he laughed.

'What about your painting? Maybe you could make a living selling your pictures to wealthy ladies, who will no doubt be charmed by you to part with their money, after all the pictures will be worth a fortune one day.'

'Ah yes,' said Howard, 'in a hundred years' time, unfortunately I won't be there to benefit from the considerable remuneration.'

'Do you still paint? 'Asked Charlotte.

'Yes, I do. I'm a very enthusiastic painter. I take a great deal of interest in natural history. I have a fondness for birds in particular.'

Charlotte interrupted, 'I love birds too, I used to keep budgerigars and I once had a pet pigeon, he was so clever and talented, he even knew how to dance.'

'Pigeons are very intelligent, very messy though, but also very friendly. Did you know the idea that a bird sleeps with its head under his wing is just a myth, for the bird really sleeps with its head under its scapular, not under the wing at all.'

'I confess I've never really thought about it.' replied Charlotte.

Back at Waterloo Station Howard was again besieged by reporters, eager to ask him about his trip to America, Howard was keen to oblige, 'The people of America and Canada were very kind to me, and I was everywhere very well received. I went to seventeen big cities, and the audiences were always large and sometimes numbered three thousand or four thousand. I was honoured with the degree of Doctor of Science at Yale University.'

'Do you intend to return to Luxor next winter?' asked a reporter.

'My work is not by any means finished,' Howard answered. 'Fifty per cent of it has still to be done, and I am going back to Luxor in November.'

'Do you think in regard to the attitude taken up by the Egyptian Government before you left the Valley of the Kings, there will be the possibility of a recurrence of the trouble?' asked another reporter.

'I do not see why there should be any further trouble.' said Howard.

'What are your future plans?' asked someone else.

'I propose taking a holiday at Madeira and in Paris and hope to resume operations in Egypt in November.'

Charlotte watched from the background, as usual. Howard was looking bronzed and very happy, unlike Charlotte who never could get beyond the red and blotchy stage. Now, she was looking very pale and feeling quite tired. The tour, the Atlantic crossing, the train ride from Southampton to Waterloo had started to catch up with her, and she felt as though all her energy had been slowly siphoned away.

CHAPTER TWENTY

England, 1924

It was time for a holiday, starting with a few days in Bath staying at the Empire Hotel. The hotel had opened in 1901; it had the rather dubious distinction of being insulted by no other than art and architectural historian, Nicholas Pevsner who called it "a monstrosity and an unbelievable piece of pompous architecture." Charlotte quite liked it, especially when the manager, Robert Lightfoot, explained the unusual style of the roof, which depicted the three classes of people, a castle on the corner for upper class, a house for the middle class, and a cottage for the lower class. The hotel was located next to the River Avon between the Pulteney Bridge and the Abbey. Fortunately, the weather was sunny and the gardens and trees looked green and lush, the view was pretty spectacular too.

'Why Bath?' Howard had asked her.

'I don't know, why not? I've never been there and I thought I'd like to go.' replied Charlotte.

Howard considered the matter, 'I've never been there either. I think I'd rather like to see it as well, I'll accompany you.' he said, not wishing to be left out of any interesting adventures that may come their way.

So, here they were in Bath, situated in the sheltered valley of the River Avon. Charlotte saw her plans for a quiet restful holiday disappear as Howard was looking forward to viewing the architecture, churches, and buildings in general, just as well she had brought stout walking shoes. Bath was first and foremost a spa, a health resort which had been famous for nearly two thousand years, its fame founded on the hot springs whose curative properties were first recognized by the people of Roman Britain. Charlotte and Howard visited the Roman Baths founded in AD75 and dedicated to the goddess of healing Sulis Minerva. The great Roman bath was uncovered in 1882. The original pavements surrounding it still remained in a good state of preservation. Architecturally Bath is essentially a Georgian city, for nowhere else is 18th century architecture and town planning seen to such good effect. The Woods, father and son, were the architects of 18th century Bath, Richard (Beau) Nash, the Master of Ceremonies, was the founder of Bath's 18th century social life. Howard and Charlotte visited the Royal Crescent, the Circus, Queen Square and the parades which are among the finest parts of the 18th century town, while many of the squares and crescents built later were modelled on the Georgian style.

Bath Abbey Church is the chief survival of the medieval city. On this site in turn a nunnery, a Saxon abbey, and a Norman Cathedral have stood. The present building was started in 1499 by Oliver King, Bishop of Bath and Wells, but was not completed for fully a century.

Charlotte didn't think she'd walked so much in her life; she had taken many photographs of Howard beaming away standing in front of whatever building they happened to be visiting that day, they even asked passers-by to take photos of them together. Charlotte would treasure these memories all her life.

In August, they went on a motoring holiday. Charlotte was quite keen to drive, Howard still having not recovered his nerves from his previous experience declined the offer and instead hired a chauffeur driven car.

They started in the market town of Tewkesbury, known for its medieval and Tudor buildings, and Tewkesbury Abbey. They visited the Black Bear pub, opened in 1308 and said to be the oldest public house in Gloucestershire, and the rather neglected Abbey cottages dating from 1410. The Battle of Tewkesbury was fought within half a mile of the town in 1641 during the Wars of the Roses between the Yorkists under Edward IV and the

Lancastrians, including a force brought from France by Margaret of Anjou to support Warwick "the kingmaker." Margaret's troops were too late; Warwick had been slain at Barnet. Now the last Lancastrian troops were utterly defeated, Margaret's son was slain, and the last attempt of the Lancastrians to gain control in England by force of arms had been crushed. This engagement, like that at Barnet, was one of the earliest in which the tide of battle was changed by artillery fire. Charlotte and Howard stood looking at the enormous field, the grass slightly brown from the heat. Apart from the odd birdcall and gentle murmur of voices, it was very peaceful now.

Travelling southwards, they arrived at the cathedral city of Gloucester. Built by the Romans and known as Glevum. When Saxon England emerged from the Dark Ages, Gloucester appeared as a religious centre with an abbey, the forerunner of the cathedral, established before the end of the 7th century. The ruins of St. Oswald's priory, Llanthony Abbey, Greyfriars and Blackfriars can still be seen. The New Inn, built in the 15th century to accommodate pilgrims to the cathedral shrines, still stands on Northgate Street, and retains its ancient galleried courtyard.

Retracing their footsteps, they travelled back up north, past Tewkesbury and onto Worcester, another cathedral city. Many of the half-timbered houses dated from the time when Worcester was the principal centre of the cloth-making industry in the 16th and early 17th centuries. Queen Elizabeth's house near the Old Corn Market has an open gallery from which Queen Elizabeth I is said to have addressed the people in 1574. Near at hand King Charles' house is the place where Charles II took refuge when he was pursued by Cromwell's soldiers. The Royal Grammar School is an ancient educational foundation, which was certainly in existence in the 13th century and was granted a charter in 1561. The King's School was endowed out of the funds made available by the dissolution of the Benedictine Monastery in 1541.

They drove eastwards to the market town, indeed the oldest market town in Warwickshire, Stratford-upon-Avon, more commonly known as the birthplace of William Shakespeare. Two bridges cross the river – the medieval stone bridge built by Sir Hugh Clopton in about 1486; and a brick-built structure which is a relic of an early 19th century tramway scheme. Clopton bridge is on or near the site of a Roman ford from which is derived the name Stratford or Street Ford. By the 12th century, it was an important market centre and a river port with a large trade in wool and corn. Shakespeare's birthplace is a half-timbered building of the early 16th century, while the church of Holy Trinity contains the poet's tomb and is an impressive combination of Gothic styles capped by an 18th century octagonal spire.

For their last visit, they travelled west, to the spa town of Malvern. Malvern stands on high ground under the eastern slopes of the range of volcanic hills known as the Malvern Hills.

During their tour of England Charlotte felt herself growing ever closer to Howard. Yes, she had already developed a friendship with him in Egypt, but over there he had been distracted with work and then the duplicitous actions of Hengel had kept him occupied. During the lecture tour of North America Howard had been busy meeting a plethora of people from all walks of society, academic colleagues, and newspapermen. The only time she really found herself alone with him was on the train travelling from one place to another.

But the last week spent travelling together had, she thought, deepened their friendship. They had visited graveyards and churches, and old houses and battlefields; they had walked along rivers and crossed ancient bridges. They had talked about history, birds, animals, and nature. They had discussed the cinema, Howard loved watching the films of Charlie Chaplin, Charlotte preferred Laurel and Hardy, she was about to say so, when it occurred to her that they may not even have been together as Laurel and Hardy in 1924. She enjoyed listening to Howard talk, he had a dry sense of humour, and she didn't always understand if he was actually joking or not, she would look at him in puzzlement and he would look back at her with the beginnings of a smile under his moustache. He seemed to enjoy teasing her; he thought she was, in some topics of conversation, quite naïve. This was only because Charlotte felt constantly on edge in case she said the wrong thing, spoke about an incident that had not yet occurred, for example.

They had enjoyed their motoring trip so much and just three days later they decided to embark upon another. They ventured further up north to the spa town of Buxton, situated over one thousand feet above sea level to the south of the Forest of the High Peak, it has the distinction of being the highest town in England. The waters were known and used by the Romans, and Roman roads connected the spa with Derby and Manchester. Medieval Buxton was founded early in the 12th century, while by the 16th century the waters long neglected, again became popular when the Chapel of St. Ann was famous for the cures effected. At the close of the 18th century the Duke of Devonshire, the lord of the manor, spent lavishly in improving the town's amenities. Many of the handsome buildings of the modern town date from that period, including the Pump Room, which was presented by the Duke of Devonshire and contains the thermal springs.

Driving 150 miles south Howard and Charlotte crossed over to Wales. They stayed in Monmouth, a town situated on the River Wye. Famous as a market and shopping centre since the Middle Ages. Henry V was born here, he was known as Harry of Monmouth. Many ancient and interesting buildings remained, including the Norman church of St. Thomas Becket and the Medieval gateway on the Monnow Bridge, an example of early bridge fortifications. Unfortunately, the castle is in ruins. They then travelled north back into England for a return visit to Malvern.

Back in London, Howard had a number of social engagements, a few days later though the pair of them were back in Malvern. Howard loved it there, the beautiful scenery, the churches, the bracing air; it really was a most beautiful part of England.

CHAPTER TWENTY-ONE

By the autumn, Howard was back on the lecture circuit. The Temple Speech Room was packed to excess. The headmaster introduced Mr. Howard Carter, ScD, to the members of Rugby School and their friends who gave Howard a very enthusiastic reception.

Howard began, 'It is nearly two years since I discovered the tomb of Tutankhamen in that awe-inspiring Valley of the Tombs of the Kings, a very remote and solitary valley dividing the foothills of Western Thebes from the Libya range of mountains which border the Sahara desert. There in that solitary valley, under a guardian peak, twenty-seven of Egypt's greatest monarchs made their eternal resting place.

'The reason which led me to suppose that Tutankhamen was buried in the valley was that some years ago Mr. Theodore Davis found beneath a rock there a small blue faience cup, which bore the cartouche of Tutankhamen, and had every quality and characteristic of coming from a tomb. There was also discovered in a small vault a number of pottery vases, containing petals of flowers used in mourning ceremonies, together with some pieces of linen and a head-dress, one of which was inscribed with the name Tutankhamen, and dated the sixth year of his reign. These objects had every appearance of coming from the ceremony of a king's burial. As a result of these and other discoveries, I persuaded Lord Carnarvon to make a search of the valley to find the tomb of the last king of that particular era, and a concession was obtained from the Egyptian Director of Antiquities to search for Tutankhamen's tomb. For some reason I selected a spot near the tomb of Rameses VI. My men had to remove 200,000 tons of rubbish deposited from previous excavations before we could begin our research work under the sub-strata.

'A heap of large flint bones, such as were frequently used for filling up entrances to the tombs of the Pharaohs and some remains of temporary workmen's huts which had been erected in connection with work on the tomb of Rameses, although we doubted whether workmen's huts would be permitted to be built over a royal tomb, we decided to excavate there. This work began in November, 1922, and on the fourth day, as I was riding into the valley, I was taken aback by the solemn silence. The 150 workmen had stopped, and on reaching the spot I was told they had discovered what appeared to be the beginning of a set of steps cut into the rock. The men were at once re-started at work, and in a few hours they had cleared away sufficient to find that it actually was the first of a series of steps leading downwards.

'You can imagine our excitement, the men would not stop mid-day for food, but worked till late in the evening, and by that time we had cleared away sufficient to see that we really had made a discovery. We re-commenced the next morning, and by evening of the fifth day we had cleared the whole of the top of the staircase, and were able to clear the actual steps themselves. At that time the work progressed quicker, and at last we exposed a doorway, blocked, plastered and sealed. Then I had hopes that at last we had found something good, if not actually a tomb, for there, in front of us, was the upper portion of a door. By the aid of the rays of the moon and a candle I examined the seals on the door. There was no name and nothing to tell us who was buried there, only the royal necropolis seal. I made a small hole in the wooden lintel of the door, and discovered that it led to a passage completely blocked with rubble and stone from top to bottom. I immediately sent a runner to Luxor with a cable for Lord Carnarvon, little knowing that, had I gone a few inches deeper, I should have found the insignia of Tutankhamen on those seals and known the secret, that that very ephemeral king was buried in a tomb of his own in the Valley of the Kings.'

Aided by a number of lantern slides, Howard went on to describe the further progress of the work and the wonderful objects found in the antechamber.

He explained that, 'We found evidence that the tomb had been entered by thieves, and sealed up again by officials, probably within fifty years of the death of the young King, at least one of the thieves must have been caught, because in one of the caskets was found, among other objects thrown in indiscriminately, a neck-cloth, which, on being unwound, revealed a number of magnificent gold rings, which evidently formed part of his booty.

'When I looked through the aperture into the antechamber, Lord Carnarvon could bear the suspense no longer, but said, "What can you see?" I could only reply, "Wonderful things." The whole of the equipment was wonderful, and for the first time in our life we realized the splendour of the Imperial age.

'Among the objects found were a number of trussed ducks in boxes, or, as a friend of mine in Chicago described them, "canned food for the underworld." Some of the miniature paintings were wonderful, and the detail and delicate finish remarkable, the colours being as brilliant as when they were painted. By the use of different alloys the gold work in some instances varied considerably in shade from bright yellow to bright scarlet. A small alabaster box proved very interesting, containing, as it did, the locks of the young King's hair, which were placed there every time they were cut.'

Howard moved on from the antechamber to the actual tomb, he said, 'the outer one of the four shrines, which enclosed the sarcophagus, completely filled the tomb chamber. The dismantling of the shrines took place during our second season's work, and proved very difficult. The shrines were built in twenty-one heavy sections, made of hard wood, heavily plated with gold. During the 3,300 years of its existence the woodwork had shrunk and the gold plating had expanded, and it was very difficult to deal with it without causing damage. In the end we carried out the work with some injury to our hands and head, but none to the shrines. The sarcophagus is 8ft. long, 4ft. 6ins. wide, and 4ft. 6ins. high; and a remarkable fact was that the sandstone lid was in two parts, and did not belong to the rest of the coffin, probably owing to the original one being broken or the king dying unexpectedly. The lid of the outer coffin contained a low relief effigy of the king, which was one of the most wonderful specimens of workmanship I have ever seen; but amid all this regal splendour the most impressive that I saw was the small wreath of flowers on the coffin, the last offering of the young Queen, which, after 3,300 years, still retained their colour tints. This little bunch of flowers made that old civilization and modern civilization akin.'

There was a huge round of applause, Charlotte joined in enthusiastically. Replying to a vote of thanks heartily accorded at the invitation of the Headmaster, Howard said, 'I have often been asked, both here and in other countries, "Why interfere with the dead?" I have asked myself that question many times, but to know an ancient people we must be intimate with them. We cannot be intimate with the living, but we can be intimate with the dead, and for that reason I think it is permissible to examine these wonderful remains, but on one condition – that is, that we don't interfere with the dead themselves.' Another loud round of applause ensued, Charlotte wasn't sure why but she found she had tears running down her face, she felt so proud of Howard and so privileged to have been given the chance of being part of his world.

Howard continued with his lecture tour visiting Norwich, Swaffham, Newbury Grammar School, Eton College and Westminster School. They then crossed the Channel and travelled by train to Paris staying one night at the Ritz, and the following day they travelled by train to Madrid. Howard delivered a lecture there to University students, the Duke of Alba presided. There were so many requests for admittance that hundreds of applicants had to be turned away

CHAPTER TWENTY-TWO

Egypt, 1924

The tour was over and Howard and Charlotte were back in Cairo. Howard had still not heard any positive news from the Egyptian Government regarding the tomb. Hengel was back in Cairo, he had allowed Egyptian officials from the Antiquities Department to visit his museum in Dresden, but they could only see the legitimate objects on display. As to the missing objects, their fate remained unknown. There was still no word regarding the reinstatement of Howard as the legal excavator of the tomb. Charlotte knew how despondent he was; he confessed to her that he felt worthless and that he may as well give up excavating altogether and hide away in London. Charlotte did her best to give him hope, she reminded him that negotiations had been continuing during his absence and there was every chance that he would be back in Luxor this autumn. 'After all,' she remarked, 'who on earth would be mad enough to take on such an enormous task?' She smiled at him, 'I think it's safe to say the tomb will be left in your capable hands.'

Howard gave her one of his looks, 'I'm happy that at least one person has confidence in my capabilities.'

'Oh, I think you're brilliant. The Government were out of their minds to think that their people would be competent enough to catalogue, preserve and document hundreds and hundreds of objects in the same meticulous manner as yourself. You and Tutankhamen were meant to meet, so to speak, it was destiny, and no Government can change that. A hundred years from now, it's your name that will be associated with King Tut, all of those pompous officials and bureaucrats who stood in your way will be completely forgotten. There'll be books and films about your great discovery, you'll never be forgotten.' Charlotte stopped to breathe.

'There's no need to over-egg the pudding.' Howard said, and then he gave her one of his nice smiles. Charlotte blushed.

Howard and Charlotte had spent the morning at the zoo. Charlotte hated seeing the animals locked up in their inadequately small cages. A bear looked at her, his eyes lifeless; he was lying down as if waiting for death to release him from his prison. Charlotte felt tears well up in her eyes, the sight made her feel very unhappy. She looked around, everyone else was enjoying their day out, even Howard was philosophical about it, claiming that as most of these people would never have the opportunity of seeing these creatures in their natural habitat, zoos were the only opportunity they would ever have of seeing magnificent lions, elephants, bears and tigers in real life. Charlotte wondered what people would think if they were the ones behind the cages being gawped out by an alien species, who laughed and teased them and threw rotten lumps of food at them, she didn't think they would enjoy it very much.

They returned to the hotel, Charlotte in a subdued mood, Howard buried in his own thoughts. While they awaited the lift, their reverie was broken by a loud voice.

'Cooee, Howard, Charlotte, my goodness I thought I might have missed you.'

Howard froze, he turned to see Araminta Fazakerley descending upon him like a giant tank, he turned back to the see if the lift had arrived, it hadn't.

'Your lady friend has found you.' said Charlotte, smiling innocently.

Plastering a smile upon his face, Howard greeted Araminta.

'Good afternoon.' he said.

'So formal, such polite manners.' said Araminta, grabbing his hand in a bone crunching grasp. 'I read all about your exploits in America, how exciting it must have been for you.' she gushed.

'Yes and Howard is a Doctor now, I sent you a postcard have you received it yet?' asked Charlotte.

'I may have done, it's probably somewhere in this wretched bag, let me see if I can find it.'

'There's no need.' said Charlotte quickly.

Too late, the contents of the bag spilled out everywhere, the lift arrive and Howard tried to sneak into it, Charlotte gave him a look, he sighed and resigned himself to spending the afternoon with Mrs. Fazakerley, reluctantly he got down on his knees and tried to retrieve her possessions.

A small dog came running over believing this to be a new game, and began to grab pieces of paper in its teeth and shake them about, growling and snapping at anyone who tried to remove them. Araminta fussed about dropping more than she picked up, the dog bit Charlotte, then a passing lady tripped over and Howard was hit in the head by her handbag.

The Hotel Manager, efficient as ever, managed to clear up and organize everybody back to their interrupted pursuits.

'Goodness me what a fuss, I could do with a cup of tea.' said Araminta. She settled herself in the seat, her grey hair looking as though it had been dragged through a bush backwards. 'I've some friends staying with me, you'll remember them Charlotte, Emily, Hettie, and Susan'. Charlotte nodded.

'That's why I'm here to take you back to my place for dinner.' Araminta added.

Howard felt the day couldn't get any worse, he had some errands to complete and supplies to buy, but that could wait until To-morrow, instead he had planned a quiet afternoon, a spot of reading and a walk later on. Now here he was in the clutches of this appalling woman, he had no desire to meet her friends, or travel in her car ever again. He looked over at Charlotte, she would be no help, she found the whole situation very amusing. He would try to think of an excuse to refuse the invitation, food poisoning, or something else along those lines.

The tea, cakes and sandwiches arrived. Araminta said she and her friends would all be arriving in Luxor within the next few days, and that they were all looking forward to visiting Tutankhamen's tomb. Howard could barely listen, he wished he could disappear and magically reappear upstairs in his nice, quiet room.

He heard somebody calling his name; it was a bellboy, 'Over here'. Howard called.

The boy handed him a message, Howard read it, and a feeling of relief and happiness came over him.

'What is it?' asked Charlotte.

'It's from M. Boivin; he wants to see me at three o'clock.'

'Why?'

'He doesn't say. I'm sorry Mrs. Faz…'

'Please call me Araminta, we're friends now, there's no need to be so formal, Howard.' she fluttered her eyes at him.

Charlotte stuffed a napkin into her mouth to stifle her giggles.

Howard glared at her, he cleared his throat, 'Araminta, I'm afraid I won't be able to keep our appointment this evening. I'm so sorry.'

'Surely you won't be gone for that long, I can wait for you. The ladies are looking forward to meeting you. You can't disappoint them Howard that would be very cruel.'

Charlotte said, 'Of course Howard will be there, he wouldn't miss it for the world.' she let out a cry as Howard kicked her.

'Are you all right my dear?' asked Araminta.

'Yes, yes, just hiccups.' said Charlotte, grabbing a glass of water and swallowing a large gulp, she choked as it went down the wrong way. Araminta gave her a hearty slap on the back, Charlotte fell forward banging her head on her plate of cakes.

'My goodness are you all right?' asked Araminta.

'Charlotte speak to me, say something.' said Howard.

Charlotte looked up dazed, a cake squashed across her face. Howard wiped it away, and gave Araminta one of his hostile stares.

'I think you'd better lay down.' he said to Charlotte.

'Where am I?' Charlotte replied.

'Cairo.' shouted Araminta, then in a quieter voice, 'Dear oh dear, I don't know my own strength, I'm so terribly sorry.'

'Never mind Mrs… I mean Araminta, I'm sure she'll be fine.' said Howard, dismissively.

'I'll be waiting for you on the terrace. Good luck with your meeting.'

Howard helped Charlotte into the lift, now he just needed a good excuse to miss dinner.

At the appointed time, Howard arrived at M. Boivin's office. He was invited to sit down and did so.

'Monsieur Carter, how good to see you looking so well. You're visit to America did you good, non.' Boivin continued, 'I wish to discuss matters concerning the tomb.'

Howard stiffened, anxiously awaiting to hear his fate.

'You will be allowed to continue your excavations and preservation work, under certain conditions.'

'What conditions?' asked Howard, his mood becoming darker.

'You will no longer have a key to the tomb; you will collect it each morning from one of the guards. Your assistants will need to be approved by myself, you will write a report to me every day. There will be no more exclusive rights to The Times. From now on, we will control the information given to the newspapers. Do you agree?'

'The matter of the key, I'm afraid I foresee problems, I need to be able to come and go as my duties demand. I may not know in advance what time I will need access to the tomb, it's far easier if I keep the key myself.'

'No, M. Carter, I would be happier if the key was kept in the possession of, shall we say, a neutral party. We do not want anything mysteriously disappearing again.'

'I hope you are not implying that I stole or plan to steal from the tomb.' said Howard, his voice rising in indignation.

'Calm yourself mon ami, it is for your own good, this way if anything happens, you cannot be accused.'

Howard gave this some thought, and then asked, 'What about Hengel, and the treasures in the museum?'

'M. Hengel is not your concern. We have no proof that he committed any crime. The items in the museum are genuine, I'm afraid you made an error when you rather rashly claimed them to be fakes. Really Monsieur Carter you ought to be more careful in what pronouncements you make, poor M. Hafez was very distressed about the situation, he had to go away for two months to recover.'

'But the photographs and film my associate Miss Hambleton showed you, that surely proves Hengel's involvement in this situation.'

'Non, it proves nothing. Your Miss Hambleton is very excitable with an overactive imagination. All she showed us were treasures in a cave, there was no picture of Hengel standing next to them, for all I know she could have staged this herself to help you.'

Howard was speechless. He just couldn't win, Hengel had money and an overbearing personality, he frightened people into thinking and doing exactly what he wanted. Howard knew there was no chance of having him arrested.

'Well M. Carter, are you agreeable to the terms of the new concession?'

'I will read it and let you know.'

'Bon, as soon as possible please. Good day.'

Boivin picked up some papers from his desk and started to peruse them, Howard stared at him, feeling heavy-hearted he left the office

CHAPTER TWENTY-THREE

Hengel was furious that the officials had insisted upon visiting his home and examining his treasures, he was not a fool, and had made allowances for such a situation as this. Nevertheless, it had caused him great inconvenience and expense, after all bribery was not cheap. He therefore vowed a terrible retribution upon Carter and especially upon the English girl, whom he felt was responsible for all the failures that had befallen him. He made plans for his revenge.

Despite covering himself from head to toe, the billowing dust invaded every nook and cranny of his body. The wind blew furiously through the valley, making it nigh on impossible to walk. Hengel forced his legs to move towards the tomb's entrance, nodding to the guard, who was safely ensconced inside his little hut, Hengel reached the stone steps and stumbled downwards. The huge electric lamps remained lit, occasionally flickering as if in harmony with the furious gusts outside.

Hengel removed his coat and scarf, and vainly tried to brush off the sand that stubbornly clung to his clothes. Even his hair felt gritty to the touch. 'This miserable country,' he said aloud, although no one else was present, 'gott im himmel, what a place, no wonder they buried their dead out here.'

Somebody else came into the tomb's antechamber, without looking Hengel said, 'Ah, Bauer, at least you managed to arrive here,' he looked Bauer up and down, 'more or less intact. Good. Are the plans progressing? You have followed my instructions I hope?'

'Yes sir, I have done everything you requested. May I ask a question?'

Hengel glared at the man, 'What?'

Bauer, shaking from nerves, said in a very nervous voice, 'What if she brings the donkey?'

'Donkey? Bauer are you losing your mind?'

'No, Herr Hengel, I just do not wish to be kicked into the stratosphere again, I have only just recovered, but I still walk with a limp.'

'Then you will shoot the wretched creature.'

'I will try sir.' replied Bauer, not feeling exactly confident, and sure that in any conflict between himself and the donkey he would probably come out worse.

'Bauer, you are meant to be my right-hand man, you are a German, you should not be running away from dumb animals. Have you no dignity?'

'No, I mean to say yes I do, but, if you don't mind my mentioning it, the donkey beat you up as well.'

Hengel gave him a very cold, steely look, 'Bauer, if you wish to continue living you will not mention anything about that to anybody, you will forget it ever happened. Do you understand?'

'I understand sir, I have forgotten everything to do with donkeys.' gulped Bauer.

Hengel looked at him; he would replace him as soon as it was convenient to do so. 'You see all of this,' Hengel pointed around the tomb, 'this should all have been mine. And thanks to idiots like you I have lost it, I have planned for years for this moment and it has been snatched away.' Hengel was shouting and his face was turning purple with rage. 'Now what am I left with, an idiot scared of a donkey. Verdammt, these Egyptian officials, Carter, that wretched girl, geh zum teufel.'

'Please calm yourself, think of your blood pressure.'

Alarmed by the bellowing coming from the bowels of the earth, one of the guards descended the steps to investigate what was going on. Reaching the antechamber the guard peered inside, his round, shiny face lit up by the bright lights, 'What is going on here?' he enquired, 'I fear you will bring down the mountains with all the noise you are making.'

Hengel glared at him, 'You are meant to be a guard, so go back

151

up the stairs and do your duty, and tidy yourself up, you are disgrace, look at the state of you.' shouted Hengel.

The poor guard was so taken aback at this barrage of abuse that in his haste to leave the tomb he tripped over his feet and fell down the stairs, landing in a dishevelled heap at Hengel's feet.

Hengel gave him a disdainful look that would very likely curdle milk and kill any sensitive flowers within a distance of two miles. Wrapping himself up, he stepped over the unfortunate guard, ascended the steps and prepared to brave the inhospitable conditions once more.

Hengel cursed everything. He was surrounded by fools, who were always finding excuses and making the simplest of tasks seem more complicated. He had planned everything so meticulously, he had got rid of Carter, or so he thought, dealt with those pompous fools from the various government departments, who had assured him of their co-operation and their faith in his ability to preserve the treasures. Yes, they had so much faith in him; yet they had returned the tomb to that fool Carter.

On top of all the stress and this blasted weather, he could feel a headache coming on. Finally reaching his car, he climbed into the back and ordered the chauffeur to take him back to the hotel.

CHAPTER TWENTY-FOUR

Arriving back at Luxor after a short stay in Cairo, Howard and Charlotte visited the Winter Palace. Here, they met Mr. Matula, who greeted them both warmly and invited them to join him for breakfast. Matula ordered a cheese omelette, bacon, sausages, pancakes with syrup, and coffee. Charlotte and Howard settled for a pot of tea.

'I hear you were a wonderful success in America. Did you enjoy your stay there?' asked Matula.

'Yes, a vast country, very friendly people, unfortunately, no whisky. Nevertheless, a very enjoyable experience.' replied Howard.

'Prohibition is a real pain, some people go on cruises to nowhere, booze cruises they're known as, ships that sail just outside of American waters allowing passengers to drink to their heart's content.' said Matula. 'And you young lady, are you well?'

'I'm very well, thank you. I've had a wonderful time, truly, truly wonderful. The places I've visited, places in my own country that I've never even seen before. I just didn't realize how beautiful everything was.' gushed Charlotte, aware that she was beginning to gabble.

'I was worried about the two of you. After you left for Cairo Hengel left here like a man with his pants on fire, I felt sure it had something to do with the pair of you.'

'He found us in Cairo,' replied Howard, 'he kidnapped Charlotte.'

'Did he harm you?'

153

'No, I'm afraid I harmed him,' said Charlotte, 'I bashed him over the head with his own crutch and made a run for it.'

'I wish I could've seen that.' said Matula, rather wistfully. 'It's a shame he's still around, I rather hoped some misfortune would have befallen him by now.'

'No, unfortunately not, the bounder escaped.' said Howard. 'I heard he's returned here and has been sniffing around the tomb.'

Harrison appeared and said, 'Hi, did I hear the name Hengel?'

'Yes, we've just been talking about him.' said Matula, 'Did you know Charlotte and Carter had an altercation with him in Cairo?'

Harrison sat down 'Yes, I know about that, he wasn't happy with you at all.' he said, looking at Charlotte.

'Have you ever been to his museum?' asked Charlotte

'Yeah, I've been to Dresden, the place where he lives is breathtaking. It's a large museum stuffed full of antiquities, some of them were bought legitimately, I guess. Probably a very small percentage he looted from various sources. When the authorities visited his home he claimed the Egyptian treasures they were interested in were actually fakes, he claimed he would never dream of stealing the real deal – he was all sweetness and politeness. You'll no doubt run into him eventually.' said Harrison.

'So, you've finally been allowed back in the tomb, where there many conditions?' said Matula to Howard.

'Everything has been amicably settled and work will begin almost immediately.' said Howard stiffly.

'That's great news.' said Matula.

They drank their tea, and turned their attention to Howard and the tomb, the weather and various other topics of interest.

Upon arrival at Howard's house Charlotte became suspicious when she noticed Howard was grinning from ear to ear, she asked him, 'Why are you so happy, what have you done?'

'I have a surprise for you.' he said.

Charlotte clapped her hands together, 'I love surprises, what is it?'

Howard nodded to a young boy who disappeared round the back of the house; curious Charlotte wondered what on earth this present could be. Suddenly there was an ear-splitting shout of 'hee-haw' and Suzy came racing round the corner, seeing Charlotte, she ran towards her almost bowling her over. Suzy nuzzled her face into Charlotte's hair, muttering and rumbling affectionately.

'Suzy,' cooed Charlotte, 'I wasn't sure I'd see you again.' She took the donkey's nose in her hands and gave her a big kiss.

Charlotte smiled at Howard, 'thank you,' she said, 'can she stay here permanently?'

'Of course, she belongs to you now.'

Charlotte almost fainted with joy; she didn't know whether to hug Suzy or Howard, she tried hugging them both, only Suzy trod on Howard's foot in the confusion, and when he cried out, the donkey, believing this was some kind of war cry, bit him on the hand. Howard cried out again. Suzy, determined to protect Charlotte, reared up, her legs flailing in the air. Charlotte ran to protect Howard not caring if she was kicked in the process and promptly received a kick on the shin, she fell to the floor, and found she did care – the pain was agonizing. Suzy, upset by this turn of events decided to charge at Howard, whom she considered the cause of all this trouble, fortunately, at this juncture, the young boy reappeared and led the irate animal back to her stable.

Howard's servants, alerted by the commotion, came out of the house; they picked up the injured parties, manhandled them inside, patched them up and dosed them with painkillers. Plus, for good measure, poured them both a stiff brandy each.

'That donkey will be the death of me.' said Howard, befuddled by pills and brandy.

Charlotte tried to answer; she opened her mouth and promptly fell unconscious, brandy glass still in hand.

Howard shook his head in disbelief; there was certainly never a dull moment when Charlotte was around. Suddenly, he felt very contented, probably from the brandy, and found he didn't care one little bit about that wretched man Hengel.

CHAPTER TWENTY-FIVE

Egypt, 1925

Tutankhamen's tomb was reopened after being closed for 11 months. The gates were unlocked in the presence of representatives of the Government, Howard, and a few tourists. The ceremony was very simple, the proceedings after the transfer of the keys to Howard being confined to a brief inspection of the contents of the tomb and of the workshop situated in the tomb of Seti II.

Everything inside was found in good order, but a sad spectacle was presented by the pall which used to cover the shrines. It was unique of its kind and Howard had expended much care on its preservation. The Antiquities Department left it all through the summer outside Seti's tomb most inadequately covered, and in consequence of this neglect it was now completely ruined. The Antiquities Department took the necessary steps to safeguard the contents of the tomb, but did not provide proper protection against exposure to the sun and air to this relic, which was now lost to archaeology. The damage greatly moved Howard, but controlling himself, he remarked, 'Well, it's a pity, for it is the only pall in the world. But anyhow, it's yours not mine.'

Howard spent weeks in the laboratory cleaning and preserving various objects, the tomb was open to visitors three mornings every week. Charlotte and Harrison often visited Howard in the laboratory and watched him and his colleagues at work. It was fascinating to see the objects come alive again after being preserved with paraffin wax, the colours looking as bold as they did when they were buried thousands of years ago.

Lurking somewhere in the mountains, Bauer and his henchmen lay in wait, spying upon the party of friends, observing the guards, noting everyone's movements.

Charlotte felt a shiver down her spine, as though someone had walked over her grave. She looked up at the clear blue sky, her sunglasses giving the world a bronze-coloured tint. Everything seemed so ordinary and quiet, no birds, or people were around. Harrison held out his arm and she took it as they walked back to the car, they would meet Howard later for dinner at the hotel.

They had a surprise waiting for them when they arrived. Amelia Fazakerley and her friends had descended en masse to Luxor, the elderly lady had been extremely disappointed that Howard and Charlotte had not visited her for dinner when they were Cairo, or written to her for that matter. Charlotte felt a wave of guilt come over her, she really ought to have made more of an effort, if she was honest with herself though, she had forgotten about Amelia in the middle of all the excitement that had surrounded her for these past weeks.

'My dear girl, there you are, we've missed you.' said Elbert Merriman, bending down to kiss her cheek, causing Charlotte to blush, she wasn't sure why though.

'Jean look who it is.'

'Charlotte, you look absolutely marvellous my dear.' Jean gave Charlotte a hug.

'Of course you've already met Mr. Maturin, yes, we're all here.' said Merriman, nodding his head in delight.

'It's Matula, we've met.' said Matula raising his eyes in defeat that Merriman would ever get his name right.

'Oh, I don't know if you've been introduced,' said Charlotte, 'this is Mrs. Araminta Fazakerley and her friends, Emily, Susan, Hettie, and err… I'm afraid I don't know all their names.'

'Never mind, most of them don't remember their names anyway.' said Araminta as she turned to shake Matula's hand, 'how do you do, what a wonderful hotel, I didn't quite catch your name.'

As she took his proffered hand her hat fell over one eye, 'Wretched thing, I don't know why I bother to wear it.' she pushed it back upon her already dishevelled head of hair.

'This is Elbert Merriman and his wife Jean,' said Matula, 'Mrs. Amelia Fazakerley.'

Elbert went pale, 'I say, Jean.' he turned helplessly to his wife.

Jean elbowed him and held out her hand, 'Very pleased to meet you Mrs. Fa…'

'Yes I know it is quite a mouthful, just call me Araminta.'

'Araminta.' said Jean, 'Why don't we all sit down.' she gestured to a large table, more chairs were brought over and the party, with much swapping of places, finally settled down.

Jean whispered to Elbert, 'At least that's one name you won't be able to mangle on your own, none of us will be able to say it.'

'How wonderful to be here, such a delightful room.' said Araminta. 'Mr. Berriman, are you a frequent visitor to Egypt?'

Merriman looked blank, Jean gave him a shove, he replied, 'Oh yes, yes, we come here every winter, Mrs. Sackerley. And yourself?'

'I live in a suburb not far from Cairo, my late husband Bartholomew built a house for us. Of course, he's been gone a long time.' Araminta sniffed, then smiled, 'At least I have my friends to keep me company, I don't know what I'd do without them.' she beamed at everyone.

Howard, who had no idea what was about to descend upon him as he entered the room, looked around for Charlotte. 'Over here Mr. Carter.' shouted a deep voice, Howard froze, it couldn't be? A large, untidy figure approached him, her arms outstretched.

'My dear, dear Howard, I can't tell you how happy I am to see you once again.' Araminta grabbed his hand and shook it vigorously. Howard winced. He was pulled over to the table and introduced to some of the elderly ladies, 'This is Emily, Hettie, Susan, well I'm sure you'll meet everyone else at some point this evening.' said Araminta.

The one called Emily, a rather dumpy looking creature, smiled shyly at him, 'Mr. Carter how wonderful to finally meet you. It's so thrilling to be in your company.' She giggled and turned red.

Susan, slightly younger and prettier than her companions, said, 'I think you ought to give us a guided tour, I can hardly wait to see the mummy.'

'Well, we haven't reached that stage yet, I expect to uncover the mummy next season.' replied Howard.

'Oh, what a shame, we won't be here next season.' Susan said petulantly.

Charlotte gave a sigh and patted to the seat next to her, Howard moved over to sit there. 'I thought it was dinner for me, you and Harrison, what earth is all this?' he gestured round the table and noticed the beaming faces observing him. He coughed, 'this is delightful, unexpected, err shall we order, perhaps?' he said.

'Oh please, let's do so, I'm starving.' said Merriman.

'You spend most of the day eating and you're always hungry, I don't know where you put it all.' replied Jean.

'The same place as everyone else I expect.' answered her husband.

Large quantities of food were consumed and liberal amounts of alcohol quaffed. They were a very noisy party, eventually ending up as the only party in the restaurant, the other diners electing to partake of their dinners in an atmosphere of quietude and serenity elsewhere.

Somebody had ordered champagne. Araminta, her grey hair resembling an oversized brillo pad, rose to her unsteady feet, 'I would like to propose a toast, to our dearest friend, Howard Carter, to congratulate him in his efforts to reclaim the tomb that was rightfully his in the first place, and for getting rid of the German fellow who would have robbed it blind. To Howard!'

Everybody raised their glasses and shouted 'To Howard!'

Howard was very touched by this display of solidarity, and thanked them all, for being here with him tonight and for helping him enjoy a jolly good dinner. Everybody clapped and cheered and those nearest shook his hand and slapped him on the back.

One man, skulking in the shadows, was not happy at all. His face was red with anger, his fists clenched by his side. To-morrow he would have his revenge.

CHAPTER TWENTY-SIX

Howard and two of his colleagues stepped out of the car and were surprised to see Hengel outside the tomb. Surrounding the tomb were twenty of Hengel's men; there was no sign of any of the official guards. Howard had a feeling that this day was not going to turn out very well at all. Waiting for Howard in the Valley were four of his workmen.

'What's going on here?' he enquired of one of the men.

'We do not know, they were here when we arrived.'

Howard was annoyed, 'Hengel,' he shouted, 'you have no right to be here, take your men and leave.'

'No Carter, by the time we have finished with you, it will be you leaving, in a box. Now take your rabble and go while you still have the chance.' bellowed Hengel.

'Authority is on my side, I only have to telephone and the guards will arrive and escort you back to Luxor.'

'I think you will find the telephone is out of order.' shouted Bauer.

'I'm sure we can settle this amicably.' said Howard, feeling a bit nervous now.

Hengel laughed, 'It is too late for that Herr Carter,' he spat the last two words out in anger. 'The tomb is mine, and I mean to take everything out of it for myself.'

'This is madness; you can't possibly complete such a task before you're discovered. Have some dignity man, leave now and we'll forget this ever happened.'

'Don't you talk to me about dignity, I have been humiliated, my home searched, my reputation besmirched, you Carter, you will pay for all of these things.'

The men slowly raised their rifles and pointed them in Howard's direction. The workmen had already disappeared with their donkeys, Howard and his party decided it was probably prudent to leave while they still could, they reentered the car and were quickly driven away.

Hengel smiled his very cruel smile, 'Cowards.' he called after them, 'Bauer, are the men in place?'

'Yes Herr Hengel.' answered Bauer.

'Good.' Hengel turned to the men, 'Keep watch, if anybody comes into sight shoot them, I don't care who they are, get rid of them.'

The men stood to attention and did their best to look vigilant.

As the car drove down the Valley road, a contingent of guards on horseback came into view. Howard explained the situation to them. He watched as they made their way towards the tombs. For about fifteen minutes, there was nothing but quietness, and then a volley of rifle shots filled the air, echoing off the valley's mountainous sides. They heard the thunderous sound of hooves and the guards came galloping back, terrified and with shocked looks upon their faces. A few of them were injured; some of them had blood streaking down their uniforms.

'We are outnumbered, we have to get reinforcements.' said one of the guards.

'There are only twenty of them.' said Howard.

'There are considerably more than twenty of them I can assure you Mr. Carter. Even worse than that, they have killed our Captain.'

The men galloped off to report the situation and to bring back more guards.

Meanwhile, the Nile ferry had docked and Araminta, her friends, the Merrimans, Mr. Matula, Mr. Harrison and Charlotte all disembarked.

'I'm not sure this is a good idea.' said Charlotte. 'Howard will be busy; I don't think he'll be very happy with us turning up unannounced.'

'He's expecting us, we told him we would visit.' said Merriman.

'Of course, he's expecting us, we're his friends, he'll be

delighted to see us.' added Araminta.

'Yes, but I don't think he was expecting everyone this morning.' said Charlotte.

'Well, I can't think what morning he would expect us to arrive, this morning's as good as any.' said Araminta.

'Can we please move on, my feet are sinking into the mud.' said Merriman.

Harrison led the way through the canals and ditches to a group of cars waiting to take them to the Valley.

'I believe I've got mildew in my feet.' said Merriman.

'Stop complaining and get into the car.' answered Jean.

'I must say it's a beautiful day, especially after all the wind we've had.' said Matula.

'Do you mind?' said an indignant Merriman.

'No, no, I meant the weather.' said Matula apologetically.

'Yes it is very hot, I must say.' said Emily, her dumpy frame squeezed into a navy jacket and matching skirt.

'I think it's very exciting, I can hardly wait to see the coffin' said Susan.

'Susan try not to sound so ghoulish.' said Hettie. 'It's not very ladylike at all.'

Hettie was smaller and tidier than Araminta, her beautifully coiffed grey hair tucked beneath her hat wouldn't dream of straying from its confines.

They were making there way towards the cars when the guards came galloping into view.

'Go back, you cannot be here To-day, it's far too dangerous, you must go back to the other side of the Nile.' said the leading guard.

'Why what's happened?' demanded Harrison.

'It is Hengel, he has gone mad, he and his men are armed, they have taken over the Valley. Nobody is allowed through. Our Captain is dead. You must turn back.'

'Where is Mr. Carter?' asked Charlotte, worried for his safety.

'He is safe, waiting at his house.'

The party stirred and a murmur of voices could be heard.

'Well that's settled then.' said Araminta.

'Good, we will help you back to the ferry.' said the guard.

'Nonsense good man, you will let us pass.' said Araminta. 'We have no intention of turning back, we're here to see the tomb, and see it we shall. Now, kindly make way.'

'Lady are you crazy? You will be killed.'

'What utter rot, we're English they wouldn't dare to kill us.' said Jean.

'Actually me and Maturin are American.' said Harrison.

'Err, it's Matula.'

'Sorry, Matula.' said Harrison, shrugging apologetically.

'We won't hold that against you, We'll look after you.' replied Araminta brandishing her umbrella.

'You English people, you are all mad.' and with that the guards galloped away, leaving a cloud of sand in their wake.

Coughing and spluttering, with murmurs of 'I say' and 'Well really', the party were encouraged, shoved and pushed in to the vehicles by their drivers, when all this was accomplished the cars made their way sedately down the road towards their destiny.

Charlotte was dropped off at Howard's house while the others continued their journey into the Valley of the Kings. Howard came out to meet her. 'What's happening?' he asked.

'We're going into battle, what does it look like?' said Charlotte.

Howard, taken aback, said, 'You mean, the guards didn't warn you?' He looked around, but couldn't see anybody. 'Please don't tell me those men are going out there unarmed.'

'Err,' said Charlotte, 'there's actually more women then men.'

Howard looked at her, a look that demanded a fuller explanation.

Charlotte shuffled her feet, 'Well… there's Harrison, Merriman, and Matula.'

'That old fool, what good will he be?'

'Yes…I see your point. But they have back up.'

'Go on.'

'Mrs. Merriman, Mrs. Fazakerley and her friends, about fifteen of them.' said Charlotte quickly.

'Good grief! Are they insane? Do they realize Hengel is armed? The man has completely lost his marbles. This is a situation the police should be involved in, not old people, some of them not altogether in this world.'

'They're very keen! I wouldn't want to face them; Mrs. Fazakerley is quite a formidable presence.'

'Not in front of a gun.'

Charlotte sighed, 'Well somebody has to do something and

we're just trying to help.'

'Then why are you here?'

Charlotte looked at him indignantly, 'If you're trying to imply that I'm hiding here then you're very much mistaken. I'm here to collect Suzy, if anyone can get rid of Hengel it's her.'

Charlotte gave Howard an emphatic nod of her head, and went round the back of the house to find Suzy. Howard was left standing, dumbfounded by the events which had overtaken him. He opened his mouth to say something, couldn't think of anything, and closed it again. He could hear Suzy's ecstatic brays as she greeted Charlotte. He sighed. Was it too much to ask for a quiet life? The donkey came galloping round the corner, Charlotte sat astride her. 'Are you coming?' she shouted.

'No, I'm going to inform the authorities.'

'Suit yourself. You'll miss all the fun.'

Howard stood enveloped in a cloud of dust, watching as they disappeared into the distance.

At the tomb, Hengel's men were beginning to relax. Hengel was not happy, the tomb was padlocked and somebody had misplaced the bolt cutters. 'I am surrounded by idiots,' he shouted, 'Do I always have to do everything myself? What do I pay for you? Dummkopf.' he stomped off with a quaking Bauer in his wake. 'You there.' he bellowed to one unfortunate man who just happened to be in the wrong place. 'Find me some bolt cutters. I want them now.'

'Yes sir.' answered the man, running around like a headless chicken, with no idea where he would find bolt cutters in the middle of the desert.

The cars had arrived at the Valley's entrance. Everybody was milling about and bumping into each other, Merriman wanted to know if there was a bar in the vicinity, and one of the ladies enquired politely if anyone knew if there were facilities nearby, as she was becoming a bit desperate. Somebody told her to go behind a rock. 'I couldn't possible do that.' she said in rather a shocked voice.

'May I have your attention please?' shouted Araminta. Everyone looked at her expectantly. 'We have a duty to perform. Over there is a mad man and his group of thugs, trying to take control of a tomb that should rightfully be in the care of our good friend Mr. Carter. The official guards have run away, typical cowardly men that they are. So it's up to us to deliver justice and to rid the world of this pestilent German man, I've forgotten his name, but that's neither here nor there. They are armed with guns and rifles. We are armed with something far better than that. Our brains, our intelligence and our wit. Yes, we will outwit these vandals and get rid of them once and for all. Now, gather round everybody, while I tell you what are strategy shall be.'

They all gathered round Araminta, 'Are we all here?' she boomed. A small voice was heard from behind the rocks, 'I'll be there in a minute.'

'Is that you Joan?'

'Yes, I'm here now'. Joan said emerging from behind a large boulder.

'You took my advice then?' said Harrison, laughing.

Joan blushed with embarrassment.

The party dispersed to take up their positions among the rocks and slopes of the valley. All was in readiness for the battle that lay ahead.

'Owww, my eye, something hit my eye.' cried Bauer.

'Bauer what are you up to now?' said Hengel.

'I think it was this rock.' said Bauer.

'You've been in the sun too long, go and sit in the tent.'

Suddenly there were shouts and cries all around Hengel, men fell down at his feet clutching various parts of their bodies as a rain of rocks hurled down at them. Hengel was about to shout something, when he was hit on the head. He fell to his knees; he felt blood trickling down his cheek. 'What on earth is going on?' he managed to say.

Everywhere men were taking cover, running, even crawling towards the valley sides, trying to avoid the barrage of rocks and stones that were falling all about them. They tried to use their weapons but it was impossible to focus without being bashed on the bonce by falling masonry.

Then all of a sudden, it became quiet. The men tentatively emerged from their hiding places. A rock knocked one of them out. Hengel looked around, 'What are you waiting for? Do something, shoot them all.' he shouted.

'There is no one to shoot at.' said one of the men.

'Always excuses, climb up there and find them, do I have to go myself?'

Some of the men started to ascend the rocky sides, only to be knocked back down by more rocks, stones and pebbles. They fell on top of each other as more bits of the valley slid down and attempted to bury them alive.

'What is that?' shouted someone.

'Quiet.' bellowed Hengel.

The sound of marching feet could be heard approaching their position. 'It can't be the guards coming back, can it?' asked Bauer.

'Shh, be quiet.' said Hengel.

'There!' called out another man, pointing towards the line of people marching towards them.

'What on earth? Is this some kind of joke?' asked an incredulous Hengel.

Araminta Fazakerley and friends were marching purposefully shoulder to shoulder, every step bringing them closer to Hengel and his battered men. They were armed with umbrellas and handbags, and all had a fierce determination in their step. There faces were in battle mode, eyes on the look out for any unexpected movement. As they came nearer, they slowed to a stop.

Araminta stepped forward; she turned back and consulted with Harrison, who reminded her of the German's name.

'She stepped forward again, 'Herr Hengel' she shouted towards him.

The man she was looking at answered 'I am Bauer, Herr Hengel is over to your right.'

'I do beg your pardon, my mistake. Where was I?' She turned to the tall fair haired man, who now sported a black eye and a face streaked with blood. 'My goodness what happened to you?' She took out her pince nez and peered at him. 'Herr Hengel, I presume?'

'You presume correctly. Now what are you doing here? Are you responsible for all of this?' his arm swept about him, the battered and bleeding men stared in disbelief at the strange sight before them.

'Of course we're responsible, who else is there? Goodness me, I thought you were an intelligent man. Now, are you going to leave this tomb or not?'

Hengel stared at the ladies before him; their ages encompassed a wide path from twenties to sixties. He shook his head. 'I think not. Now kindly turn around and go back to your knitting and your afternoon tea and leave us to get on with our work.' he mistakenly turned his back on them, and suddenly fell to his knees as he was whacked over the head by a handbag. The ladies charged. Hengel's men didn't know what to do or where to go. They ran about aimlessly, they were assaulted by handbags, and tripped by umbrellas. Some of them were knocked unconscious by rocks. Merriman's voice came drifting down into the valley, 'Good shot, that's five I've hit.'

Bauer stuck his head round the tent flap and was hit by a handbag; he fell to the rock-strewn floor. Some men began to regroup, rifles in hand; the ladies began to back away. There was a rumble in the distance; everybody looked to see what it was. Donkeys! Suzy and Charlotte, with Jabari and his friends together with their donkeys descended en masse upon the scene. The battle recommenced.

Emily had hidden herself inside a tent and leaning upon the floor with her umbrella sticking out of the flap she managed to trip up quite a few of Hengel's fleeing men. Araminta was busy wielding her handbag bashing heads left, right and centre, 'Hey steady on you nearly knocked me unconscious.' 'I do beg your pardon Mr. Harrison.'

'This is so exciting!' exclaimed Susan throwing a rock at an approaching enemy, who went down with a satisfying thump.

Suzy was having a wonderful time, Charlotte had left her to her own devices, and she was kicking all the men she could see, then trampling upon them for good measure, she liked to do things properly. Jabari and his friends, who had weighed into the fray with enthusiasm, yelled and threw sticks and bits of stones, and the occasional basketful of sand. Donkeys were braying and kicking, men were shouting, women were calling out 'Good shot', 'Let him have it' and so on and so forth, boys were yelling encouragement to each other. A fierce looking man spotted Araminta and with a gap-toothed leer approached her; he was holding a baton and passing it from one hand to the other. Araminta, her head held high, firmly stood her ground. From seemingly out of nowhere a large rock came swinging through the air and hit the man squarely upon the back of his head. He collapsed in front of Araminta, 'Well aimed Susan.' Susan blushed and went off to find another victim.

Jean and Elbert along with Matula were standing at the top of the cliff, throwing stones and rocks and anything they could find down into the melee below. 'That must be about twenty-five hits for me now.' said Merriman.

'I'm afraid that last one doesn't count.' said Matula.

'Why on earth not, perfectly legitimate hit.' said Merriman.

'You old fool,' said Jean, 'you hit one of ours.'

'Oh, I'm so sorry.' Merriman shouted downwards.

'Honestly, fat lot of help you are.' said Jean.

'I do my best. Oh, there's another one, that's definitely not one of ours.' Merriman lobbed a rock and watched as it just clipped the back of the man's head. The man turned and stared upwards.

'Hengel himself, I think I'm the winner.'

'It doesn't count either, he's still standing.' said Matula.

'Honestly, Patula you really are a party pooper.'

'Sorry.'

'Humph,' said Merriman, sulkily grabbing some more stones.

'Shoot, use your rifles, you fools.' shouted Hengel over the din of battle.

'We are trying, it is not easy, I have a donkey standing on my foot and he is eating my shirt.' replied one of the men.

Hengel grabbed a rifle from the ground and fired a shot into the air, he yelled as a donkey bit him. Suddenly boys and fierce looking animals surrounded him. 'Go away.' he shouted. The boys looked at him and a large stone came flying through the air and hit him squarely in the chest, winding him, he dropped the rifle. 'Oh my gott, this is a nightmare. Bauer where are you.' he tried to shout but couldn't, there was so much noise no one could hear him.

Bauer emerged bruised and battered from his tent and was about to walk over to Hengel, when Araminta stepped in front of him. With a shaking hand he held up his revolver and pointed it at her head. Araminta stood still, staring at him. Unbeknownst to Bauer, creeping up behind him was Emily, who smashed him over the head with a wooden chair. 'Good shot.' said Araminta.

'I always try to do my best, Araminta.' said Emily smiling.

Suzy had spotted Hengel, and with a look of fury approached him. Hengel recognized her, 'You, you are the miserable creature who caused so much destruction at the cave.'

Hengel looked directly into Suzy's eyes; he aimed his rifle squarely at her head. The donkey's eyes bored into his soul, she pawed the ground ominously. Hengel became aware that it was very quiet, everybody had stopped and were now watching the two protagonists as they squared up to each other. Charlotte saw her brave friend, and the rifle aimed at her, she cried out, 'Noooo.' and ran in front of Suzy.

Hengel pulled the trigger, the shot echoed loudly throughout the valley. Charlotte dropped like a stone to the ground. A second or so later an ear-splitting scream broke the silence, Suzy upset and not fully understanding what had happened to Charlotte, tried to nudge her and brayed gently into her head, there was no movement. The donkey whimpered softly. Hengel raised his rifle and pulled the trigger once more, this time the rifle remained silent; he pulled the trigger again, before realizing it was out of cartridges. Suzy catching his movement from the corner of her eye stared at him with such hatred that Hengel found he was unable to move his feet from fear. Suzy gave a great bellowing 'hee-haw' and charged. Hengel tried to make a run for it, but his legs were rooted to the spot. The donkey butted him and sent him flying through the air with such immense force that he almost landed atop the cliff; he came crashing down upon one of the guard's tents. The sound of breaking chairs and broken crockery echoed around the valley. There was a moment's silence and then a huge cheer went up from Jabari and his friends, who ran over towards the tent, to restrain what was left of the stricken man.

Araminta and Emily rushed over to Charlotte, but Suzy refused to allow anyone to come near her. She stood guard over her friend, her nose buried in Charlotte's neck. Howard and the relief force arrived. Not that there was anything for the guards to accomplish, the ladies had all the men tied up, Bauer included, and Jabari had Hengel under his watchful eye. Howard looked around for Charlotte; Araminta approached him, 'I'm afraid there's been a rather nasty incident.'

'Where's Charlotte? What's happened?' Howard asked, he was feeling nervous and apprehensive, something awful had happened. 'Please tell me she's not dead.'

'I'm so sorry.' said Araminta, putting a hand on his shoulder.

Howard felt as though his heart had stopped, this couldn't be, he had only seen her a couple of hours ago. He warned her that this silly venture could turn out to be dangerous, he should have gone with her. Why didn't he go with her? He berated himself, fool he thought, it's all my fault, I should have stopped her.

'Where is she?' he asked.

Araminta pointed, 'Over there.'

Howard looked; he saw a donkey standing over a body. 'Oh my god.' He put his hand to his mouth in shock.

'We can't get near her, the donkey won't allow it.' said Araminta. 'Perhaps you have some influence over the creature?'

Howard looked a bit stunned.

'Mr. Carter, Howard, you have to move the donkey.'

'Yes, sorry.' Howard walked over towards Charlotte and Suzy. The donkey stared balefully at him. Howard cleared his throat, 'Err, Suzy,' he coughed, 'you have to let us help Charlotte, we have to see if she's still alive. We may need to take her to hospital.' The donkey continued looking at him. Howard looked around, everybody was watching him, he suddenly felt a bit foolish trying to explain to a donkey the need for urgency. He tried again. 'Err, please Suzy, if we don't help her she may die.' If she's not dead already he thought, and tried not to think about that.

Suzy nuzzled Charlotte's head, and gave a quiet bray, then moved aside to allow Howard to bend over and check if she was still breathing, he felt her pulse, it was very faint, but at least he could feel it. 'She's alive.' he called out. There was a collective sigh of relief.

The guards rounded up the miscreants; Bauer, who was stammering how he had been forced to help Hengel and how innocent he really was, after all he was just the valet. The unconscious Hengel was extricated from the ruins of the tent and stretchered away to hospital under police custody.

The ladies, Howard, Jabari and friends, the donkeys including Suzy, along with the Merrimans, Matula and Harrison all departed. Araminta and the ladies to go back to the hotel to fortify themselves with sherry for their nerves. The Merrimans, Matula and Harrison accompanied a distressed Suzy back to Howard's house. Howard accompanied Charlotte to the hospital.

The valley was left alone, rocks and stones were strewn all over the ground, tents lay crushed and broken. A lone man came hurrying along urging his donkey to go faster. The donkey stopped, the man dismounted and looked around in stunned disbelief. He called out, 'Herr Hengel, are you here? I have found the bolt cutters.'

CHAPTER TWENTY-SEVEN

Charlotte's wound turned out to be a badly grazed head. As the doctor had said, it was lucky Hengel was a bad shot. Howard sat by her bedside, she asked him about Suzy.

'She's pining for you, she barely eats anything. However, Jabari is with her now and he's taken a tough stance with her, he told her that if she didn't eat she would never see you again. She seemed to understand, so she's finally begun to eat a bit each day.'

'What about Hengel?'

'He's still in hospital, the authorities have abandoned him and he's been banished from ever entering Egypt again. Bauer has spilled the beans, and the treasure has been recovered.'

'So it's over then, the tomb's yours once more.'

'Yes, I can finally get back to work without any further disturbances, I hope.'

Charlotte slowly recovered and Howard invited her to stay in his spare room so she could be near Suzy. Araminta fussed around, Emily, who was rather taken with Howard had a tendency to flutter about him whenever he made an appearance, causing him no end of discomfort. Since the shooting, Suzy had steadfastly refused to be parted from Charlotte, she followed her all over Howard's house, even on board the ferry when Charlotte and Howard crossed the Nile to the Winter Palace. The ladies spoiled her dreadfully, Suzy, not Charlotte, and a young boy discreetly cleaned up the deposits left by the donkey. The hotel manager, Mr. Nashat turned a blind eye to this, after all everyone knew how eccentric English people were, if they wanted to take tea with a donkey who was he to say no, as long as they took tea out on the terrace of course. Unfortunately, after an accident involving Suzy and two rather large potted palms - apparently donated to the hotel by Mr. Nashat's mother ten years ago and the pride of Mr. Nashat's reception area, Suzy was forbidden entry to the hotel. It was only because Howard had paid a large sum of money for clearing up the damaged pots, scattered earth and shredded and half-chewed palms, that Mr. Nashat allowed Suzy anywhere near the terrace.

Howard, meanwhile, had been busy working in the laboratory, despite suffering from a troublesome cold. Working quietly, he was able to forward another large consignment of treasures from the tomb to the Cairo Museum, where many of them were already on view.

It was decided to have a celebratory picnic at an old burial site approximately two hours away from Qurna. Howard, Charlotte, the Merrimans, Harrison, Matula, Suzi and Jabari piled into the bus, the back seats having been removed to allow space for Suzy. The donkey, initially unsure about this mode of transport decided she quite liked it once the bus was underway. Her observant eyes noted that everyone appeared to have their own seats, Suzy looked around for her seat, there wasn't one. She thought she would like to try one though and sat down upon the nearest one, a muffled voice shouted something that sounded like 'help.'

'What's going on down there?' asked Jean. Peering down the bus, she said sternly, 'Elbert, for goodness sake will you put that donkey down. Can't leave that man alone for five minutes before he's up to no good.' She walked up to Suzy, 'There, there, my dear you come to Auntie Jean, is that dreadful man bothering you?' Suzy was all too happy to leave, the seat was lumpy, bumpy and wriggled around a lot, she was happier standing at the back.

Merriman gasped for air, 'I thought it was my last hour, wretched creature sat on me.'

'Stop making such a fuss, here, read your book.' said Jean, shoving the book in his hands and knocking his glasses off his lap.

'I can't read without my glasses.' said Merriman.

'For goodness sake, where are they?' asked Jean.

There was the sound of crunching glass, both Merrimans looked at each other and then at Suzy, she had sat on them.

Merriman sighed, 'Now what, I shan't be able to see anything properly.'

'You'll just have to manage without, now try to stay out of trouble.'

Nothing but sand could be seen in all directions, the sky was hazy with heat. Surrounding the area were the remains of burial mounds, over to the left were the ruins of a mud-brick structure, only two walls and a partial roof remaining. Nearby stood an impressive mastaba constructed using sandstone and granite.

The party set up their camp within the mud-brick structure. Tables and chairs were set out for their picnic. Canvas awnings were erected for shade. There were no birds or creatures of the desert to be seen, they were all taking shelter from the sun's intense heat. The air was heavy with silence. The food, packed safely in its boxes was hidden away in the shade of the awning. The fare consisted mainly of sandwiches, along with salads and raw vegetables also lemonade, cold tea, and water to quench their thirst.

It was decided to explore the mastaba first. Howard made sure that everyone was armed with a torch, and warned them to stay together, although the construction had been previously excavated, nevertheless it was very derelict and could be dangerous. There was a frisson of excitement among the group, a feeling as though they were true explorers setting off into the unknown. They located the entrance at the far side of the tomb complex, a succession of passages led downwards to the subterranean chambers. The floor was uneven; the plaster having long since come away, the walls were covered with granite. A strange smell emanated from the interior, the smell of a long unvisited and undisturbed structure. Charlotte felt a shiver down her spine, she thought it was a very creepy place and was glad she was not alone.

The passage descended at a gentle angle and became steeper as they continued along it. Matula lost his footing and managed to slide right down to the bottom.

'Goodness me, he's in a hurry.' said Merriman.

The others caught up with him, Jean dusted him down and told him not to worry about his ripped jacket, you could barely see the tear she reassured him. They found themselves in a chamber; doorways leading to other chambers could be seen in the murky dimness. The large space was devoid of wall paintings and whatever it once contained had long since disappeared. They wondered around, their footsteps echoing spookily about them. Harrison produced a very loud sneeze, scaring everyone almost to death. 'Sorry, it's this dust.' he said, producing a handkerchief and blowing his nose loudly. 'Can't you be more subtle?' Said Howard, 'you'll have the roof down upon us.'

'Sorry.' replied Harrison. 'Who was buried here?'

'No one knows,' answered Howard, 'it was discovered in the middle of last century, only a broken sarcophagus remained, nothing else was found.'

'Such a strange place,' said Jean, 'it almost seems haunted. So bare, so much hard work digging this structure deep underground and now it's just an empty hollow shell.'

'I'm going to see what's through here.' said Merriman.

The others stayed a few more minutes contemplating the bare chamber before following Merriman through the left-hand door. This chamber was more dilapidated; Howard warned them to be very careful where they put their feet, as the floor had some decidedly unsafe looking gaps patterned across it. They began to fan out, suddenly there was a scream and everyone turned to look. A small fissure had opened up and a pair of hands could be seen clinging desperately to an old rope attached to the top.

'Help,' shouted Charlotte, 'I'm not sure I can hold on for much longer.'

'Quick grab her hands.' said Harrison.

Matula bent down, there was a loud rip, 'Oh, no!' he exclaimed, 'my trousers!'

'Never mind about that.' said Howard, pushing Merriman out of the way.

'I hate to bother you,' said a voice from the depths of the fissure, 'some assistance would be appreciated.'

'Hold on, Charlotte, I'm coming.' said Howard, running towards the gap and bumping into Harrison who was coming from the opposite direction.

'Honestly,' said Jean, 'men, leave this to me.' She bent down and looked into the fissure.

'I'm sinking, the rope's beginning to fray.' cried Charlotte.

'Someone bring another rope, there should be one in the bus.' said Harrison.

'I'll go.' called out Matula, running as fast as he could, trying to protect his dignity as he went.

'Matula's gone to find a rope, hold on Charlotte.' called Howard.

'I wasn't planning to let go.' said Charlotte. 'But I don't think I can hold on any longer, my hands are slipping, the rope's disintegrating fast and there's nothing else to hold on to.'

Jean bent down, 'Nonsense girl, you can't possible let go, how will we explain your absence to the authorities, not to mention the effect it will have upon that donkey. Do your best to hang in there, Matula will be back eventually.'

Matula burst out into the sunshine, drenched in sweat; he managed to make his way to the mud-hut, where Jabari and Suzy were waiting.

Matula tried to speak, he gasped for air, but the words just wouldn't come out.

Jabari looked at him, the man was covered in dust he had a large rip in his trousers and a torn jacket. 'What has happened, have you had an accident?'

'Rope. Need a rope.' Matula gasped, 'Charlotte fell down a hole, need to help her out.'

'You stay here, I will find rope.' Jabari found the rope and calling Suzy they ran through the mastaba's entrance and down the passageway, colliding with Merriman at the bottom, who found himself sitting at the opposite end of the chamber.

'Hee-haw.' bellowed Suzy, and a ton of plaster and brick fell on top of them.

'Keep that donkey quiet.' shouted Howard, and more plaster and dust fell on top of him.

'I have the rope,' said Jabari, in a whisper.

'Pardon.' shouted Jean.

'Quiet,' hissed Howard, as a shower of dust settled at their feet.

Jabari peered down the fissure, 'I cannot see her, Charlotte are you there?'

'Of course I'm still here, where else would I be?' replied Charlotte.

'I will throw the rope to you, tie it under your arms.' said Jabari.

'Tie a weight to the end, it'll make it easier for her to catch it.' suggested Jean.

Jabari found a small rock and tied the rope around it. 'I am throwing it now.'

There was a clunk, as if a stone had hit a piece of wood.

'Oww, are you trying to kill me?' shouted Charlotte.

'Shhh, not so loud.' said Howard, as more bits of brick came down.

'Stop messing around down there, this whole place is going to come down on top of us any moment now.' said Harrison.

'Charming. Thank you for your concern.' answered Charlotte.

'Get on with it' hissed Howard.

'All right, I'm ready, pull me up please, my arms are killing me.'

Jabari tied the rope to Suzy, and slapped her on the rump, 'Go Suzy, go.'

Suzy, always willing to do her best, did go, she charged through the chambers and up the passageway. Charlotte came out of the fissure like a cork popping out of a champagne bottle.

'Stop, Suzy. Somebody do something to help me.' Charlotte called out.

Everyone stood stupefied, and then charged after the disappearing pair. More bricks fell from the roof, muffled shouts of 'Stop Suzy, stop!' echoed round the chambers. Merriman, who had just managed to get back on his feet, found himself swept along the passageway.

Finally they reached daylight, Suzy stopped, her mission accomplished. She turned about and wondered over to Charlotte, 'Suzy, why didn't you stop?' Suzy nuzzled Charlotte's head.

'Charlotte are you all right?' cried Howard in alarm as he picked her up, untied the rope, and tried to remove the bits of plaster and stone still adhering to her clothes. 'Look at the state of you, you're filthy.'

'I'm all right, I think.' replied Charlotte. 'Never mind though, I've had a wonderful day.'

'Good, I'm glad you enjoyed it.' said Howard absent-mindedly.

The rest of the party appeared, covered in dust and bits of plaster, Matula with his ruined trousers and jacket, joined them. Merriman looked like something from a horror film, his pale face and sparse hair sticking up in muddy spikes. Jean looked like she was going to faint. Harrison looked as though he could do with a stiff whisky. Howard's hair was doing its best to resemble a thorny bush. Suzy beamed upon them all. Jabari shouted, 'Photo, smile everyone!' He ran over to join them, a huge grin on his face as the timer on the camera clicked the shutter and took the picture.

They sat down and ate their picnic, afterwards they wondered about the rest of the burial site. Soon it was time to go. Piling back into the bus, they drove back towards Luxor. A few days after their return stories began to circulate about the tragic fate of a mastaba, whose interior had completely collapsed in a heap, leaving behind a mountain of rubble; people wondered if an underground tremor or earthquake had caused the structure to cave in. Howard swore everyone to secrecy on pain of death, he'd only just restored his reputation and he wasn't going to jeopardize his return to Tutankhamen's tomb by being thought of as a destroyer of ancient tombs.

CHAPTER TWENTY-EIGHT

England, 1925

All too soon, the season ended, Howard returned to London, where despite suffering from a heavy cold, he gave a speech at the Royal Institution on the Tomb of Tutankhamen. His speech dealt mainly with the work of the second and third seasons upon the tomb and the investigation of the burial chamber. He described the task of demolishing the partition wall that divided the anteroom from the burial chamber; the dismantling of the four golden shrines erected one within the other, and the unmasking of the magnificent yellow quartzite sarcophagus containing the mortal remains of the boy king.

That undertaking, he said, required some 84 days of heavy manual labour. The four shrines comprised some 80 sections and panels, and from the fact that the woodwork of the shrines had shrunk in the course of 3,300 years the overlaying gold work had slightly expanded, with the result that a space was left between the basic wood and the ornamental surface, which, when touched, tended to crush and fall away.

Among the funerary furniture discovered was a unique palace lamp carved out of pure semi-translucent alabaster, a triple lamp of floral design, which would appear to be a prototype of the three-branched candlestick, golden emblems of Anubis, and a perfume vase of the king and queen, a cosmetic jar still containing its cosmetic plastic and fragrance, the gold stick of the king, the gorgeous fans similar to those in use at the Vatican, and among other objects a wine jar bearing the vintage, "Year five, wine of the House of Tutankhamen, from the western river, Chief of the vinterers Kla."

An account was given of the great yellow quartzite sarcophagus discovered, with its winged goddesses Isis, Nephthys, Neith, and Selk, sculptured at the four corners in high relief, and so designed that their full spread wings and outstretched arms encircled the sarcophagus with their protective embrace.

The discourse ended with the description of the raising of the lid of the sarcophagus and of the wondrous golden coffin found within. Upon the forehead of the effigy of the King was a touching tribute from the girlish widowed Queen, a tiny wreath of flowers that had retained their tinge of colour throughout 30 centuries. The golden coffin, yet to be examined, is no doubt the centre shell of a series of coffins, one within the other, the last containing the mortal remains of the young Pharaoh, placed there fourteen centuries before Christ.

Charlotte, having managed to tear herself away from Suzy's affections arrived in London a few weeks later. It was quite a wrench to leave her friend behind, she could still see the donkey's sad eyes and bowed head as she kissed her goodbye, Suzy turning her back on her broke Charlotte's heart. She tried to explain that she would be back in a few months time, but Suzy went back to her stable and refused to look at her. Just thinking about it Charlotte felt a stabbing pain in her heart, she felt so cruel. May be she should have stayed, everyone she knew had left though, so she would have been alone. Poor Suzy, Jabari would look after her, at least that thought comforted her.

One of Charlotte's highlights was a visit with Howard to the London Pavilion at Piccadilly Circus, to see a revue presented by Charles Cochran. She hadn't seen a revue before and very much looked forward to it. It was called "On with the Dance," with a book and lyrics by Noel Coward; there were also two ballet sequences presented by Leonide Massine, no less. It was certainly an eclectic series of selections from staged ballets, production numbers and sketches. Nigel Bruce appeared as an old clubman lamenting that things had altered for the worse in a quite realistic Paris café scene. Various songs followed, then a vivid impression of Hogarth's "The Rake's Progress" choreographed by Leonide

Massine who appeared therein, this proved to be one of Charlotte's favourite pieces, closely followed by the brilliantly presented Hungarian Wedding. Afterwards there was some jazz music, another Massine ballet, "Crescendo." Russian dancing, acrobatics, a dancing violinist, a comedy about a Vicarage Tea Party featuring Hermione Baddeley, and much, much more. Charlotte's head was spinning, she enjoyed every single moment of it. Howard was quite blasé about it, having seen all this before in one form or another.

Afterwards, Mr. Cochran invited them to a private reception, various other people were there, but Charlotte had no idea whom any of them were, she was a bit disappointed that Noel Coward hadn't turned up.

Howard and Charlotte travelled back to Shropshire to the beautiful town of Oswestry. 15th and 16th century inns still stood, looking very elegant with their timber framing and slate roofs. Howard was here to give a lecture on Tutankhamen. He told the audience that in October next he and his colleagues proposed to examine the mortal remains of the King, not with the intention of interfering with them, but to examine and enjoy the wonderful things that had been bequeathed. It would not be necessary even to remove the body.

With regard to the cosmetics discovered still in plastic and fragrant condition in the tomb, experts were still examining them, and hoped to be able to produce for the women of To-day cosmetics like those used by women three thousand years ago.

Howard's next engagement took place at the New Oxford Theatre in London. For hundreds of years, he explained to the audience, Egyptologists had been trying to find out how the Ancient Egyptians illuminated their homes, and in their excavations in the Valley of the Kings, they came across several lamps. They were executed in beautiful designs in translucent alabaster, and one of them stood about three feet in height with a large central cup. There was no decoration either on the exterior or the interior of the cup, but immediately a light was placed in the vessel their could be seen a picture of the young King and Queen in colours. This effect was produced by another cup being turned inside the outer vessel, and the two being fitted so well that the joints could not be detected.

'We are just beginning to use alabaster for electric lamps,' said Howard, 'but in Egypt, 1,350 years before Christ, it was done even more finely than we do it To-day.'

Speaking of the opening of the casket, Howard said it was a wondrous sight after the removal of linen shrouds darkened with age. There lay the golden effigy of the boy-King, of magnificent workmanship, filling the whole of the interior of the sarcophagus. Upon the forehead of the effigy were two emblems encrusted with brilliant inlay.

Most touching of all was the fact that around these emblems lay a tiny wreath of flowers, probably the last farewell offering of the girlish widowed Queen. Among all that regal splendour, that royal magnificence, everywhere the glint of gold, there was nothing so charming as those few withered flowers, still retaining their tinge of colour. They told what a short period 3,300 years really was – but yesterday and the morrow. In fact, this little touch of nature made that ancient and our modern civilization kin. There was a feeling of awe, Howard said, when they entered the antechamber and beheld for the first time the splendour of the Imperial Age in Egypt of the fourteenth century before Christ. The gorgeousness of the sight, its sumptuous splendour, made it appear more like the confused magnificence of those counterfeit splendours heaped together in the property room of some modern theatre than any possible reality surviving from antiquity.

'It would be difficult to describe our emotions,' said Howard, 'when for the first time, the light from our powerful electric lamps flooded that tomb chamber – that silent seat of a Lord of the West – illuminating as it did the walls on which were painted representations of Amentît, the West, and the immense shrine overlaid with gold, inlaid with brilliant blue faience tiles, filling nearly the entire area of the chamber.'

Referring to the difficulties of his work, Howard said they had to squeeze in and out of the tomb like weasels. 'We bumped our heads,' he continued, 'nipped our fingers, and spilt hot wax upon our bare skin. I think I remember how one of the eminent chemists, who kindly assisted us in the preservation work, when taking records of various phenomena in the tomb, found that he had also recorded a certain percentage of profanity! Nevertheless, I am glad to say that in the conflict we did more harm to ourselves than to those wonderful shrines.'

Howard's next lecture took place at the Assembly Rooms Agricultural Hall in Norwich. The Lord Mayor (Dr. G. S. Pope) introduced Howard as a native of Swaffham, who, said Dr. Pope would unfold what we have read of as being one of the greatest romances of the age in which we live. Mr. Carter was a marvellous explorer, who, like all good Norfolk men, had been endowed with singular luck.

Howard described the discovery of the tomb, the clearing of the antechamber and the moment when they were able to penetrate and solve the mystery of the inner sealed door which proved to be the entrance of the King's burial chamber. Though a shrewd guess anticipated what might be beyond that mysterious sealed door, guarded by two imposing sentinel figures of the King, little did they expect the impressive sight revealed as stone by stone the masonry which blocked the doorway was removed. First, to all appearances, a wall of gold met their gaze, with no clue as to its meaning; then as the aperture in the masonry became larger, they realized that that which barred their view was no less than an immense golden shrine, and that they were now at the entrance of the actual burial chamber of Tutankhamen.

Howard went on to say that the fourth season's work was about to begin, and he hoped to leave next week for Egypt. They would first examine the Royal mummy, opening the great sarcophagus, and unwrapping the mortal remains, whereupon, he thought, they would probably find the Royal regalia and also religious documents.

'We shall then,' added Howard, 'immediately re-wrap these mortal remains and replace them in the sarcophagus, where they will be left, so far as I can tell, for ever. We shall then commence upon the investigation of one of the smaller chambers of the tomb, wherein there are numbers of shrines, a flotilla of boats, boxes containing jewellery, and thirty-five great black boxes, sealed. We do not know their contents. In fact, imagination falters at what they may contain.'

Referring to the finding within the sarcophagus of a coffin in the form of an effigy of the young King, Howard said the decoration was rendered in fine bas-relief, the head and the hands of the King were in the round, in massive gold, and of the finest sculpture. The hands, crossed over the breast, held the royal emblems – the crook and the flail – encrusted with deep blue faience. There was a touch of realism, for while the rest of the coffin was of brilliant yellow gold, that of the face and hands seemed different, the gold of the flesh was of different alloy, which gave the impression of the greyness of death.

Thanking Howard at the close of the lecture, the Lord Mayor said criticism had been raised by some people of what they considered to be the desecration of a tomb for idle curiosity; but he thought it would be agreed by all who had heard Mr. Carter that he had approached his subject with real reverence and a desire to acquire knowledge of the ages for the use of ourselves and our descendants

CHAPTER TWENTY-NINE

Egypt, then England, 1925

The little donkey was so overjoyed her friend was back, every time she saw Charlotte she brayed and ran around in circles, then head butted Charlotte, then nuzzled her face in Charlotte's hair. Charlotte had brought her some treats and a new red rope, which she placed around Suzy's neck, it made the donkey look very smart. Suzy seemed quite pleased with it and paraded about and showed it off to Jabari. Charlotte had bought him some presents as well, a new tea towel, with Oswestry printed along the side of it. Jabari seemed very happy with it, he considered it quite a unique word, and said he would wear the towel with pride. They sat and chatted and played with Suzy, who was in her element, Jabari was of the opinion that Charlotte would have a hard time settling the donkey for the night, 'Oh, that's all right,' said Charlotte, 'I'll just sing to her.'

Jabari looked puzzled, 'She likes you to sing to her?'

'No, nobody likes me to hear me sing, I was thrown out of the school choir, the chorus master said I put everyone off key.'

'Then I don't understand.'

'It's because my singing is so terrible, Suzy will do anything I ask just as I long as I stop making that awful noise.'

'I see! Yes, that is a very useful talent to possess. Of course, it wouldn't work for me, I sing like an angel.' Jabari said, giving Charlotte a very angelic smile.

'Shut up and eat your chocolate.' said Charlotte indignantly.

Howard arrived and re-opened the tomb, with the object of investigating the mummy of Pharaoh itself. The linen covering was removed from the second sarcophagus, together with the bouquets reposing on it, and this revealed another sarcophagus, the chief feature of which was a representation of the god Osiris. This sarcophagus was richly decorated, being entirely covered with painted designs and vari-coloured glass, with a layer of gold on a marble ground.

Further investigations brought to light a human-shape, gilt-covered, and wearing a necklace. Flowers were tied to a head bandage, and also resting on the breast. At the head part of the form was also painted a face representing a young pharaoh. The figure was covered with a tightly fitting linen shroud, and when this was removed the actual coffin of the Pharaoh was exposed. This was covered with gold ornamentation, of beautiful workmanship, but, unfortunately, most of the detail was concealed by a black glutinous layer, the result of the libations poured out at the funeral services.

In the presence of Government and scientific representatives, Howard began the examination of the mummy of King Tutankhamen, which was carried on in situ, since the mummy could not be removed from the coffin without injury.

The outer surfaces of the wrappings, which were in a very fragile condition, were first consolidated by means of a thin coating of melted paraffin wax, after which a longitudinal incision was made from the mask to the feet.

The outer coverings, on being turned back, exposed a layer of wrappings, which were equally carbonized and decayed. In these circumstances any orderly unwrapping was manifestly impossible.

As the work proceeded a large number of interesting and beautiful objects were gradually revealed. At each stage of the proceedings both written and photographic records were taken.

Among the objects brought to light, the more important were amuletic collarettes, a superb gold dagger with a crystal handle, bracelets of intricate workmanship, a large number of finger rings of diverse materials, some having scarabs bearing the King's names for their bezels; a second dagger even more beautiful than the first, several large inlaid pectorals, beadwork, ornaments, gold circlets, etc.

The work of uncovering the mummy proceeded only so far as to expose the lower part of the body and limbs.

According to the opinion of anatomical experts, the evidence up to the present reveals no doubt that the body is that of a male, not yet adult, and in a much-emaciated condition. Carbonized on the feet are golden sandals, and upon each toe and finger golden stalls. So far, no trace of documents have been discovered. Both the forearms were loaded with magnificent jewels.

The jewellery discovered on the King, who lies in his coffin of solid gold, is far beyond expectations.

A few days after Christmas Tutankhamen's gold coffin, the most extensive piece of solid gold work which archaeological research has ever brought to light, left the Valley of the Kings.

Borne on the shoulders of eight men to the railway station at Luxor – a strange contrast with that day some three thousand years ago when it was conveyed with all the Royal funereal pomp of ancient Egypt to the tomb.

Howard and an armed guard accompanied the coffin on the train, Charlotte had insisted on going as well, there was no way she was going to miss this spectacle. The train left Luxor at six o'clock that evening and arrived in Cairo the next day.

King Fuad honoured Howard for his splendid work in connection with the Tutankhamen discoveries, by conferring upon him the Order of the Nile (Third Class).

General Sir John Maxwell expressed himself quietly but forcibly on the subject of the Tutankhamen controversy.

'More than twelve thousand people have been to see the tomb this year already,' he said, 'and it costs 180 piastres – nearly £2 – to go in. In addition to that, each tourist must have spent at least £100 in Egypt on the visit to the tomb. And what does the Government do for Carter? They present him with the Third Class Order of the Nile – the sort of thing they give to stationmasters. And not only that, they practically accuse him of theft. He actually had to pay the railway fare for the golden effigy of Tutankhamen from Luxor to Cairo – as well as for himself.'

At lunch one day Charlotte asked Howard what or who he planned to look for next. Howard smoked his cigarette and gave some thought to the question.

'If I had time to spare from the work of clearing Tutankhamen's tomb I would probably discover two or three tombs of the queens,' he declared. 'The valley of the kings is now almost entirely cleared, and contains no other royal tombs.' He took a sip of tea.

'Hasn't that been announced before? Belzoni claimed there were no more tombs to be found in the Valley and the same sentiments were expressed by Theodore Davis, yet years later look what you discovered.' said Charlotte.

Howard gave Charlotte an indulgent smile, 'There is a possibility that a few ancient Egyptian notables were granted the signal honour of burial among the kings. The valley of the queens, on the other hand, has not yet been thoroughly explored, and certainly holds the remains of a number of royal wives.'

'So what's going to be happening next season?'

'I'm quite enthusiastic about the prospects of next winter's work.' said Howard as he took another puff of his cigarette.

'The two outer chambers have been cleared of their contents, and they will shortly be exhibited in the Cairo Museum. I plan to begin immediately clearing out the two chambers as yet untouched.

'I think that both contain valuable treasure, and greatly hope to discover papyrus which might reveal historical information of the greatest value.'

Howard was invited to join the Society of Authors; there was a dinner at the St. George's Hotel, Margate to welcome the new members, amongst whom were Lord Berners, Viscount Burnham, Lord Riddell, The Earl of Arran, Sir D. Plunket Barton, and Sir Bruce Bruce-Porter. Distinguished company indeed, thought Charlotte, feeling immensely proud that Howard was part of this illustrious company.

William Carter's portrait of his brother Howard was exhibited at Burlington House, unfortunately the portrait exhibition garnered lukewarm reviews, the portrait of Howard being described by an unknown critic, "...though unpretentious, is interesting."

Howard enjoyed frequenting the auction houses of London, and on this day, together with Charlotte, he was visiting Sotheby's, where the late Lord Carmichael's collection of Greek, Roman, Egyptian and other antiquities were up for sale. Charlotte had never attended an auction, she felt a frisson of excitement upon entering the room, many distinguished people were there, including General Sir John Maxwell.

The auction began and Charlotte was intrigued by the auctioneer, how on earth did he know who was bidding? The bidding for each item happened so quickly, she was grateful she wasn't buying anything, in fact she sat on her hands worried that any slight movement may end up in the purchase of some very expensive piece of sculpture.

Howard was his usual calm self, he radiated self-confidence, nodding to acquaintances, and looking as if he owned the establishment. As it turned out he paid the highest price of the afternoon, £610, for a late eighteenth dynasty bronze figure of Hesmeref, 9¾in. high, an unusually fine and rare ushabti. Howard also bought a cat in bronze, 5½in. high, twenty-fifth dynasty - £64.

At the auction General Sir John Maxwell had invited Howard to a luncheon hosted by himself and his wife, Lady Maxwell. The guest of honour was Princess Beatrice, the fifth daughter and the youngest of the nine children of Queen Victoria and Prince Albert.

Howard was also invited to a variety of dinner parties, sometimes allowing Charlotte to accompany him, although she felt a bit out of her comfort zone amongst these rich society people. She slowly became used to this life style, and began to rather enjoy it, who would have thought that she would be moving in such high society.

CHAPTER THIRTY

Egypt, then England, 1926

The first work of the new season at Luxor was to return the body of Tutankhamen to its place in the great stone sarcophagus. In an inner store-room beyond the burial-chamber now in the process of exploration, were discovered models of boats of every kind, a chariot, decorated caskets, numerous black shrines of wood, all sealed save one, and finally a gilded chest containing the four canopic jars in which the internal organs of the King had been placed by the embalmers when removed from the body. This chest, with its cornice of cobras and its freestanding figures of the four guardian goddesses at the corners, made a big impression upon Howard.

Several gilded statuettes, each in its own casket, with folding doors, and a number of sacred boats gilded and ornamented with precious stones and having on their prows figures of Tutankhamen, throwing-stick in hand, engaged in duck-hunting, were also discovered.

Many of the articles discovered required chemical treatment before their removal, and consequently the atmosphere in the chamber was bad, and made the work difficult.

Crossing the desert with an armed escort to Luxor, King Fuad paid his first visit to the tomb, over which he was personally conducted by Howard. His Majesty's deep interest was enhanced by the fact that he had just recently visited the Cairo Museum, and had there beheld, not without awe, the wonderful treasures that had been removed from the tomb.

While Howard worked at the tomb, Charlotte and Suzy spent their time wondering around the hills and valleys, exploring caves and crevices and stopping for picnics. They strolled through fields green with grain and rich with sugar canes, they entered desolate valleys, surrounded by hills, standing gaunt and arid amongst the blue sky.

They visited Howard at the laboratory; Suzy had been banned from entering so Charlotte found a shady spot for her and left her with some snacks and water. She found Howard repairing a gorgeous collarette that had belonged to Tutankhamen. On a table, there stood four exquisite statuettes, perhaps two feet high, carved of oak and covered in gold leaf. These represented the King holding a long crook, and as a harpooner in a boat. There were other statuettes already packed up and waiting to be sent to the Museum at Cairo. A ceremonial fan, unique in its gracefulness, the ostrich feathers still looking wonderful, Howard told her he had only had to spray them with a chemical preservative. The paints and writing box of the King when he was a boy was an interesting find, as was his underwear. Beautiful and artistic jewellery, some of which had fallen to pieces.

Three other guests were also visiting the laboratory, and Howard transformed himself into a delightful showman, he didn't look like a conventional showman, he had remarkable patience and his enthusiasm was contagious, he spoke in words that any layperson could understand. He talked of the history and symbolism of the various things he showed to them. They saw what was not fastened down in the boxes for removal and then he carefully lowered the steel gates, locked the great gates and they all went down into the tomb.

Descending the flight of 16 steps cut out of the limestone, they entered the first chamber. Howard, allowed them to look inside the storehouse and see in it the superbly gorgeous cabinet containing the four Canopic jars, and other magnificent works of Egyptian art.

Returning to London, Howard and Charlotte were back at Sotheby's for a two-day sale of the collection of Egyptian antiquities belonging to General Sir John Maxwell. Howard had contributed an interesting preface to the sales catalogue concerning the growth of the collection. On this first day, Howard paid £35 for the lid of a box, 3¼in. diameter, in light green faience modelled in the form of a conventionalized lotus flower.

On the second day Howard created a buzz of excitement around the auction room when an electrum mummy mask of an Egyptian princess was put up, the auctioneer asked, 'Now, gentlemen, what am I bid for this magnificent relic?' There was silence for about thirty seconds. Then, from beneath the auctioneer's rostrum, where he was sitting next to Charlotte, Howard called out, 'Five bob.'

The bidders began to laugh, and then someone said 'Two hundred pounds.' That bid was capped by one of five hundred, outbid by a thousand.

Another would-be purchaser stood up and offered 'Two thousand.' Howard never even turned a hair. 'Three thousand,' he said, with the same inflection as he had uttered the words of his opening bid.

In the taxi on the way home, Howard was in a jolly mood. Turning to Charlotte he said, 'What is it that a cat has that no other animal has?'

Charlotte, who was never any good at finding answers to jokes like this, gave it some consideration, 'I have no idea.' She replied.

Howard smiled and gave the answer, 'Kittens.'

Charlotte smiled indulgently, 'Very funny, Howard, you've brightened my day. What would I do without you?'

'My dear Charlotte, I fear you would find your life to be extremely dull indeed.' he said.

Charlotte leaned over and kissed him on the cheek, 'I'm so glad I met you.'

Howard smiled, he was quite glad he had met her too, but he didn't say it aloud.

CHAPTER THIRTY-ONE

Egypt, 1932

The seasons past and the work at the tomb continued. Ninety cases of treasures, representing two year's restoration work by Howard arrived at Cairo from Luxor and were now exhibited in the Cairo Museum. They included a wonderful bed made of gold, an alabaster boat, four head-rests, two of them in blue faience and one in ivory, the first real sickle sword ever found, a gaming board on an ebony sled, and two ivory boxes of games, not unlike dice, of exquisite workmanship.

Elbert and Jean Merriman came to stay as Howard's guests for several days.

'Carter, do you ever see that elderly lady with the funny name, Caramel, or something?' Merriman asked.

'Not very often.' replied Howard, feeling a bit guilty, as he had been deliberately avoiding Araminta.

'No. I can't say I blame you dear boy. Rather an overpowering presence, one doesn't like to speak ill of a friend but I do rather worry that she may squash me flat one day.'

'Why on earth should she do that?' asked Jean.

'Well, my dear she's rather prone to absent-mindedness, and she does hover about so. I fear one day I may find her sitting on top of me.'

'Why would she want to sit on you?' Jean asked incredulously.

'There I'll be minding my own business sitting in a comfortable armchair, and Mrs. whatshername will come sailing in, oblivious to everything and without noticing, sit down on top of me. It has happened before you know.'

'Oh yes, I remember.' said Charlotte. 'Suzy sat on you in the coach when we went on that picnic.'

'I've never got over it, I still have nightmares about the whole wretched affair.' said Merriman.

'Yes, well…' said Jean, and then changing the subject, 'Howard I think you're home is wonderful.'

Howard was very proud of his house and was pleased with the comment, until Merriman went and spoilt the moment.

'Yes, it is a wonderful Arab house, but isn't there an important thing lacking?' Merriman said, giving a genial smile.

'What's that?' asked Howard anxiously.

'Oh, just the harem.' Merriman quietly replied, chuckling to himself.

Charlotte laughed to herself as an image of her dressed as a harem girl dancing for Howard came into her head; she quickly dismissed it when she saw Howard's non-plussed expression.

Jean glared at her husband, turning to Howard she asked him what he proposed to do once the work on the tomb had finished.

Howard often talked to Charlotte about making an effort to locate and explore the tomb of Alexander the Great. He said 'Alexander was believed to be buried by Ptolemaeus at Alexandria in 323 B.C. in a golden coffin, subsequent to his death at Babylon. Should his tomb be found, the discoveries will be of much greater importance than those resulting from the unveiling at Tutankhamen, for Alexander had as great an influence on western as on eastern history. I also hope that some remnants of the famous Alexandria library, which was destroyed by fire, may also be discovered.'

The last finds from the tomb were dispatched to the Egyptian Museum, after ten years' work the last treasures were now gone, Howard's labours had finally come to an end. Charlotte stood with her hero and friend in the empty antechamber.

Howard recalled that day when he had discovered the entrance to the tomb, the clearing of the rubble-filled passage and the discovery of the second sealed door.

'Using a steel probe I began to work it through the plaster to find out whether there was a space beyond. There was.' Howard turned to Charlotte, 'You've heard me tell this story many times.'

Charlotte didn't mind hearing it again, she knew how proud he was, that he, a boy with no formal education, had been the one destined to find the lost tomb of Tutankhamen, 'You know I love listening to you, carry on.'

Howard carried on, 'My hands trembling a little, now widened the aperture so I could see into the void beyond. But first, as a precaution, I took a lighted candle and held it in the gap to test for possible dangerous gases.

'Then, while my companions hardly dared breathe, I peered into the darkness by the light of the flickering candle. For some moments I said nothing. Then, unable to bear the suspense any longer, Carnarvon asked if I could see anything. Still I remained silent.

'At last I answered. "Yes, wonderful things..."

'At first I could see nothing, the hot air escaping from the chamber causing the candle to flicker. But, presently, as my eyes grew accustomed to the light, details of the room within emerged slowly from the mist, strange animals, statues, and gold – everywhere the glint of gold.

'It was the day of days, the most wonderful I have ever lived through, and certainly one whose like I can never hope to see again.'

Charlotte held his hand; they stood and looked towards the burial chamber. All that remained inside was the magnificent stone sarcophagus containing the mortal remains of Tutankhamen.

'You found him, and now you'll both be remembered, your lives inextricably entwined for all eternity.' said Charlotte.

Standing quietly they both stared at the sarcophagus each buried deep within their own thoughts. 'It's time to go.' said Howard.

They climbed the sixteen steps back to daylight, Howard retrieved his hat and stick, he offered Charlotte his arm and they walked along the pathway of the Valley of the Kings to Howard's car.

CHAPTER THIRTY-TWO

1932-1935

A few weeks later, Howard gave an afternoon lecture at University College, Gower Street, London, describing some of the more remarkable of the objects found in the tomb. Little, he said, was actually known of Tutankhamen in comparison with what the world had heard of him! Howard talked in a quiet, unassuming manner, painting a wonderful picture of the desert tomb gradually yielding up its treasures.

Howard and Charlotte payed a visit to the Loan Exhibition of the Treasure of the Cathedral of Mainz at Spink and Sons Galleries in St. James's. There eyes feasted upon beautiful treasures of religious art from the late middle ages including paintings, drawings, stone and wooden sculptures, manuscripts, sacred art, and textiles.

Mrs. Saïde-Ruete gave a musical reception at 36, Cheniston-gardens. Miss Betsy De La Porte sang "Allmacht" by Schubert, "Aria: Air des Adieux," by Tchaikovsky, and "Songs of the East," by Granville Bantock. Mr. Victor Babin, the young pianist, played some Chopin and Mendelssohn. Charlotte enjoyed the concert very much.

On another memorable occasion, the Egyptian Prime Minister gave a dinner party followed by a reception at the Egyptian Legation in London. At the reception, Mmes. Danilova, Tchernicheva and Doubrovska, and M. Serge Lifar, of the

Diaghileff Ballet, danced "Les Sylphides" to the music of Chopin, and Mr. Dettmar Dressel played the violin, accompanied by Mr. Ivor Newton. Charlotte loved ballet and was thrilled to see these legendary dancers in real life.

Howard took Charlotte on a cruise around the Greek Islands. They boarded their ship in Piraeus, her name was Byzantium and she carried 49 passengers in 25 cabins. Charlotte thought she was lovely, so very homely and the crew and their fellow passengers were all very friendly, the whole experience was unforgettable.

They had spent the previous days exploring Athens, following the typical tourist trail - visiting the Parthenon, temple to Poseidon and Athena. Exploring the Acropolis, Hadrian's Arch, the Academy of Plato and the Monastery of Daphne, the ancient sites of the Roman Tower of the Winds and the Hill of the Muses where Socrates was said to have drunk hemlock. They ate moussaka and Greek salad, and drank wine and ouzo, although not at the same time.

They sailed across the Aegean Sea to Rhodes, with its fabulous historic buildings and atmospheric cobbled streets, the 14th century Palace of the Grand Masters and Hospital of the Knights of St. John, and the pink domed 16th century Mosque of Suleyman.

The next port of call was Santorini, with its dazzling white houses clinging to the edge of vertical rocky cliffs and considered by many to be the site of the "Lost City of Atlantis".

They travelled along the azure sea to Souda Bay and visited the charming old Venetian town of Chania, its cobbled streets lined with colourful Venetian townhouses.

Their last stop was Heraklion, where they visited the remains of Knossos, the Palace of King Minos and the island's capital under the Minoans. With its endless maze of salons, staircases and courtyards Charlotte could easily understand how the legend of the Labyrinth, housing the evil Minotaur at its centre, came alive.

Charlotte had been very relieved when 23rd February 1928 had past by and Howard had not died. She often wondered how much longer she had before she found herself transported back to her time. But the years had passed by and she was still here. Charlotte was very happy living in this time and she had no wish to return to the 21st century. She loved Howard; she loved him as a person, and as a close friend. Although she knew he would never say anything to her about his feelings, she felt that he had a great fondness for her company, he always said that he had never met anyone quite like her.

The 1934 exhibition of the Royal Academy of Miniature Painters, which was held at the Arlington Gallery in London, included some works of peculiar interest. Mrs. Winifred Brunton, wife of Mr. Guy Brunton, the well-known Egyptologist, had been given permission by Howard to paint miniatures of the jewels unearthed from Tutankhamen's sepulchre. Mrs. Brunton was a most accomplished miniaturist, and her copies of these historic relics had attracted widespread attention.

The Tutankhamen jewels are extremely beautiful, as well as interesting from the historical point of view; and Mrs. Brunton's miniature studies, done with patient clarity and exactness, enabled people to see more realistically than otherwise some of the gems of the Tutankhamen tomb.

Howard also lent his support to the present day revival of needlework. The needlework craze had swept Mayfair, and a large gathering of society hostesses attended a lecture given by Dr. Carter in the Victoria and Albert Museum, which has the largest collection of embroideries in the world. The lecture was organized by the Embroiderers' Guild, which has Queen Mary as its patron. Dr. Carter talked on "Colour." He has considerable knowledge of embroideries, and presented to the Embroiderers' Guild a wonderful piece of work done in Egypt in the tenth century. Charlotte loved it when people addressed Howard as Doctor Carter, she knew he appreciated it as well, he was enormously proud of his title. She would sometimes send him letters just so she could write Dr. Howard Carter upon the envelope.

Howard had recently moved to 49 Albert Court, and he had helped Charlotte find herself a lovely flat in Kensington. She was fascinated by this London; it seemed to have more charm than the London she knew. She loved the cars and buses, and trams too. One of her favourite things to do was travelling on the Underground; the tube stock was a delight. The seats were large and far more comfortable than on the modern day tube.

They still visited Egypt every year, Howard would show the occasional privileged tourist around the tomb and Charlotte would be able to see Suzy and Jabari, who had grown into a handsome young man.

On one memorable occasion when departing for home, Howard had booked passage aboard the famous RMS Aquitania.

In what she thought of her as her 'proper life', the life she was born into, which was far away in the future, Charlotte had a passion for ocean liners. She didn't care much for the modern cruise ship, they looked like floating boxes, but an ocean liner was elegant and beautiful. With Howard, she had already travelled upon the famous Berengaria and Mauretania. Now she was about to embark upon the ship known as "the ship beautiful". On boarding at Port Said, Charlotte could see why.

The ship's first class Grill Room was decorated in Jacobean style, the main restaurant was in the style of Louis XVI, there was even a garden lounge designed to resemble an English country garden.

The ship had entered service in 1914 on the transatlantic route, initially alongside Mauretania and Lusitania, then after the war with Berengaria and Mauritania. Aquitania was the last survivor of the four-funnelled liners; she would also be the only liner to serve in both world wars and would stay in service until 1950. She was now used for cruising, visiting Mediterranean ports. During her current cruise, the liner had called at Madeira and Gibraltar and then made a spring tour of the Mediterranean during which she had visited Algiers, Barcelona, Villefranche, Athens, Istanbul, Rhodes, Haifa, Port Said, Catania and Naples.

The voyage home had been a leisurely one, and nothing out of the ordinary had happened until that is they reached the English Channel. A heavy west-south-west wind was blowing at a rate of about 35 miles an hour and this caught the ship at an unlucky moment and forced her on the bank. At the point where the Aquitania stuck the channel leading up to Southampton describes an "S" bend, and is a well-known danger spot for shipping. Thorne Knoll lies between the Bramble Bank and Calshot Spit, where the channel is from 800 to 1,000 yards wide.

Some of the passengers, including Charlotte and Howard, were landed at Southampton Docks by tender.

Howard told a reporter, "The liner was simply thrown onto the bank by the wind. I felt a slight shudder and knew we were aground. But then I have done that before because boats on the Nile are always running aground on the sandbanks. I doubt, however, if very many of the passengers realized that anything unusual had happened."

One of Howard's favourite places was the Kulm Hotel in St. Moritz. On every occasion he visited a great reception would be given to him upon his arrival, which of course, pleased him no end and he couldn't take the smile off his face.

He was asked to give a lecture illustrated by lantern slides, on his discovery of the tomb of Tutankhamen. The proceeds were given to the Engadine Hospital at Samadan.

CHAPTER THIRTY-THREE

Egypt, 1937

Howard had spent over 40 years, off and on, in the East. As soon as the cold winds of winter arrived in England, he hurried back to Egypt. Now Howard and Charlotte were back once more, but this time there was no Suzy to greet Charlotte. Jabari had met a very nice girl called Chione and they were getting married the following year. As he was no longer free to look after Suzy, he had tried to find another carer for her. Rather unexpectedly, he had bumped into Araminta on one of her rare visits to Luxor. During their conversation, Jabari had mentioned his problem, and Araminta had told him she would take Suzy to live with her. Charlotte was relieved having feared the worst, and was already planning a trip back to Cairo to visit her friends.

The days were quiet without Suzy and Charlotte felt lonely, they're old friends the Merrimans no longer visited Egypt but preferred to stay in Portugal over the winter months. Harrison and Matula had both returned to their respective lives in America.

One evening sitting in Howard's house, watching him read a book, Charlotte thought that he must be about 63 years of age, but she thought he didn't look much older than 40. She was thinking that he was still a very handsome man, when he looked up at her. Removing his glasses, he rubbed his eyes and smiled at her. She felt warm and happy in his company, and she wanted to stay with him forever. She walked over to him, knelt down, and hugged him. I love you, she thought, but she couldn't bring herself to tell him. She let go and he kissed her on the forehead.

They took the overnight train to Cairo, and then a taxi to Araminta's house, Howard was adamant he wasn't going to be driven by that crazy lady. Upon arrival at the little house, Charlotte noticed a special area in the garden had been set up just for Suzy, with a little stable, a water trough, and a place for her food. As soon as the donkey heard the taxi she let out a bellow, the taxi driver, under the impression the end of the world was nigh, sped off at full throttle, it was only when he found himself in the middle of desert that he realized he had sped off in the wrong direction.

Suzy, not being one for the niceties in life, such as opening the gate, charged through the fence and raced around Charlotte and Howard at such a frantic pace that Howard thought she would bury them in the dust cloud she was kicking up. Coughing and spluttering, they finally managed to calm Suzy down, Charlotte hugged her and the donkey nuzzled into her friend's ear. Araminta came out, all in a tizzy, hugging first Howard, then Charlotte, then Suzy.

'Oh my dears, how wonderful it is to see you. I wish you'd told me you were arriving To-day, I haven't got anything ready.'

'Don't worry, Araminta.' said Charlotte. 'We've brought lots of food with us.'

'I'm afraid it seems to be covered in sand.' Said Araminta, peering over at a dust heap.

'Unfortunately, Suzy was rather over enthusiastic with her greetings. Never mind, Howard can dig it out, he's had a lot of experience you know.' said Charlotte.

Howard glared at Charlotte and she smiled innocently back at him.

'My dear Howard, how well you look, so tanned and handsome.' Said Araminta, 'Charlotte, don't you agree?'

Charlotte, blushing, said 'Yes, very handsome indeed.'

Howard, deciding enough was enough, went towards the house; he wanted to freshen up and try to get the dust out his clothes and wash his face. Of course, he would have to trip over the broken bit of paving. 'Howard, oh my goodness, are you hurt?' asked Charlotte, running to help him.

Araminta started fussing, 'Oh, my, how dreadful, I should have fixed that wretched thing years ago, here let me help you.'

Araminta ran towards Howard as well.

Suzy, observing these goings on and not wishing to be left out of any family business, decided to run over as well. All three of them descended upon Howard, who looked up in astonished surprise, just seconds before the lights went out.

Buried beneath two people and a donkey was not Howard's idea of a relaxing holiday, he struggled to extricate himself. 'Will you please let me out of here?' he asked in a plaintive cry.

'I'm trying,' said Charlotte, 'Suzy is sitting on me, I can't move.'

Suzy sat on top of her friends, believing this to be a new game, and was feeling very content, she had even found a dusty old hat and was chewing amiably upon it.

Araminta, who now gave the impression of a rather neglected scarecrow with her clothes all askew managed to get to her feet. Suzy stared at her and wasn't quite sure if this was friend or foe. Charlotte managed to call Suzy's name. The donkey looked around wondering where the voice had come from. Charlotte tried to shake herself free, and just when she thought she would suffocate, Suzy stood up.

'Oh my,' said Charlotte gasping for air, 'Where's Howard?'

'I'm here. Help me up.'

Charlotte helped him up and Araminta handed him his hat.

'Someone's eaten my hat.' said Howard, looking over at Suzy, whose expression was one of complete innocence. 'My favourite hat, that donkey, she'll kill us all one day.'

'Never mind Howard, you can always buy another one.' said Charlotte, ushering him into the house. 'Here have a drop of brandy; it'll make you feel better.'

The days went by, Charlotte and Suzy went for rides in the countryside, they sat and ate their picnic and admired the changing scenery, from canals and trees to the desert and rocks. Charlotte adored Suzy, she had no idea how long a donkey's lifespan was or for that matter, how old Suzy was. However, she vowed she would come and visit her every year. She had thought about bringing her back to England, but where would she keep her? She doubted Suzy would be happy there, no it was better to leave her in the climate she was used to. Araminta would look after her, for now, but she was an elderly lady, what would happen to Suzy then? Charlotte supposed she would have to come and live here permanently, but then of course she would miss Howard. Oh dear, her head was spinning now, she decided not to think about it anymore, the days were too gorgeous and Suzy was by her side.

Howard had not been well for the last few days and Charlotte was worried about him. She hoped he would be all right on the long journey home as the time had come for them to return to London. Charlotte said her farewells to Suzy, the little donkey, sensing her friend was leaving, put her head upon Charlotte's shoulder, Charlotte hugged her and told her she loved her very much.

Araminta insisted upon driving them to Cairo, and Charlotte thought it would be churlish not to accept her offer, but only if she promised to drive carefully, Araminta, slightly affronted, she thought of herself as a very competent driver, after all she'd never had an accident, as far as she could remember.

The car started and Charlotte turned to wave goodbye to Suzy, Suzy shouted 'hee-haw', and Charlotte's heart broke, and she started to cry.

'Why on earth are you crying?' asked Howard. 'You'll see her in a few months time.'

'I know, it's silly really, it's just I've got this feeling that I won't see her again.'

Araminta got them to Cairo, without mishap. At the station Howard and Charlotte boarded the train, leaning out of the window to wave goodbye to their friend. The venerable lady clutching a vast handkerchief, dabbed delicately at her tearful eyes, she begged them to look after themselves, they shouted their goodbyes and thank yous, and promised to keep in touch. With a blast of its whistle, the train began to move slowly out of the station.

CHAPTER THIRTY-FOUR

London, 1939

Back at Howard's flat, Charlotte spent the days looking after him, not wishing to leave him alone, she spent the nights sleeping upon a sofa, just in case he should need her. Howard slept a lot and when he was awake, Charlotte would read him the news, one day she found an obituary for Elbert Merriman, she was going to mention it to Howard, but decided not to.

Howard was still his irascible old self, there had been a story doing the rounds for a year or so about peas. Peas supposedly found in Tutankhamen's tomb, having been there for over three thousand years, had apparently been cultivated and actually produced green peas. This story, having come to Howard's attention, had made him so indignant that he had instructed his solicitor to write a letter to The Times, refuting in the fullest terms that no peas were found in the tomb, that if there had been they were not his property to give away, and that physically it would be impossible that the peas after thousands of years would have any reserve of life force.

Howard would sit up in bed chatting to Charlotte about the adventures they had had, about her crazy donkey Suzy, whom Charlotte suspected Howard was actually quite fond of. They occasionally discussed Ottomar Hengel and all the trouble he had caused them. They talked about their holidays and spent hours looking through their photograph albums, remembering the happy times they had spent and the sad ones as well.

'Don't leave me, please.' said Charlotte suddenly, tears in her eyes.

'Charlotte my dear, of course I'm not going to leave you. My life would be very boring indeed without you by my side.'

Charlotte sniffed; she never seemed to have a handkerchief when she needed one. Howard passed one over to her and she blew her nose with it. She looked at him and blurted out 'I love you, Howard.' There, she had told him at last.

Taking her hand, he smiled at her, 'I love you too.' squeezing her hand in his, he leant forward and kissed her gently on the lips.

Howard died later that night.

The funeral was held four days later at Putney Vale Cemetery. Apart from Charlotte, nine other people attended, including Howard's brother William, his nephew Samuel, and Lord Carnarvon's daughter, Lady Evelyn Beauchamp.

After Howard's funeral, Charlotte had sat by the grave long after the others had departed. She missed him so much it hurt. She couldn't believe that this once vibrant, clever man, whom she had shared so much with, was gone.

EPILOGUE

During the Second World War Charlotte worked as a clippie on the No. 9 bus travelling from Hammersmith through Kensington and ending at Aldwych. Later, she worked in the booking office at Hammersmith Station. After the war, Charlotte returned to Egypt to spend time with Araminta and Suzy. Araminta was by now a shadow of her former self, she had lost a great deal of weight and spent most of her time in the garden lying upon a sun bed.

Charlotte and Suzy would walk together and eat their picnics as they had done in days past. One day when they came home, Charlotte called out to Araminta, only to find her friend had died in her sleep. Now there was only Suzy left to keep Charlotte company. They remained living at Araminta's house, but in 1952, shortly before the Egyptian Revolution, Charlotte took Suzy back to England.

Howard had left Charlotte some money and with the sale of her flat she was able to buy a property in a village in Exeter. There was plenty of space for Suzy to run around and get up to mischief. Although Suzy refused to sleep in her stable and insisted on sleeping in the house, Charlotte didn't have the heart to turn her out. During the winter months, the two of them would occupy Charlotte's sitting room, watching television or listening to music. Suzy was very keen on classical music, for some reason she especially liked the opera, Tosca, and would go into ecstasies of braying whenever she heard "E lucevan le stelle."

Charlotte enjoyed her life; she worked at Exeter Station in the booking office. She had a small circle of friends with whom she went to the cinema or theatre. They all adored Suzy, and spoilt her dreadfully. Suzy had even been allowed to visit the Station to say 'Hello' or rather 'hee-haw' to Charlotte's boss, Mr. Hardy, although he had drawn the line at allowing Suzy to travel by train to Dawlish.

Suzy died in 1971, leaving Charlotte heart-broken, she didn't know how she would continue to live. Suddenly she felt completely alone. A few years later, Charlotte moved back to London. One day she had been to a matinee performance of a West End musical called "Irene". Afterwards, she took the tube back to South Kensington and when she emerged from the subway into Exhibition Road, she suddenly felt the urge to visit Howard's grave. She hadn't visited it once since his burial, as she couldn't bring herself to see it, until now.

The afternoon was beautiful and unusually warm for March. A little boy was running down the path too busy playing with his ball to notice the elderly lady walking slowly towards him. He bumped into her, and mumbled sorry before running off again. Charlotte smiled to herself; she slowly continued her walk, her stick tapping along the path. She arrived at the tomb and was pleased to see a shining new headstone; peering through her glasses, she read the epitaph.

Howard Carter
Egyptologist
Discoverer of the Tomb of Tutankhamun
Born 9 May 1874
Died 2 March 1939
May your spirit live, may you spend millions of years, you who love Thebes, sitting with your face to the north wind, your eyes beholding happiness.

That night Charlotte remembered her life, she thought of her beloved Howard and Suzy, her friends, Araminta, Elbert and Jean, Harrison, and Matula. All of them were now long gone, their bodies just piles of dust and bare bones. Their thoughts, their feelings, their personalities, all disappeared in the mist of time.

Tears ran down her cheeks, she wanted to be back with Howard and Suzy; she wanted to be part of their world once more.

She looked at her photographs, until her eyes became gritty with tiredness; she closed the lid of the album and placed it upon the table together with the other albums, next to them lay her diaries detailing all of her adventures that had taken place so many years ago. There was a letter as well, asking who ever found her to make sure her treasured possessions went to a good home, a museum perhaps, or a collector of Howard Carter memorabilia. She hoped her precious collection of memories would find a new home, for she had no one to leave them to.

Charlotte made her way slowly to bed, upon her bedside table stood her precious framed photograph, a black and white image of Howard, Suzy and herself, taken by Jabari outside Howard's domed house, all three of them were smiling, looking happy and carefree, and that's how Charlotte would always remember them. Holding the photograph tightly in her hands, Charlotte lay down, and looked at it one last time, for she knew that she would not see it again, she closed her eyes and slept the sleep of eternity.

THE END

SOURCES THAT HELPED ME WRITE THIS BOOK

British Newspaper Archives

Carter, Howard, *The Tomb of Tutankhamun*
Volumes 1, 2, and 3. (Cassell & Company Ltd., London, 1923, 1927 and 1933)

James, T. G. H., *Howard Carter, The Path to Tutankhamun* (Kegan Paul International Ltd., London, 1992)

Reeves, Nicholas and John H. Taylor, *Howard Carter before Tutankhamun* (British Museum Press, London, 1992)

Printed in Great Britain
by Amazon